HEAT WAVE

ALSO BY RICHARD CASTLE

Naked Heat

HEAT WAVE

RICHARD CASTLE

HYPERION

NEW YORK

Premium Mass Market ISBN: 978-0-7868-9141-2

Hyperion books are available for special promotions and pre-
miums. For details contact the HarperCollins Special Markets
Department in the New York office at 212-207-7528, fax 212-
207-7222, or email spsales@harpercollins.com.

Book design by Shubhani Sarkar

FIRST PREMIUM MASS MARKET EDITION

10 9 8 7 6 5 4 3 2 1

To the extraordinary KB
and all my friends at the 12th

HEAT WAVE

ONE

It was always the same for her when she arrived to meet the body. After she unbuckled her seat belt, after she pulled a stick pen from the rubber band on the sun visor, after her long fingers brushed her hip to feel the comfort of her service piece, what she always did was pause. Not long. Just the length of a slow deep breath. That's all it took for her to remember the one thing she will never forget. Another body waited. She drew the breath. And when she could feel the raw edges of the hole that had been blown in her life, Detective Nikki Heat was ready. She opened the car door and went to work.

The wallop of one hundred degrees almost shoved her back in the car. New York was a furnace, and the soft pavement on West 77th gave under her feet like she was walking on wet sand. Heat could have made it easier on herself by parking closer, but this was another of her rituals: the walk up. Every crime scene was a flavor of chaos, and these two hundred feet afforded the detective her only chance to fill the clean slate with her own impressions.

Thanks to the afternoon swelter, the sidewalk was nearly empty. The neighborhood lunch rush was over, and tourists were either across the street cooling in the American Museum of Natural History or seeking refuge in Starbucks over iced drinks ending in vowels. Her disdain for the coffee drinkers dissolved into a mental note to get one herself on the way back to the precinct. Ahead she clocked a doorman at the apartment building just her side of the barrier tape that encircled the sidewalk café. His hat was off and he was sitting on the worn marble steps with his head between his knees. She looked up at the hunter green canopy as she passed him and read the building name: The Guilford.

Did she know the uniform flashing her the smile? She rapid-fired a slideshow of faces but stopped when she realized he was just checking her out. Detective Heat smiled back and parted her linen blazer to give him something else to fantasize about. His face rearranged itself when he saw the shield on her waistband. The young cop lifted the yellow tape for her to duck under, and when she came up she caught him giving her a sex-ray again, so she couldn't resist. "Make you a deal," she said. "I'll watch my ass, you watch the crowd."

Detective Nikki Heat entered her crime scene past the vacant hostess podium of the sidewalk café. All the tables at La Chaleur Belle were empty except one where Detective Raley of her squad sat with a distraught family with sunburned faces struggling to translate German into a statement. Their uneaten lunch swarmed with flies. Sparrows, avid outdoor diners themselves, perched on seat backs and made bold dives for *pommes frites.* At the service door Detective Ochoa looked up from his notebook and quick-nodded her while he questioned a busboy in a white apron flecked with blood.

The rest of the serving staff was inside at the bar having a drink after what they had witnessed. Heat looked over to where the medical examiner knelt and couldn't blame them one bit.

"Male unknown, no wallet, no identification, preliminary age range sixty to sixty-five. Severe blunt force trauma to head, neck, and chest." Lauren Parry's gloved hand peeled back the sheet for her friend Nikki to have a look at the corpse on the sidewalk. The detective glanced and quickly looked away. "No face, so we'll comb the area for any dental; otherwise not much to ID from after that impact. Is this where he landed?"

"There." The M.E. indicated the café busing station a few feet away. It had caved in from the top so hard it was split in half. The violent splash of ice and blood had already baked into the sidewalk in the minutes since the fall. As Heat stepped over there, she noted that the café umbrellas and the stone walls of the building also wore dried blood, ice spatter, and bits of tissue. She got as close to the wreckage as she dared without contaminating the scene and looked straight up.

"It's raining men."

Nikki Heat didn't even turn. She just sighed his name. "Rook."

"Hallelujah." He held onto his smile until she finally looked at him, shaking her head. "What? It's OK, I don't think he can hear me."

She wondered what sort of karma payback it was for her to be saddled with this guy. It wasn't the first time that month she had wondered it, either. The job was hard enough if you were doing it right.

Add a reporter with a mouth playing make-believe cop and your day just got a little longer. She backed up to the long flower boxes that defined the perimeter of the outdoor café and looked up again. Rook moved with her. "I would have been here sooner except somebody didn't call me. If I hadn't phoned Ochoa, I would have missed this."

"It's just tragedy upon tragedy, isn't it?"

"You wound me with your sarcasm. Look, I can't research my article on New York's finest without access, and my deal with the commissioner specifically states—"

"Trust me, I know your deal. I've been living day and night. You get to observe on all my homicides just like real-life detectives who work for a living."

"So you forgot. I accept your apology."

"I didn't forget, and I didn't hear any apology. At least not from me."

"I kind of inferred it. You radiate subtext."

"Someday you're going to tell me what favor you did for the mayor to get this ride-along pushed through."

"Sorry, Detective Heat, I'm a reporter and that's strictly off the record."

"Did you kill a story that made him look bad?"

"Yes. God, you make me feel cheap. But you'll get nothing more."

Detective Ochoa wrapped his busboy interview and Heat beckoned him over. "I passed a doorman for this building who looked like he was having a very bad day. Go check him out, see if he knows our Doe."

When she turned back, Rook had curled his hands to form skin binoculars and was sighting up the building overlooking the café. "I call the balcony on six."

"When you write your magazine article, you can make it any floor you like, Mr. Rook. Isn't that what you reporters do, speculate?" Before he could reply, she held her forefinger to his lips. "But we're not celebrity journalists here. We're just the police, and darn it, we have these pesky things called facts to dig up and events to verify. And while I try to do my job, would it be too much to ask that you maintain a little decorum?"

"Sure. No problem."

"Thank you."

"Jameson? Jameson Rook?!" Rook and Heat turned to see a young woman behind the police line waving and jumping up and down for his attention. "Oh my God, it's him, it's Jameson Rook!" Rook gave her a smile and a wave, which only made his fan more excited. Then she ducked under the yellow tape.

"Hey, no, get back!" Detective Heat signaled to a pair of uniforms, but the woman in the halter and cutoffs was already inside the line and approaching Rook. "This is a crime scene, you have to go."

"Can I at least get an autograph?"

Heat weighed expediency. The last time she tried to chase off one of his fans, it had involved ten minutes of arguing and an hour writing up an answer to the woman's official complaint. Literate fans are the worst. She nodded to the uniforms and they waited.

"I saw you on *The View* yesterday morning. Oh my God, you're even cuter in person." She clawed through her straw bag but kept her eyes on him. "After the show I ran out and bought the magazine so I could read your story, see?" She pulled out the latest issue of *First Press*. The cover shot was Rook and Bono at a relief center in Africa. "Oh! I have a Sharpie."

"Perfect." He took the marker and reached for her magazine.

"No, sign this!" She took a step closer and tugged aside the cup of her halter.

Rook smiled. "I think I'm going to need more ink."

The woman exploded with laughter and clutched Nikki Heat's arm. "See? This is why he's my favorite writer."

But Heat was focused on the front steps of the Guilford, where Detective Ochoa clapped a sympathetic hand on the shoulder of the doorman. He left the shade of the canopy, did a limbo under the tape, and crossed to her. "Doorman says our vic lived in this building. Sixth floor."

Nikki heard Rook clear his throat behind her but didn't turn. He was either gloating or signing a groupie's breast. She wasn't in the mood to see either one.

An hour later in the solemn hush of the victim's apartment, Detective Heat, the embodiment of sympathetic patience, sat in an antique tapestry chair across from his wife and their seven-year-old son. A blue reporter's-cut spiral notebook rested closed on her lap. Her naturally erect dancer's posture and the drape of her hand on the carved wooden armrest gave her a look of regal ease. When she caught Rook staring at her from across the room, he turned away and studied the Jackson Pollock on the wall in front of him. She reflected on how much the paint splatters echoed the busboy's apron downstairs, and though she tried to stop it, her cop's brain began streaming its capture video of the mangled busing station, the slack faces of traumatized waitstaff, and the coroner's van departing with the body of real estate mogul Matthew Starr.

Heat wondered if Starr was a jumper. The economy, or, more accurately, the lack of it, had triggered scores of collateral tragedies. On any given day, the country seemed one turn of a hotel maid's key away from discovering the next suicide or murder-suicide of a CEO or tycoon. Was ego an antidote? As New York real estate developers went, Matthew Starr didn't write the book on ego, but he sure did the term paper. A perennial also-ran in the race to slap his name on the outside of everything with a roof, you had to credit Starr with at least staying in the chase.

And by the looks of his digs, he had been weathering the storm lavishly on two luxury floors of a landmark building just off Central Park West. Every furnishing was either antique or designer; the living room was a grand salon two stories high, and its walls were covered up to the cathedral ceiling by collectible art. Safe bet nobody left take-out menus or locksmith brochures at this front door.

A trace of muffled laughter turned Nikki Heat's attention to the balcony where Detectives Raley and Ochoa, a duo affectionately condensed to "Roach," were working. Kimberly Starr rocked her son in a long hug and didn't seem to hear it. Heat excused herself and crossed the room, gliding in and out of ponds of light beaming down from the upper windows, casting an aura on her. She sidestepped the forensics tech dusting the French doors and went out onto the balcony, flipping her notebook to a blank page.

"Pretend we're going over notes." Raley and Ochoa exchanged confused looks then drew closer to her. "I could hear you two laughing in there."

"Oh, jeez . . . ," said Ochoa. He winced and the sweat bead clinging to the tip of his nose fell onto her page.

"Listen to me. I know to you this is just another crime scene, right? But for that family in there, it's the only one they've ever experienced. Are you hearing me? Good." She half turned to the door and turned back. "Oh. And when we get out of here? I want to hear that joke. I could use it."

When Heat came back in, the nanny was ushering Kimberly's son out of the room. "Take Matty outside for a while, Agda. But not out front. Do you hear me? Not out front." She pulled another tissue and dabbed her nose.

Agda stopped in the archway. "It is so hot in the park today for him." The Scandinavian nanny was a looker and could have been Kimberly's coed sister. A comparison that made Heat ponder the age had the most rage to siphon off. Or was she just recalling herself back when she was the one in The Loss Chair, nineteen years old with her world suddenly imploding around her? Had she really siphoned off all her rage, or merely clamped a lid on it?

"It's summer, damn it, we should be in the Hamptons. This wouldn't have happened if we were at Stormfall." Now, that's money. You don't just buy an estate in East Hampton, you name it. Stormfall was beachfront, secluded, and Seinfeld-adjacent with a partial Spielberg view. "I hate this city," Kimberly shouted. "Hate it, hate it. What is this, like, murder number three hundred so far this year? As if they even matter to you people after a while." She panted, apparently finished. Heat closed her notebook and circled around the coffee table to sit beside her on the sofa.

"Please hear me. I know how difficult this is."

"No, you don't."

"I'm afraid I do." She waited for the meaning of that to sink in on Kimberly, then continued. "Murders are not numbers to me. A person died. A loved one. Someone you thought you were eating dinner with tonight is gone. A little boy has lost his father. Someone is responsible. And you have my promise I will see your case through."

Mollified or maybe just shock-worn, Kimberly nodded and asked if they could finish this later. "Right now I just want to go to my boy."

She left them in the apartment to continue their investigation. After she left, Rook said, "I always wondered where all those Martha Stewarts came from. They must breed them on a secret farm in Connecticut."

"Thank you for not interrupting while she was spewing."

Rook shrugged. "I'd like to say that was sensitivity, but it was really because of the chair. It's hard for a man to sound authoritative surrounded by toile. OK, now that she's gone, can I tell you I get a vibe off her I don't like?"

"Uh-huh, I'm not surprised. That was a hell of a shot she took at your 'profession.' Accurate though it was." Heat turned, in case her inner smile leaked onto her face, and started back to the balcony.

He fell in with her. "Oh, please, I have two Pulitzers, I don't need her respect." She gave him a side glance. "Although, I did kind of want to tell her that the series of articles I wrote about my month underground with the Chechen rebels are being optioned for a movie."

"Why didn't you? Your self-aggrandizement might have been a welcome distraction from the fact that her husband just died a violent death."

They stepped out into the afternoon scorch, where Raley and Ochoa's shirts had soaked clean through. "What have you got, Roach?"

"Definitely not liking suicide," said Raley. "A, check out the fresh paint chips and stone dust. Somebody banged open those French doors pretty hard, like during a struggle."

"And B," Ochoa picked up, "you've got your trail of scuff marks leading from the doors across the . . . what is this?"

"Terra-cotta tile," said Rook.

"Right. Shows the marks pretty good, huh? And they go all the way to here." He stopped at the balustrade. "This is where our man went over."

All four of them leaned to look below. "Wow," said Rook. "Six floors down. It is six, isn't it, fellas?"

"Let it go, Rook," said Heat.

"But here's our telltale." Ochoa got on his knees to indicate something on the railing with his pen. "You'll have to get close." He backed up to make room for Heat, who knelt to see where he was pointing. "It's torn fabric. Forensics geek says it'll test out as blue denim after he runs it. Our vic wasn't wearing jeans, so this came from someone else."

Rook knelt down beside her to look. "As in someone who shoved him over." Heat nodded, as did Rook. They turned to face each other, and she was a little startled by his proximity but didn't pull back. Nose-to-nose with him in the heat, she held his gaze and watched the dance of reflected sunlight playing off his eyes. And then she blinked. Oh shit, she thought, what was that? I can't be attracted to this guy. No way.

Detective Heat quickly rose to her feet, crisp and all business. "Roach? I want you to run a background on Kimberly Starr. And check out her alibi at that ice cream place on Amsterdam."

"So," said Rook, rising beside her, "you got a vibe off her, too, huh?"

"I don't do vibes. I do police work." Then she hurried away to the apartment.

Later, on the elevator ride down, she asked her

detectives, "OK, what was so funny that I could have killed you both with my bare hands? And so you know, I am trained to do that."

"Aw, nothing, just letting the giddy out, you know how it gets," said Ochoa.

"Yeah, nothing at all," said Raley.

Two floors of silence passed and they both started a low hum of "It's Raining Men" before they cracked up.

"That? That's what you were laughing at?"

"This," said Rook, "may be the proudest moment of my life."

As they stepped back out into the blast furnace and gathered under the Guilford canopy, Rook said, "You'll never guess who wrote that song."

"I don't know songwriters, man," from Raley.

"You'd know this one."

"Elton John?"

"Wrong."

"Clue?"

A woman's scream cut through the rush-hour noise of the city, and Nikki Heat bounded onto the sidewalk, her head swiveling to search up and down the block.

"Over there," called the doorman, pointing toward Columbus. "Mrs. Starr!"

Heat followed his gaze to the corner, where a large man gripped Kimberly Starr by the shoulders and jammed her against a store window. It thundered on impact but did not break.

Nikki was off in a sprint, with the other three close behind. She waved her shield and hollered at pedestrians to move as she wove through the after-work crowd. Raley fisted his two-way and called for backup.

"Police, freeze," called Heat.

In the assailant's split second of alarm, Kimberly went for a groin kick that missed wildly. The man was already on the move and she torqued herself down to the pavement. "Ochoa," said Heat, pointing at Kimberly as she passed. Ochoa stopped to attend her while Raley and Rook followed Heat, dodging cars into the crosswalk on 77th. A tour bus making an illegal turn blocked their path. Heat ran around the bus's rear end, through a puff of hot diesel exhaust, emerging on the cobblestone sidewalk that surrounded the museum complex.

There was no sign of him. She slowed to a jog and then a race-walk across from the Evelyn at 78th. Raley was still on his walkie behind her, calling in their location and the man's description: ". . . male cauc, thirty-five, balding, six feet, white short-sleeve shirt, blue jeans . . ."

At 81st and Columbus Heat stopped and turned a circle. A sheen of perspiration glistened on her chest and fed a darkened V-pattern down the front of her top. The detective showed no sign of fatigue, only alertness, seeing near and far at the same time, knowing all she needed was a glimpse of any piece of him to put her back on the run.

"He wasn't in that good a shape." Rook sounded a little winded. "He couldn't have gotten far."

She turned to him, a little impressed he had kept up. And a little annoyed that he had. "What the hell are you doing here, Rook?"

"Extra set of eyes, Detective."

"Raley, I'll cover Central Park West and circle the museum. You take 81st to Amsterdam and loop back on 79th."

"Got it." He cut against the grain of the downtown flow on Columbus.

"What about me?"

"Have you noticed I might be too busy to baby-sit you right now? If you want to be helpful, take that extra set of eyes and see how Kimberly Starr is doing."

She left him there on the corner without looking back. Heat needed her concentration and didn't want her focus pulled, not by him. This ride-along was getting tired enough. And what was with that business back there on the balcony? Pulling up next to her face like some perfume ad in *Vanity Fair*, those ads that promise the kind of love that life just never seems to deliver. Lucky she shook herself out of that little tableau. Still, she wondered, maybe she had just bitch-slapped the guy a little too hard.

When she turned to check on Rook, she didn't see him at first. Then she spotted him halfway down Columbus. What the hell was he doing crouching behind that planter? He looked like he was spying on something. She hopped the fence of the dog park and cut across the lawn toward him at a jog. That's when she saw White Shirt–Blue Jeans climb out of the Dumpster at the rear entrance to the museum complex. She kicked it up to a sprint. Ahead of her, Rook stood up behind his planter. The guy made him and took off down the driveway, disappearing into the service tunnel. Nikki Heat called out to him, but Rook was already running into the underground entrance after her perp.

She cursed and leaped over the fence at the other end of the dog park, chasing after them.

TWO

Nikki Heat's footsteps echoed back at her off the concrete tunnel as she ran. The passage was wide and high, big enough to truck in exhibits for both museums in the complex: the American Museum of Natural History and the Rose Center for Earth and Space, aka the planetarium. The orange cast of sodium-vapor lamps gave good visibility, but she couldn't see ahead around the curve of the wall. She also didn't pick up any other footfalls, and coming around the bend, she saw why not.

The tunnel came to a dead end at a loading dock and nobody was there. She bounded up the steps to the landing, from which a pair of doors fed off—one to the natural history museum on the right, the other to the planetarium on her left. She made a Zen choice and hit the push bar to the natural history door. It was locked. To hell with instinct; she went for the process of elimination. The door to the planetarium service bay popped open. She drew her gun and went in.

Heat entered in the Weaver stance, keeping her back to a line of crates. Her academy trainer had drilled her to use the more square and sturdy Isosceles, but in tight quarters with lots of pivoting, she made her own call and assumed the pose that let her flow and present less target area. She cleared the room quickly, startled only once by an Apollo space suit dangling from an old display. In the far corner she found an internal staircase. As she approached, somebody upstairs threw a door open against a wall. Before it slammed shut, Heat was climbing steps two at a time.

She emerged into a sea of visitors roaming the lower level of the planetarium. A camp counselor passed by leading a herd of kids in matching T-shirts. The detective holstered-up before young eyes could freak out at her gun. Heat waded through them, squinting in the blinding whiteness of the Hall of the Universe, speed-scanning for Rook or Kimberly Starr's attacker. Over by a rhino-sized meteorite she spotted a security guard on his two-way, pointing at something: Rook, vaulting a banister and clambering up a ramp that curved around the hall and spiraled to the floor above. Halfway up the incline, her suspect's head popped over the railing to backcheck on Rook. Then he raced on with the reporter in pursuit.

The sign said they were on the Cosmic Pathway, a 360-degree spiral walkway marking the timeline of the evolution of the universe in the length of a football field. Nikki Heat covered thirteen billion years at a personal best. At the top of the incline, quads protesting, she stopped to make another scan. No sign of either of them. Then she heard the screams of the crowd.

Heat rested a hand on her holster and orbited under the giant central sphere to see the guest lineup for the space show. The alarmed crowd was parting, backing away from Rook, who was on the ground taking a rib kick from her man.

The attacker drew back for another kick, and during the most vulnerable part of his balance shift, Heat came up behind him and used her leg to sweep his out from under him. All six feet of him dropped hard onto the marble. She cuffed him rodeo quick and the crowd broke into applause.

Rook sat himself up. "I'm fine, thanks for asking."

"Nice work slowing him down like that. Is that how you rolled in Chechnya?"

"The guy jumped me after I tripped." He pointed under his foot to a bag from the museum store. "On that." Rook opened it up and pulled out an art glass paperweight of a planet. "Check it out. I tripped on Uranus."

When Heat and Rook entered the Interrogation Room, the prisoner snapped upright at the table the way fourth-graders do when the principal walks in. Rook took the side chair. Nikki Heat tossed a file on the table but stayed on her feet. "Stand up," she said. And Barry Gable did. The detective walked a circle around him, enjoying his nervousness. She bent low to examine his blue jeans for any rips that could match the fabric shard the killer had left on the railing. "What did you do here?"

Gable arched himself to look at the scuff she was pointing to on the back of his leg. "I dunno. Maybe I scraped them on the Dumpster. These are brand-new," he added, as if that might put him in a more favorable light.

"We're going to want your pants." The guy started to unhitch them right there, and she said,

"Not now. After. Sit down." He complied, and she eased into the seat opposite, all casual, all in charge. "You want to tell us why you attacked Kimberly Starr?"

"Ask her," he said, trying to sound tough but shooting nervous looks at himself in the mirror, a giveaway to her he had never sat in Interrogation before.

"I'm asking you, Barry," said Heat.

"It's personal."

"It is to me. Battery like that against a woman? I can get very personal about that. You want to see how personal?"

Rook chimed in, "Plus you assaulted me."

"Hey, you were chasing me. How did I know what you were going to pull? I can tell a mile away you're not a cop."

Heat kind of liked that. She arched an eyebrow at Rook and he sat back to stew. She turned back to Gable. "Not your first assault, I see, is it, Barry?" She made a show of opening the file. There weren't many pages in it, but her theater made him more uneasy, so she made the most of it. "Two thousand six scrape with a bouncer in SoHo; 2008, you pushed a guy who caught you keying the side of his Mercedes."

"Those were all misdemeanors."

"Those were all assaults."

"I lose it sometimes." He forced a John Candy chuckle. "Guess I should stay out of the bars."

"And maybe spend more time at the gym," said Rook.

Heat gave him a cool-it glance. Barry had turned

to the mirror again and adjusted his shirt around his gut. Heat closed the file and said, "Can you tell us your whereabouts this afternoon, say around one to two P.M.?"

"I want my lawyer."

"Sure. Would you like to wait for him here or down in the Zoo Lockup?" It was an empty threat that only worked on newbies, and Gable's eyes widened. Underneath the hard-ass face she fixed on him, Heat was loving how easily he caved. Gotta love the Zoo Lockup. Works every time.

"I was at the Beacon, you know, the Beacon Hotel on Broadway?"

"You do know we will check your alibi. Is there anyone who saw you and can vouch for you?"

"I was alone in my room. Maybe somebody at the front desk in the morning."

"That hedge fund you operate pays for a mighty nice address on East 52nd. Why book a hotel?"

"Come on, are you going to make me say this?" He stared at his own pleading eyes in the mirror then nodded to himself. "I go there a couple times a week. To meet somebody. You know."

"For sex?" asked Rook.

"Jeez, yeah, sex is part of it. It goes deeper than that."

"And what happened today?" asked Heat.

"She didn't show."

"Bad for you, Barry. She could be your alibi. Does she have a name?"

"Yeah. Kimberly Starr."

———

When Heat and Rook left Interrogation, Detective Ochoa was waiting in the observation booth, staring through the magic mirror at Gable. "Can't believe you wrapped this interview and didn't ask the most important question." When he had their attention, he continued, "How did that swamp doofus get a babe like Kimberly Starr into the sack?"

"You are so superficial," said Heat. "It's not about looks. It's about money."

———

"Weird Al," said Raley when the three of them entered the squad room. " 'It's Raining Men'? My guess is Al Yankovic."

"Nope," said Rook. "The song was written by . . . Ah, I could tell you, but where's the sport in that? Keep trying. But no fair Googling."

Nikki Heat sat at her desk and swiveled to face the bullpen. "Can I break up tonight's episode of *Jeopardy!* for a little police work? Ochoa, what do we know about Kimberly Starr's alibi?"

"We know it doesn't check out. Well, I know, and now you do, too. She was at Dino-Bites today but left shortly after she got there. Her kid ate his tar pit soup with the nanny, not his mom."

"What time did she leave?" asked Heat.

Ochoa flipped through his notes. "Manager says around one, one-fifteen."

Rook said, "I told you I got a vibe off Kimberly Starr, didn't I?"

"You like Kimberly Starr as a suspect?" asked Raley.

"Here's how it spins for me." Rook sat on Heat's desk. She noticed him wince from the rib kicks he'd taken and wished he would get himself checked out. "Our adoring trophy wife-and-mother has been getting sweet lovin' on the side. Her punch pal Barry, no looker he, claims she dropped him like a sack of hammers when his hedge fund cratered and his money supply pinched off. Hence today's assault. Who knows, maybe our dead gazillionaire kept the little missus on a short money leash. Or maybe Matthew Starr found out about her affair and she killed him."

Raley nodded. "Does look bad that she was cheating on him."

"I have a novel idea," said Heat. "Why don't we do this thing called an investigation? Gather evidence, assemble some facts. Somehow that might sound better in court than, 'Here's how it spins for me.'"

Rook took out his Moleskine notebook. "Excellent. This is all going to be swell in my article." He clicked a pen theatrically to needle her. "So what do we investigate first?"

"Raley," said Heat, "check out the Beacon, see if Gable's been a regular there. Show them a picture of Mrs. Starr while you're at it. Ochoa, how soon can you pull together a background check on our trophy widow?"

"How's first thing tomorrow?"

"OK, but I was kind of hoping for first thing tomorrow."

Rook raised his hand. "Question? Why not just

pick her up? I would love to see what happens when you set her down in your hall of mirrors."

"Much as I live my day to provide you with top entertainment, I'm going to hold off until I learn a little more. Besides, she's not going anywhere."

———

The next morning, amid flickering lights, City Hall put out the word for New Yorkers to curtail air-conditioning use and strenuous activity. For Nikki Heat that meant her close-quarter combat training with Don, the ex-SEAL, would be done with the gym windows open. His brand of training combined Brazilian jujitsu, boxing, and judo. Their sparring began at five-thirty with a round of grapples and rolls in eighty-two degrees and humidity to match. After the second water break Don asked her if she wanted to call it. Heat answered with a takedown and a textbook blood choke and release. She seemed to thrive on the adverse weather, fed on it, really. Rather than wearing her down, the gasping intensity of morning combat pushed out the noise of her life and left her in a quiet inner place. It was the same way when she and Don had sex from time to time. She decided if she had nothing going, maybe next week she'd suggest another after-hours session to her trainer, with benefits. Anything to get her heart rate up.

Lauren Parry led Nikki Heat and her reporter tag-along through the autopsy room to the body of Matthew Starr. "As always, Nik," said the medical examiner, "we don't have the tox work yet, but barring lab surprises, I'm writing up cause of death as blunt force trauma due to a fall from an unreasonable height."

"And what box are you going to check, suicide or homicide?"

"That's why I called you down. I found something that indicates homicide." The M.E. circled to the other side of the corpse and lifted the sheet. "We've got a series of fist-sized contusions on the torso. These tell me he got worked over sometime day of. Look closely at this one here."

Heat and Rook leaned in at the same time and she drew away to avoid a repeat of the balcony perfume ad. He stepped back and gestured a be-my-guest. "Very distinct bruising," said the detective. "I can make out knuckles, and what's this hexagonal shape from, a ring?" She stepped out to let Rook in and said, "Lauren, I'd like to get a photo of that one."

Her friend was already holding out a print to her. "I'll put it up on the server so you can copy it, and what did you do, get in a bar fight?" She was looking at Rook.

"Me? Oh, just a little line-of-duty action yesterday. Cool, huh?"

"Way you're standing, my guess is intercostal injury right here." She touched his ribs without pressing. "Does it hurt when you laugh?"

Heat said, "Say 'line-of-duty action' again, that's funny."

———

Detective Heat taped autopsy blowups on the bull pen whiteboard to prep for her unit case meeting. She drew a line with a dry-erase marker and wrote the names of the Forensics print matches off the balcony doors at the Guilford: Matthew Starr, Kimberly Starr, Matty Starr, and Agda the nanny. Raley arrived early with a bag of donut holes and confirmed Barry Gable's regular hotel bookings at the Beacon. Reception and service staff had identified Kimberly Starr as his steady guest. "Oh, and the lab work came in on Barry the Beacon Beefcake's blue jeans," he added. "No match to those balcony fibers."

"No surprise," Heat said. "But it was fun to see how fast he was willing to drop his pants."

"Fun for you," said Rook.

She smiled. "Yeah, definitely one of the perks of the job watching sweaty clods shimmy out of their knockoff jeans."

Ochoa rushed in, speaking as he crossed to them. "I'm late, it was worth it, shut up." He pulled some printouts from his messenger bag. "I just finished the background check on Kimberly Starr. Or shall I say Laldomina Batastini of Queens, New Yawk?"

The unit drew close as he read bits from the file. "Our preppy Stepford Mom was born and raised in Astoria above a mani-pedi salon on Steinway. About as far from the Connecticut girls' schools and riding academies as you can get. Let's see, high school dropout . . . and she's got a rap sheet." He handed it to Heat.

"No felonies," she said. "Juvie busts for shoplifting, and later for pot. One DUI . . . Oh, and, here we go, busted twice at nineteen for lewd acts with customers. Young Laldomina was a lap dancer at numerous clubs near the airport, performing under the name Samantha."

"I always said *Sex and the City* fostered poor role modeling," said Rook.

Ochoa took the sheet back from Heat and said, "I talked to a pal in Vice. Kimberly, Samantha, whatever, hooked up with some guy, a regular at the club, and she married him. She was twenty. He was sixty-eight and loaded. Her sugar daddy was from Greenwich old money and wanted to take her to the yacht club, so he—"

"Let me guess," said Rook, "he got her a Henry Higgins," drawing blank stares from Roach.

"I speak musical theater," Heat said. Right up there with animated films, Broadway was Nikki's great escape from her work on the other streets of New York—when she could swing a ticket. "He means her new husband got his exotic dancer a charm tutor for a presentability makeover. A class on class."

Rook added, "And a Kimberly Starr is born."

"The husband died when she was twenty-one. I know what you're thinking, so I double-checked. Natural causes. Heart attack. The man left her one million dollars."

"And a taste for more. Nice work, Detective." Ochoa popped a victory donut hole, and Heat continued. "You and Raley keep a tail on her. Loose one. I'm not ready to show my hand until I see what else shakes free on other fronts."

Heat had learned years ago that most detective work is grunt work done pounding the phones,

combing files, and searching the department's database. The calls she had made the afternoon before,
to Starr's attorney and detectives working com-
plaints against persons, had paid off that morning
with a file of people who'd made threats on the real
estate developer's life. She grabbed her shoulder bag
and signed out, figuring it was about time to show
her celeb magazine writer what fieldwork was all
about, but she couldn't find him.

She had almost left Rook behind when she came
upon him standing in the precinct lobby, very occupied. A drop-dead-stunning woman was smoothing the collar of his shirt. The stunner barked out a
laugh, shrieked, "Oh, Jamie!" then pulled her designer sunglasses off her head to shake her raven
shoulder-length hair. Heat watched her lean in close
to whisper, pressing her D-cups right against him.
He didn't step back, either. What was Rook doing,
making a perfume ad with every damn woman in
the city? Then she stopped herself. Why do I care?
she thought. It bothered her that it even bothered
her. So she blew it off and walked out, mad at herself for her one look back at them.

"So what's the point of this exercise?" Rook
asked on the drive uptown.

"It's something we professionals in the world of
detection call detecting." Heat picked the file out
of her driver's door pocket and passed it to him.
"Somebody wanted Matthew Starr dead. A few
you'll see in there made actual threats. Others just
found him inconvenient."

"So this is about eliminating them?"

"This is about asking questions and seeing where

the answers lead. Sometimes you flush out a suspect, sometimes you're getting information you didn't have that takes you somewhere else. Was that another member of the Jameson Rook fan club back there?"

Rook chuckled. "Bree? Oh, hell, no."

They rode another block in silence. "Because she seemed like a big fan."

"Bree Flax is a big fan, all right. Of Bree Flax. She's a freelancer for the local glossy mags, always on the prowl for the true crime piece she can upsell into an instant book. You know, ripped from the headlines. That operetta back there was all about getting me to cough up some inside stuff on Matthew Starr."

"She seemed . . . focused."

Rook smiled. "By the way, that's F-l-a-x, just in case you want to run a check."

"And what's that supposed to mean?"

Rook didn't answer. He just gave her a smile that made her blush. She turned away and pretended to watch cross traffic out her side window, worried about what he saw on her face.

Up on the top floor of the Marlowe Building there was no heat wave. In the enveloping coolness of his corner office, Omar Lamb listened to the recording of his threatening phone call to Matthew Starr. He was placid, his palms rested flat and relaxed on his leather blotter as the tiny speaker on the digital recorder vibrated with an enraged version of him spouting expletives and graphic descriptions of what he would do to Starr, including where on his body he would insert an assortment of weapons, tools, and firearms. When it was over, he turned it off and said nothing. Nikki Heat studied the real estate developer, his gym-rat body, sunken cheeks, and you're-dead-to-me eyes. A surplus of refrigerated air whispered from unseen vents to fill the silence. She was chilly for the first time in four days. It was a lot like the morgue.

"He actually recorded me saying that?"

"Mr. Starr's attorney provided it when he put the complaint on the record."

"Come on, Detective, people say they're going to kill people all the time."

"And sometimes they do it."

Rook observed from a perch on the windowsill, where he divided his attention between Omar Lamb and the lone blader braving the heat in the Trump Skating Rink in Central Park thirty-five stories below. So far, Heat thought, thank God he seemed content to follow her instructions not to butt in.

"Matthew Starr was a titan of this industry who will be missed. I respected him and deeply regret that phone call I made. His death was a loss to us all."

Heat had known on sight that this guy was going to take some work. He didn't even look at her shield when she walked in, didn't ask for his lawyer. Said he had nothing to hide, and if he did, she sensed he was too smart to say anything stupid. This was not a man to fall for the ol' Zoo Lockup routine. So she danced with him, looking for her opening. "Why all the bile?" she asked. "What got you so lathered up about a business rival?"

"My rival? Matthew Starr didn't have the skill set to qualify as my rival. Matthew Starr needed a stepladder just to kiss my ass."

There it was. She'd found an open sore on Omar Lamb's tough hide. His ego. Heat picked at it. She laughed at him. "Bull."

"Bull? Did you just say 'bull' to me?" Lamb jerked to his feet and hero-strode from behind the fortress of his desk to face her. This was definitely not going to be a perfume ad.

She didn't flinch. "Starr had title to more property than anyone in the city. A lot more than you, right?"

"Garbage addresses, environmental restrictions, limited air rights . . . What does more mean when it's more crap?"

"Sounds like rival talk to me. Must have felt bad to unzip and flop 'em on the table and come up short."

"Hey, you want to measure something?" This was good. She loved it when she rattled the tough boys into talking. "Measure all the properties Matthew Starr stole from under my nose." With a manicured finger, he poked her shoulder to punctuate each item on his list: "He fudged permits, he bribed inspectors, he underbid, he oversold, he underdelivered."

"Gee," said Heat, "it's almost enough to make you want to kill him."

Now the developer laughed. "Nice try. Listen. Yeah, I made threats to the guy in the past.

Operative word: past. Years ago. Look at his numbers now. Even without the recession Starr was a spent force. I didn't need to kill him. He was a dead man walking."

"So says his rival."

"Don't believe me? Go to any of his job sites."

"And see what?"

"Hey, you expect me to do all your work?"

At the door, as they were leaving, Lamb said, "One thing. I read in the *Post* he fell six stories."

"That's right, six," said Rook. The first thing he said and it was a shot at her.

"Did he suffer?"

"No," said Heat, "he died instantly."

Lamb grinned, showing a row of laminates. "Well, maybe in hell, then."

———

Their gold Crown Victoria rolled south on the West Side Highway, the AC blasting and humidity condensing into wisps of fog around the dashboard vents. "So what's your take?" asked Rook. "Think Omar offed him?"

"Could have. I've got him on my list, but that's not what that was about."

"Glad to hear it, Detective. No rush, there's only, what, three million more people to meet and greet in New York. Not that you aren't a charming interviewer."

"God, you're impatient. Did you tell Bono you were tired of relief stations in Ethiopia? Did you push the Chechen warlords to pick up the pace? 'Come on, Ivan, let's see a little warlord action?'"

"I just like to cut through, is all."

She was glad for this sea change. It got her off his personal radar, so she ran with it. "You want to actually learn something on this ride-along project of yours? Try listening. This is police work. Killers don't walk around with bloody knives on them, and the home invasion crews don't dress like the Hamburglar. You talk to people. You listen. You see if they're hiding something. Or sometimes, if you pay attention, you get insight; information you didn't have before."

"Like what?"

"Like this."

As they pulled up, the Starr construction site on Eleventh Avenue on the lower west side was dead. Almost noon, and no sign of work. No sign of workers. It was a ghost site. She parked off the street, on the dirt strip between the curb and the plywood construction fence. When they got out, Nikki said, "You hear what I hear?"

"Nothing."

"Exactly."

"Yo, miss, this is a closed site, you gotta go." A guy in a hard hat and no shirt kicked up dust on his way to meet them as they squeezed in the chain-link gate. With that swagger and that gut, Heat could picture whooping New Jersey housewives sticking dollar bills in his Speedo. "You, too, buddy," he said to Rook. "*Adios.*" Heat flashed tin and Shirtless mouthed the F-bomb.

"*Bueno,*" said Rook.

Nikki Heat squared herself to the guy. "I want to talk to your foreman."

"I don't think that's possible."

She cupped a hand to her ear. "Did you hear me ask? No, I definitely don't think it was a question."

"Oh, my God. Jamie?" The voice came from across the yard. A skinny man in sunglasses and blue satin warm-ups stood in the open door of the site trailer.

"Heyyy," called Rook. "Fat Tommy!"

The man waved them over. "Come on, hurry up, I'm not air-conditioning the Tri-State Area, you know."

Inside the double-wide, Heat sat with Rook and his pal, but she didn't take the chair she was offered. Although there were no current warrants on him, Tomasso "Fat Tommy" Nicolosi ran enforcement for one of the New York families, and caution dictated she not get wedged in between the table and the Masonite wall. She took the outside seat and angled it so her back wasn't to the door. Through his smile, the look she got from Fat Tommy said he knew exactly what she was doing.

"What happened to you, Fat Tommy? You're not fat."

"The wife's got me doing NutroMinder. God, has it been that long since I saw you?" He took off his tinted glasses and turned his pouchy eyes to Heat. "Jamie was doing this article a couple of years ago on 'the life' on Staten Island. We got to know each other, he seemed OK for a reporter, and what do you know, he ends up doing me a little favor." Heat smiled thinly and he laughed. "Don't worry, Detective, it was legal."

"I just killed a couple guys is all."

"Kidder. Have you noticed he's a kidder?"

"Oh, Jamie? He has me going all the time," she said.

"OK," said Fat Tommy, "I can see this ain't no social call, so go ahead. The two of us can catch up later."

"This is Matthew Starr's project, right?"

"It was until yesterday afternoon." The wiseguy had one of those faces that was perennially balanced between menace and amusement. Heat could have read his answer as a joke or a fact.

"Mind if I ask what your role is here?"

He sat back, relaxed, a man in his element. "Labor consultation."

"I notice there's no labor taking place."

"Damn straight. We shut it down a week ago. Starr stiffed us. You know, nonpayment on our, ah, agreement."

"What sort of agreement was that, Mr. Nicolosi?" She knew full well what it was. They called it lots of things. Mostly the unofficial construction tax. The going rate was two percent. And it didn't go to the government.

He turned to Rook. "I like your girlfriend."

"Say that again and I'll break your knees," she said. He looked at her and decided she could, then smiled. "Not, huh?" Rook affirmed that with a mild shake of his head.

"Huh," said Fat Tommy, "fooled me. Anyways, I owe Jamie a solid, so I'll answer your question. What sort of agreement? Let's call it the expediting fee. Yeah, that works."

"Why did Starr stop paying, Tommy?" Rook

was asking questions, but she found herself glad for his participation, tag-teaming from angles she couldn't take. Call it good cop/no cop.

"Hey, man, the guy was strapped. He said he was and we checked. Underwater so deep he was sprouting gills." Fat Tommy laughed at his joke and added, "We don't care."

"Do guys ever get killed for that?" asked Rook.

"For that? Come on. We just shut it down and let nature take its course." He shrugged. "OK, sometimes guys get dead for that, but not this time. At least not at this early stage." He crossed his arms and grinned. "For real. Not his girlfriend, huh?"

———

Over *carnitas burritos* at Chipotle, Heat asked Rook if he still felt like they were wheel-spinning. Before he answered, Rook slurped the ice cubes with his straw, vacuuming for more Diet Coke. "Well," he said, finally, "I don't think we've met Matthew Starr's killer today, if that's what you mean." Fat Tommy drifted in and out of her mind as a possible, but she kept it to herself. He read her though, adding, "And if Fat Tommy tells me he didn't do Matthew Starr, that's all I need."

"You, sir, are an investigative force unto yourself."

"I know the guy."

"Remember what I said before? Ask questions and see where the answers lead? For me they've led to a picture of Matthew Starr that doesn't fit the image. What did he put out there?" She drew a frame in the air with both hands. "Successful, respectable, and most of all, well funded. OK, now ask yourself this. All that money and he couldn't pay his mob tax? The spiff that kept concrete pouring and iron rising?" She balled up her wrapper and stood. "Let's go."

"Where to?"

"To talk to Starr's money guy. Look at it this way, it's another chance for you to see me at my charming best."

———

Heat's ears popped on the express elevator to the penthouse floor of Starr Pointe, Matthew Starr's headquarters on West 57th near Carnegie Hall. When they stepped into the opulent lobby, she whispered to Rook, "Do you notice this office is one floor higher than Omar Lamb's?"

"I think it's safe to say that, even up to the end, Matthew Starr was acutely aware of heights."

They announced themselves to the receptionist. As they waited, Nikki Heat perused a gallery of framed photos of Matthew Starr with presidents, royals, and celebrities. On the far wall, a flat screen soundlessly looped Starr Development's corporate marketing video. In a glass trophy case, beneath heroic scale models of Starr office buildings and gleaming replicas of the corporate G-4 and Sikorsky-76, stretched a long row of Waterford crystal jars filled with dirt. Above each, a photograph of Matthew Starr breaking ground from the site that had filled the jar.

The carved mahogany door opened, and a man in shirtsleeves and a tie stepped out and extended his hand. "Detective Heat? Noah Paxton, I am . . . Rather, I was Matthew's financial advisor." As they shook hands, he gave her a sad smile. "We're all still in shock."

"I'm very sorry for your loss," she said. "This is Jameson Rook."

"The writer?"

"Yes," he said.

"OK . . . ," said Paxton, accepting Rook's presence as if recognizing there was a walrus on the front lawn but not understanding why. "Shall we go to my office?" He opened the mahogany door for them and they entered Matthew Starr's world headquarters.

Heat and Rook both stopped. The entire floor was empty. Glass cubicles to the left and right were vacant of people and desks. Phone and Ethernet cables lay disconnected on floors. Plants sat dead and dying. The near wall showed the ghost of a bulletin board. The detective tried to reconcile the posh lobby she had just left with this vacant space on the other side of the threshold. "Excuse me," she said to Paxton, "Matthew Starr just died yesterday. Have you already begun to close the business?"

"Oh this? No, not at all. We cleared this out a year ago."

As the door closed behind them, the floor was so deserted the snap of the metal tongue latch actually echoed.

THREE

Heat and Rook trailed two steps behind Noah Paxton as he led them through the vacant offices and cubicles of Starr Real Estate Development's headquarters. In stark contrast to the go-go opulence of its lobby, the penthouse floor of the thirty-six-story Starr Pointe tower had the hollow sound and feel of a foreclosed grand hotel after the creditors had swarmed it for everything that wasn't nailed down. The space had an eerie, post-biodisaster feel. Not merely empty, abandoned.

Paxton gestured to an open door and they entered his office, the only functioning one Heat had seen. He was listed as the corporation's financial officer, but his furniture was a combo plate of Staples, Office Depot, and hand-me-down Levenger. Neat and functional but not the trappings of a Manhattan corporate head, even for a midsize firm. And certainly not befitting the Starr brand of swank and swagger.

Nikki Heat heard a small chuckle from Rook and followed the reporter's line of sight to the poster of the kitty dangling from the branch. Under its rear paws was the caption "Hang in there, baby." Paxton didn't offer coffee from his four-hour-old pot; they just took seats in mismatched guest chairs. He established himself in the inner curve of his horseshoe workstation.

"We came to ask for your help understanding the financial state of Matthew Starr's business," said the detective, making it sound light and neutral. Noah Paxton was edgy. She was used to that; people got spooked by the badge same as they were by doctors' white coats. But this guy couldn't hold eye contact, a basic red flag. He looked distracted, like he was worried he'd left his iron plugged in at home and wanted to get there, and right now. Play it out mellow, she decided. See what tumbles when he lets himself relax.

He looked again at her business card and said, "Of course, Detective Heat," once more trying to hold her look but only half making it. He made a deal of studying the card again. "There's one thing, though," he added.

"Go ahead," she said, alert for the dodge or the call to the bull pen for a shyster.

"No offense, Mr. Rook."

"Jamie, please."

"If I have to answer police questions, that's one thing. But if you're going to quote me for some exposé in *Vanity Fair* or *First Press*—"

"Not to worry," said Rook.

"—I owe it to Matthew's memory and to his family not to air his business in the pages of some magazine."

"I am only here on background for an article I'm doing on Detective Heat and her squad. Whatever you say about Matthew Starr's business will be off the record. I did it for Mick Jagger, I can do it for you."

Heat could not believe what she'd just heard.

The bald ego of a celebrity journalist at work. Not only name-dropping but favor-dropping. And it sure didn't help get Paxton in the mood.

"This is a horrible time to do this," he said, trying her now that Rook had met his terms. He turned away to study whatever was on his flat-screen and then brought it back to her. "He hasn't even been dead twenty-four hours. I'm in the middle of . . . Well, you can imagine. How about tomorrow?"

"I only have a few questions."

"Yes, but the files are, well, I'm saying I don't keep everything," he snapped his fingers, "right at hand. Tell you what. Why don't you tell me what you need, and I can have it ready when you come back?"

All right. She had tried smooth 'n' soothe. He was still dodgy, and now he had it in his head that he could stiff-arm her out of there in lieu of an appointment at his convenience. Time, she decided, to switch tactics.

"Noah. May I call you Noah? Because I want to keep this friendly while I tell you how this is going to go. OK? This is a homicide investigation. I am not only going to ask you some questions right here and right now, I expect you to answer them. And I'm not worried about whether you have your figures," she snapped her fingers, "right at hand. Know why? I'm going to have our forensic accountants go through your books. So you can decide right now how friendly this can be. Do we understand each other, Noah?"

After the smallest pause, the man put it right

out there for her in a headline. "Matthew Starr was broke." A calm, measured statement of fact. What else was it Nikki Heat heard behind it? Candor, for sure. He was looking her directly in the eye when he said it; there was no aversion now, only clarity. But there was something else, like he was reaching out to her, showing some other feeling, and when she struggled to grasp the word for it, Noah Paxton said it as if he were in her mind with her. "I feel so relieved." There it was, relief. "Finally, I can talk about this."

For the next hour Noah did more than just talk. He unfolded the story of how a personality-branded wealth machine had been flown to great heights piloted by the flamboyant Matthew Starr, amassing capital, acquiring key properties, and building iconic towers that indelibly shaped the world's view of the New York skyline, and then had rapidly been imploded by Starr's own hand. It was the tale of a boom-to-bust crash in a sharp downward spiral.

Paxton, who corporate records said was thirty-five, had joined the firm with his newly minted MBA near the peak of the company's upswing. His sure handling of creative financing to greenlight construction of the avant-garde StarrScraper in Times Square had cemented him as Matthew Starr's most trusted employee. Perhaps because he was forthcoming now, Nikki looked at Noah Paxton and saw a trustworthiness about him. He was solid, capable, a man who would get you through the battle.

She didn't have much experience with men like

him. She had seen them, of course, on the Metro-North train to Darien at the end of the day, with ties loosened, sipping a can of beer from the bar car with a colleague or neighbor. Or with wives in Anne Klein at *prix fixe* dinners before curtain on Broadway. That might have been Nikki in the candlelight with the Absolut cosmo, filling him in on the teacher conference and planning the week at the Vineyard, if things had gone differently for her. She wondered what it must be like to have that lawn and the reliable life with a Noah.

"That trust Matthew had in me," he continued, "was a two-edger. I got to know all the secrets. But I also got to know all the secrets."

The ugliest secret, according to Noah Paxton, was that his Midas-touch boss was driving his company into the ground and couldn't be stopped.

"Show me," said the detective.

"You mean, like, now?"

"Now or in a more . . . ," she knew this dance and let her pause do its work, "formal setting. You choose."

He opened a series of spreadsheets on his Mac and invited them inside the U of his workstation to view them on the big flat-screen. The figures were startling. Then came a progression of graphs chronicling the journey of a vital real estate developer who was practically laser-printing money until he plummeted off a red-ink cliff, well ahead of the mortgage meltdown and ensuing foreclosure debacle.

"So this isn't about hard times in a bad economy?" asked Heat, pointing over his shoulder at what looked to her like an escalator to the basement painted red.

"No. And thank you for not touching my monitor. I never understood why people have to touch computer screens when they point."

"I know. The same people who need to mime telephones with their fingers when they say call me." When they laughed, she got a whiff of something citrus-y and clean off him. L'Occitane, she guessed.

"How did he manage to stay in business?" asked Rook when they retook their seats.

"That was my job and it wasn't easy." And then, with a disclosure look to Nikki, "And I promise you it was all legal."

All she said was "Just tell me how."

"Simple. I started liquidating and divesting. But when the real estate bust came along, it ate our lunch. That's when we ran into the buzz saw with financing. And then we hit a snag maintaining our labor relations. You may not know it, but our sites are not working these days." Nikki nodded and swept her glance to Fat Tommy's champion. "We couldn't service our debt, we couldn't keep construction going. Here's a simple rule: no building, no rent."

Heat said, "It sounds like a nightmare."

"To have a nightmare, you have to be able to sleep." On the office couch she noted the folded blanket with the pillow resting on it. "Let's call it a living hell. And that's just the business finances. I haven't even told you about his personal money problems."

"Don't most CEOs build a firewall between their corporate and personal finances?" asked Rook.

Damn good question. He's finally acting like a reporter, thought Nikki, so she jumped aboard. "I always thought the idea was to structure things so a failure in business doesn't wipe out the personal and vice versa."

"And that's how I built it when I took over his family finances, too. But, you see, both sides of the firewall were blazing cash. You see . . ." A sober look came over him and his young face gained twenty years. "Now, I truly need assurance this is off the record. And won't leave this room."

"I can promise that," said Rook.

"I can't," said Detective Heat. "I told you. This is a homicide investigation."

"I see," he said. And then he took the plunge. "Matthew Starr indulged some personal habits that compromised his personal fortune. He did damage." Noah paused then took the plunge. "First, he was a compulsive gambler. And by that, I mean losing gambler. He not only hemorrhaged cash to casinos from Atlantic City to Mohegan Sun, he bet the horses and on football with local bookies. He was in debt to some of these characters for serious money."

Heat wrote a single word on her spiral pad: "Bookies."

"And then, there were the prostitutes. Matthew had certain, um, tastes we don't need to get into— unless you say so, I mean—and he satisfied them with very expensive, high-end call girls."

Rook couldn't help himself. "Now, that's a

marriage of terms that always tickles me, 'high-end' and 'call girl.' Like, is that your job status or a sexual position?" He earned their silent stares and muttered, "Sorry. Go on."

"I can detail the burn rate of the money for you, but suffice it to say these and a few other habits ate away at him financially. Last spring we had to sell the family estate in the Hamptons."

"Stormfall." Nikki reflected on Kimberly Starr's upset that the murder never would have happened if they had been away in the Hamptons. Now she understood its depth and irony.

"Yes, Stormfall. I don't need to tell you about the bath we took on that property in this market. Sold it to some reality show celebrity and lost millions. The cash from the sale barely made a dent in Matthew's debt. Things got so bad he ordered me to stop payments on his life insurance, which he let lapse against my advice."

Heat jotted two new words. "No insurance." "Did Mrs. Starr know about that?" In the periphery of her vision, she saw Rook lean forward in his chair.

"Yes, she did. I did my best to shelter Kimberly from the seedier details of Matthew's spending, but she knew about the life insurance. I was there when Matthew told her."

"And what was her reaction?"

"She said . . ." He paused. "You have to understand, she was upset."

"What did she say, Noah? Her exact words, if you remember."

"She said, 'I hate you. You're not even any good to me dead.'"

————

In the car on the ride back to the precinct, Rook went right to the grieving widow. "Come on, Detective Heat, 'No good to me dead'? You talk about gathering information that paints a picture. What about this portrait we're seeing of Samantha the Lap Dancer?"

"But she knew there was no life insurance. Where's the motive?"

He grinned and needled her again. "Gee, I don't know, but my advice is to keep asking questions and see where they lead."

"Bite me."

"Oh, are you talking tough with me now that you have other irons in the fire?"

"I'm talking tough because you are an ass. And I don't get what you mean by other irons."

"I mean Noah Paxton. I didn't know whether to throw a bucket of water on you or fake a cell phone call to leave you two alone."

"This is why you're a magazine writer who only *plays* cop. Your imagination is greater than your grasp of facts."

He shrugged. "Guess I was wrong." Then he smiled that smile, the one that made her face flush. And there she was again, feeling this torment over Rook for something she should have laughed off. Instead, she popped in her earbud and speed-dialed Raley.

"Rales, it's me." She angled her head toward Rook and sounded brisk and formal, so he wouldn't miss her meaning, even though she did radiate subtext. "I want you to run a background on Matthew Starr's financial guy. Name's Noah Paxton. Just see what kicks out, priors, warrants, the usual."

After she hung up, Rook looked amused. This was going nowhere she liked, but she had to say it. "What." And when he didn't answer, "What?"

"You forgot to have him run a check on Paxton's cologne." And then he opened a magazine and read.

———————

Detective Raley looked up from his computer when Heat and Rook came into the bull pen. "That guy you wanted me to run, Noah Paxton?"

"Yeah? You got something?"

"Not so far. But he called for you just now."

Nikki avoided the playground look she was getting from Rook and surveyed the stack of messages on her desk. Noah Paxton's was on top. She didn't pick it up. Instead, she asked Raley if Ochoa had checked in. He was on Kimberly Starr surveillance. The widow was spending the afternoon at Bergdorf Goodman.

"I hear shopping is a balm for the bereaved," said Rook. "Or maybe the merry widow is returning a few designer rags for ready cash."

When Rook disappeared into the men's room, Heat dialed Noah Paxton. She had nothing to hide from Rook; she just didn't want to deal with his preadolescent taunts. Or see that smile that chapped her ass. She cursed the mayor for whatever payback made her have to deal with him.

When Paxton got on the line, he said, "I located

those life insurance documents you said you wanted to see."

"Good, I'll send someone over."

"I also got a visit from those forensic accountants you were talking about. They copied all my data and left. You weren't kidding."

"Your tax dollars at work." She couldn't resist adding, "You do pay your taxes?"

"Yes, but you don't have to take my word for it. Your CPAs with badges and guns look like they'll be able to tell you."

"Count on it."

"Listen, I know I wasn't the most cooperative."

"You did all right. After I threatened you."

"I want to apologize for that. I'm finding I don't do well with grief."

"You wouldn't be the first, Noah," said Nikki. "Trust me."

———

She sat alone that night at the center row of the movie theater laughing and munching popcorn. Nikki Heat was transfixed, swept up in an innocent story and spellbound by the eye candy of digital animation. Like a house tied to a thousand balloons, she was transported. Just over ninety minutes later she carried the weight again on her walk home in the mugginess of the heat wave, which brought fusty odors up out of subway grates and, even in the dark, radiated the day's swelter off buildings as she passed them.

At times like these, without the work to hide in, without the martial arts to quiet it, the replay always came. It had been ten years, and yet it was also last week and last night and all of them thatched together. Time didn't matter. It never did when she replayed The Night.

It was her first Thanksgiving break from college since her parents divorced. Nikki had spent the day shopping with her mother, a Thanksgiving Eve tradition transformed into a holy mission by her mom's new singleness. This was a daughter determined to make this not so much the best Thanksgiving ever, but as close to normal as could be achieved given the empty chair at the head of the table and the ghosts of happier years.

The two squeezed around each other as they always had in the New York apartment–sized kitchen that night, making pies for the next day. Over tandem rolling pins and chilled dough, Nikki defended her desire to change majors from English to Theater. Where were the cinnamon sticks? How could they have forgotten the cinnamon sticks? Ground cinnamon never flew in her mother's holiday pies. She grated her own from a stick, and how could they have overlooked that on their list?

Nikki felt like a Lotto winner when she found a jar of them on the spice aisle at the Morton Williams on Park Avenue South. For insurance, she took out her cell phone and called the apartment. It rang and rang. When the message machine kicked on, she wondered if her mom couldn't hear the phone over her mixer. But then she picked up. Over the squeal of recorder feedback she apologized but she had been wiping butter off her hands. Nikki hated the sharp reverb of the answering machine, but her mother never knew how to turn that damn thing off without disconnecting. Last call before closing, did she need anything else from the market? She waited while her mom carried the portable to check on evaporated milk.

And then Nikki heard glass crash. And her mother's scream. Her limbs went weak and she called for her mom. Heads turned from the check stands. Another scream. As she heard the phone on the other end drop, Nikki dropped the jar of cinnamon sticks and ran to the door. Damn, the in door. She brute-forced it open and ran out in the street, nearly getting clipped by a delivery guy on a bicycle. Two blocks away. She held the cell phone to her ear as she ran, pleading for her mom to say something, pick up the phone, what's wrong? She heard a man's voice, sounds of a scuffle. Her mother's whimper and her body dropping next to the phone. A *tah-tang* of metal bouncing on the kitchen floor. One block to go. A clink of bottles in the fridge door. The snap-hiss of a pop top. Foot-steps. Silence. And then, her mother's weak and failing moan. And then just a whisper. "Nikki . . ."

FOUR

Nikki didn't go home following the movie after all. She stood on the sidewalk in the warm, spongy air of the summer night looking up at her apartment, the one where she had lived as a girl and that she had left to go to college in Boston, and then left again on an errand to buy cinnamon sticks because ground wouldn't do. The only thing up there in that two-bedroom was solitude without peace. She could be nineteen again walking into a kitchen where her mother's blood was pooling under the refrigerator, or, if she could bat the image balloons away, she could catch some news on the tube and hear about more crimes—heat-related, the Team Coverage would say. Heat-related crime. There was a time when that had made Nikki Heat smile.

She weighed texting Don, to see if her combat trainer was up for a beer and some close-quarter bedroom grapples, against the alternative of letting some late night comic in a suit help her escape without the crowded bathroom in the morning. There was another alternative.

Twenty minutes later, in her empty precinct squad room, the detective swiveled in her chair to contemplate the whiteboard. She already had it burnished in her head, all the elements-to-date pasted and scrawled inside that frame which did not yet reveal a picture: the list of fingerprint matches; the green five-by-seven index card with its bullet points of Kimberly Starr's alibis and prior lives; photos of Matthew Starr's body where he hit the sidewalk; photos from the M.E. of the punch bruising on Starr's torso with the distinctive hexagonal mark left by a ring.

She rose and walked up to the ring mark photo. More than studying its size and shape, the detective listened to it, knowing that at any time any piece of evidence could gain a voice. This photo, above all other puzzle pieces on the board, was whispering to her. It had been in her ear all day, and its whisper was the song that had drawn her to the squad room in the stillness of night so she could hear it clearly. What it whispered was a question: "Why would a killer who tossed a man over a balcony also beat him with nonlethal blows?" These bruises weren't random contusions from any scuffle. They were precise and patterned, some even overlapping. Don, her combat boxing instructor, called it "painting" your opponent.

One of the first things Nikki Heat had implemented when she took command of her homicide unit was a system to facilitate information sharing. She logged on the server and opened the read-only file OCHOA. Scrolling through pages, she came to his witness interview with the doorman at the Guilford. Love that Ochoa, she thought. His keyboard skills are crap, but he took great notes and asked the right questions.

Q: Had vic lef bdg anytm drng curse of morng?
A: N.

Nikki closed Ochoa's file and looked at the clock. She could text her boss, but he might not see it. Like if he was sleeping. Drumming her fingers on the phone was only making it later, so she punched his number. On the fourth ring Heat cleared her throat, preparing to leave a voice mail, but Montrose picked up. His hello was not sleepy and she could hear the TV blasting the weather forecast. "Hope it's not too late to call, Captain."

"If it is too late, it's too late to hope. What's up?"

"I came in to screen that surveillance cam video from the Guilford and it's not here yet. Do you know where it is?"

Her boss covered the phone and said something muffled to his wife. When he came back to Nikki, the TV sound was off. He said, "I got a call tonight during dinner from the attorney representing their residents board. This is a building with wealthy tenants sensitive about privacy issues."

"Do they have issues with their fellow tenants hurtling past their windows?"

"You trying to convince *me*? For them to give it up it will take a court order. I'm looking at the clock and thinking we'll wait to find a judge to issue one in the morning." He heard her sigh because she made sure he did. Heat couldn't stand effectively losing another day waiting for a court order. "Nikki, get some sleep," he said with his usual gentle touch. "We'll get it for you sometime tomorrow."

Of course the skipper was right. Waking a judge to cut a warrant was capital you spent on high-priority matters against a ticking clock. To most judges this was just another homicide, and she knew better than to push Captain Montrose to squander a chip like that. So she switched her desk lamp off.

Then she switched it back on. Rook was pals with a judge. Horace Simpson was a poker pal at the weekly game she always ducked when Rook invited her. Simpson was not as sexy a name drop as Jagger, but last she heard, none of the Stones was issuing warrants.

But hang on, she thought. Eager was one thing, owing a favor to Jameson Rook was another. And besides, she had overheard him boasting to Roach he had a dinner date with that groupie in the halter who crashed Nikki's crime scene. At this hour, Heat might be interrupting the application of his autograph to a new and more exciting body part.

So she picked up the phone and dialed Rook's cell.

"Heat," he said with no surprise. It was more a shout-out, like on *Cheers* when they'd holler, "Norm!" She listened for background noise, but why? Did she expect Kenny G and a champagne cork?

"Is this a bad time?"

"The caller ID says you're at the precinct." Evasion. Writer Monkey wasn't answering her question. Maybe if she threatened the Zoo Lockup.

"A cop's work is never done, and all that. Are you writing?"

"I'm in a town car. Just had an awesome meal at Balthazar." Then silence. She had called to screw with him, how did her head end up being the one messed with?

"You can give me your Zagat rating some other time, this is a business call," she told him, even as she wondered if his halter groupie knew not to wear cutoff jeans to a bistro, SoHo hip or otherwise. "I called to tell you don't come in for the morning meeting. It's off."

"Off? That's a first."

"The plan was for us to prep for a sit-down with Kimberly Starr tomorrow morning. That meeting's in question now."

Rook sounded beautifully alarmed. "How come? We need to get with her." She loved the urgency in his voice more than she felt guilty for playing him.

"The whole reason to see her is to screen surveillance pictures from the Guilford yesterday, but I can't get access to the surveillance tape without a warrant, and good luck reaching a judge tonight." Heat envisioned underwater video of a big mouth bass opening wide for the miracle lure on one of those sport fishing infomercials she saw too many of on her sleepless nights.

"I know a judge."

"Forget it."

"Horace Simpson."

Now Nikki was up, pacing the length of the bull pen, trying to keep the grin out of her voice as she said, "Listen to me, Rook. Stay out of this."

"I'll call you back."

"Rook, I am telling you no," she said in her best command voice.

"I know he's still up. Probably watching his

soft-core porn channel." And then Nikki heard the woman giggle in the background just as Rook hung up. Heat had gotten just what she wanted, but it somehow didn't feel like the win-win she'd envisioned. And why did she care? she asked herself yet again.

———

At ten o'clock the next morning, in the stickiness of what the tabloids were calling "The Summer of Simmer," Nikki Heat, Roach, and Rook met under the Guilford canopy holding two sets of twelve still frames from the lobby surveillance camera. Heat left Raley and Ochoa to show one array to the doorman while she and Rook entered the building for their appointment with Kimberly Starr.

As soon as the elevator doors closed, he started in. "You don't have to thank me."

"Why should I thank you? I specifically told you not to call that judge. As usual, you do what you please, meaning the opposite of what I say."

He paused to absorb the truth of that and said, "You're welcome." Then he broke out that shiteater of his, "It's the subtext thing. Oo, the air is thick with it this morning, Detective Heat." And was he even looking at her? No, he was tilted back enjoying the up-count of LED numbers, yet she still felt all X-rayed and naked and at a loss for words. The soft bell chimed a rescue signal on six. Damn him.

When it was Noah Paxton who opened the front door of Kimberly Starr's apartment, Nikki made a mental note to find out if the widow and the accountant were sleeping together. On an open murder case everything went on the table, and what belonged more on the "What If" list than a trophy wife with an appetite for cash and the man who handled the money hatching a pillow-talk conspiracy? But she let it go by saying, "This is a surprise."

"Kimberly's running late from her beauty appointment," said Paxton. "I was dropping off some documents for her to sign and she called to see if I'd keep you entertained until she got here."

"Nice to see she's focused on finding her husband's killer," said Rook.

"Welcome to my world. Trust me, Kimberly doesn't do focus." Detective Heat tried to read his tone. Was it true exasperation or cover?

"While we're waiting, I want you to look at some pictures." Heat found the same tapestry chair as she had on her last visit and took out a manila envelope. Paxton sat opposite her on the sofa, and she dealt two rows of four-by-six prints on the red lacquer coffee table in front of him. "Look carefully at each of these people. Tell me if any of them looks familiar."

Paxton studied each of the dozen photos. Nikki did what she always did during a photo array, studied the studier. He was methodical, moving right to left, top row, then bottom, no inordinate pauses, all very even. Without any sense of desire, she wondered if he was like that in bed and once again thought about her untaken road to the suburbs and more pleasant routines. When Paxton was done, he said, "I'm sorry, but I don't recognize any of these people." And then he said what everybody said when they came up empty. "Is one of these the killer?" And he looked again, as they all did, wondering which one did it, as if they could tell by looking.

"Can I ask an obvious question?" said Rook as Heat slid her photos back in the envelope. As usual, he didn't wait for permission to shoot his mouth off. "If Matthew Starr was so broke, why didn't he just sell off some of his stuff? I'm looking around at all this antique furniture, the art collection . . . That chandelier alone could fund an emerging nation for about a year." Heat looked at the Italian porcelain chandelier, the French sconces, the floor-to-cathedral-ceiling display of framed paintings, the gilded Louis XV mirror, the ornate furniture, and thought, Then again, sometimes Writer Monkey came out with a gem.

"Look, I don't feel comfortable talking about this." Then he glanced over Nikki's shoulder as if Kimberly Starr might come walking in.

"It's a simple question," said the detective. She knew she'd regret giving the props to Rook but added, "And a good one. And you're the money man, right?"

"I wish it were that simple."

"Try me. Because I hear you telling me how broke the man was, company imploding, personal money leaking like an Alaskan oil tanker, and then I look at all this. What's this worth, anyway?"

"That I can answer," he said. "I.T.E., forty-eight to sixty million."

"I.T.E.?"

Rook answered that. "In today's economy."

"Even at a fire sale, forty-eight mill solves a lot of problems."

"I've opened the books to you, I've explained the financial picture, I've looked at your pictures, isn't that enough?"

"No, and you know why?" With her forearms on her knees, she leaned forward to him and bored in. "Because there is something you're not wanting to say, and I will hear it here or at the precinct."

She gave him space to have whatever his internal dialogue was, and after a few seconds he said, "It just feels wrong to dump on him in his own home after he just died." She waited again and he let go. "Matthew had a monster ego. You have to have one to accomplish what he did, but his was off the chart. His narcissism made this collection bulletproof."

"But he was in financial quicksand," she said.

"Which is exactly the reason he ignored my advice—advice hell, my hounding—to piece it off. I wanted him to sell before bankruptcy creditors went after it, but this room was his palace. Proof to him and the world he was still king." Now that it was out, Paxton became more animated and paced along the walls. "You saw the offices yesterday. No way Matthew would meet a client there. So he brought them here so he could negotiate from his throne surrounded by his little Versailles. The Starr Collection. He loved big shots standing over one of these Queen Anne chairs and asking if it was OK to sit. Or looking at a painting and knowing what he paid for it. And if they didn't ask, he made sure to tell them. Sometimes I hid my face, it was so embarrassing."

"So, what happens to all this now?"

"Now, of course, I can start liquidation. There are debts to pay, not to mention Kimberly's tastes to support. I think she'll be more prone to lose a few knickknacks to maintain her lifestyle."

"And after you pay the debts, will there be enough to make up for her husband not having life insurance?"

"Oh, I don't think Kimberly will need to throw any telethons," said Paxton.

Nikki processed that as she wandered the room. Last time she visited, it was a crime scene. Now she was simply taking in its opulence. The crystal, the tapestries, the Kentian bookcase with fruit and flower carvings . . . She saw a painting she liked, a Raoul Dufy yachting scene, and leaned in for a closer look. The Boston Museum of Fine Arts was a ten-minute walk from her dorm when Nikki attended Northeastern. Although the hours she spent there as an art lover did not qualify her as an art expert, she recognized some of the works Matthew Starr had collected. They were expensive, but to her eye, the room was a two-story grab bag. Impressionists hung beside Old Masters; 1930s German poster art rubbed elbows with an Italian religious triptych from the 1400s. She lingered before a John Singer Sargent study for one of her favorite paintings, *Carnation, Lily, Lily, Rose*. Though it was a preliminary sketch in oil, one of the many Sargent made before each finished painting, she found herself transfixed by the familiar little girls, so wonderfully innocent in their white play dresses, lighting Chinese lanterns in a garden in the delicate glow of twilight. And then she wondered what it was doing beside the brash Gino Severini, a pricey, no doubt, but gaudy canvas of oil and crushed sequins. "Every other collection I've seen has a . . . I don't know, theme to it, or a common feel or, what am I trying to say . . . ?"

"Taste?" said Paxton. Now that he'd crossed his line, it was a free-fire zone. Even so, he lowered his voice to a hush and looked around as if he would be ducking lightning bolts for speaking ill of the dead. But speak ill he did. "If you're looking to see rhyme or reason to this collection, you won't, due to one unavoidable fact. Matthew was a vulgarian. He didn't know art. He knew price."

Rook came up beside Heat and said, "I think if we keep looking we'll find a *Dogs Playing Poker*," which made her laugh. Even Paxton indulged himself a chuckle. They all stopped when the front door opened and Kimberly Starr breezed in.

"Sorry I'm late." Heat and Rook stared at her, barely masking disbelief and judgment. Her face was swollen from Botox or some other series of cosmetic injections. Redness and bruising highlighted the unnatural swelling of her lips and smile lines. Her brow and forehead were marked with deep pink speed bumps that filled wrinkle lines and seemed to be growing before their eyes. The woman looked as if she had fallen face-first into a hornet's nest. "The traffic lights were out on Lexington. Damn heat wave."

"I left the papers on the desk in the study," said

Noah Paxton. He already had his briefcase in one hand and the other on the doorknob. "I have a lot of loose ends to attend to at the office. Detective Heat, if you need me for anything, you know how to find me." The eye roll he gave Nikki behind Kimberly's back threw water on Heat's trophy wife/accountant sleeping together hypothetical, although she would still check it out.

Kimberly and the detective took their identical seats in the living room from the day of the murder. Rook avoided the toile wingchair and sat on the couch with Mrs. Starr. Probably so he wouldn't have to look at her, thought Nikki.

The face work wasn't the only change. She was out of her Talbots and into Ed Hardy, a black tank dress with a large tattoo print of a red rose and the legend "Dedicated To The One I Love" in biker scroll. At least the widow was in black. Kimberly came at her brusquely, like this was some intrusion on the rest of her day. "Well? You said you have something for me to look at?"

Heat didn't personalize. Her style was to assess, not judge. Her assessment was that, personal grief modality aside, Kimberly Starr was treating her like the hired help, and she needed to reverse that power dynamic and fast. "Why did you lie to me about your whereabouts at the time of your husband's murder, Mrs. Starr?"

The woman's swollen face was still capable of registering some emotions, and fear was one of them. Nikki Heat liked the look. "What do you mean? Lie? Why would I lie?"

"I'll get to that when I'm ready. First, I want to

know where you were between one and two P.M. since you were not at Dino-Bites. You lied."

"I didn't lie. I was there."

"You dropped your son and nanny off and left. I already have witnesses. Should I ask the nanny, also?"

"No. That's true, I left."

"Where were you, Mrs. Starr? And this time I'd advise you to be truthful."

"All right. I was with a man. I was embarrassed to tell you."

"Tell me now. What do you mean with a man?"

"God, you're a bitch. I was sleeping with this guy, OK? Happy?"

"What's his name?"

"You can't be serious."

The face Nikki gave her could still show the full range of expression. It told her she was quite serious. "And don't say Barry Gable, he says you stood him up." Heat watched Kimberly's mouth go slack. "Barry Gable. You know, the man who assaulted you on the street? The one you told Detective Ochoa must have been a purse snatcher and that you didn't know him?"

"I was having an affair. My husband just died. I was embarrassed to say."

"So if you're over your shyness, Kimberly, tell me about this other affair so I can verify your whereabouts. And, as I'm sure you just figured out, I will check."

Kimberly gave her the name of a doctor, Cory Van Peldt. Yes, it was the truth, she said, and yes, it was the same doctor she had seen this morning.

Heat had her spell his name and wrote it on her pad along with his number. Kimberly said she met him when she went in for a facial assessment two weeks ago, and they had this magic thing. Heat was betting the magic was in his pants and was his wallet, but she knew better than to say so. She prayed Rook had the same sense.

As long as things were in a hostile vein, Nikki decided to press on. In a few minutes she would need Kimberly's cooperation with the photos and wanted her to think twice about lying, or be so rattled she'd do it poorly if she did. "A lot of things can't be taken at face value with you."

"What's that supposed to mean?"

"You tell me, Laldomina."

"Excuse me?"

"And Samantha."

"Hey, don't you start with that, nuh-uh."

"Wow, that's cool. You sounded pure Long Island." She turned to Rook. "See what stress does? All that preppy posing falls away."

"First of all, my legal name is Kimberly Starr. There's no crime in changing a name."

"Help me out: Why Samantha? I'm picturing you with your natural color and see you more as a Tiffany or Crystal."

"You cops, you always loved to give us girls a hard time for getting by any way we could. People do what they gotta do, ya know?"

"That's why we're having this conversation. To find out who did what."

"If that means did I kill my husband . . . God, I can't believe I just said that . . . The answer is no."

She waited for some response from Heat, and Nikki didn't give it. Let her wonder, she thought.

"My husband changed his name, too, did you know that? In the eighties. He took a branding seminar and decided what was holding him back was his name. Bruce DeLay. He said the words construction and DeLay weren't the best selling tool, so he researched names that would be brand-positive. You know, upbeat and inspiring confidence. He made a list, names like Champion and Best. He picked Star and added the extra r so it wouldn't sound fake."

Much as she had the day before, when she'd crossed from his opulent lobby into his ghost-town offices, Heat watched another chunk of Matthew Starr's public image crack and drop off. "How did he end up with Matthew?"

"Research. He did focus groups to see what name people trusted that went with his looks. So what if I changed mine, too? BFD, ya know?"

Detective Heat decided she had gotten as much as she was going to get out of this line of questions and was happy at least to have a fresh alibi to check. She took out her photo array. As she began to lay down the pictures and tell her to take her time, Kimberly interrupted her on the third shot.

"This man here. I know him. That's Miric."

Nikki felt the tingle she got when a domino was tipping, ready to fall. "And how do you know him?"

"He was Matt's bookie."

"Is Miric a first or last name?"

"You're all about names today, aren't you?"

"Kimberly, he might have killed your husband."

"I don't know which name. He was just Miric. Polish dude, I think. Not sure."

Nikki had her examine the rest of the array, without any other hits. "And you're positive your husband placed bets with this man."

"Yeah, why wouldn't I be sure of that?"

"When Noah Paxton looked at these pictures, he didn't recognize him. If he's paying the bills, wouldn't he know him?"

"Noah? He refused to deal with the bookmaking. He had to give Matthew the cash but looked the other way." Kimberly said she didn't know Miric's address or phone number. "No, I only saw him when he came to the door or showed up at a restaurant."

The detective would double-check Starr's desk and personal diary or his BlackBerry for some coded entry or recent call list. But a name and face and occupation was a good start.

As she squared her stack of photos to put away, she told Kimberly she had thought she didn't know about her husband's gambling.

"Come on, a wife knows. Just like I knew about his women. Do you want to know how much Flagyl I took in the last six years?"

No, Nikki did not care to know. But she did ask her for any names she recalled of her husband's past lovers. Kimberly said most of them seemed casual, a few one-nighters and weekends at casinos, and she didn't know their names. Only one got serious, and that was with a young marketing executive on his staff, an affair that lasted six months and ended about three years ago, after which the executive left the company. Kimberly gave Nikki the woman's name and got her address off a love letter she had intercepted. "You can keep that if you want. I only held onto it in case we got divorced and I needed to squeeze his balls." With that, Nikki left her to grieve.

They found Roach waiting for them in the lobby. Both had their coats off, and Raley's shirt was soaked through again. "You've got to start wearing undershirts, Raley," said Heat as she walked up.

"And how about switching to an Oxford?" added Ochoa. "Those polyester things you're wearing go see-through when you sweat."

"Turning you on, Ochoa?" asked Raley.

His partner jabbed back. "Much like your shirt, you see right through me."

Roach reported the same hit off the photo array when they showed it to the doorman. "We had to sort of pry it out of him," said Ochoa. "Doorman was a little embarrassed Miric slipped into the building. These guys always call up to the apartment before letting anybody in. He said he was taking a leak in the alley and must have missed him. But he did catch him coming out." Quoting from notes, the doorman described Miric as a "scrawny little ferret" who came by to see Mr. Starr from time to time but whose visits had become more frequent over the past two weeks.

"Plus we scored a bonus," said Raley. "This gentleman was coming out with ferret dude that day."

He peeled off another shot from the array and held it up. "Looks like Miric brought some muscle."

Of course, Nikki's instincts had already been crackling about this other guy, the brooder, when she screened the lobby video that morning. He was in a loose shirt, but she could tell he was a body-builder or at least spent a lot of his day at the weight rack. Under any other circumstances, she wouldn't have thought twice and would have assumed he was delivering air conditioners, probably one under each arm, from the looks of him. But the serene lobby of the Guilford wasn't the service entrance, and a grown man had been tossed off his balcony there that day. "Did the doorman give a name for this guy?"

Ochoa looked at his notes again. "Only the nickname he gave him. Iron Man."

While the precinct ran Miric and Iron Man Doe through the computer, digitals of the pair were blast-sent to detectives and patrols. It was impossible for Heat's small unit to canvass every known bookie in Manhattan, even assuming Miric was a known, and wasn't from one of the other boroughs, or even Jersey. Plus a man like Matthew Starr might even use an exclusive betting service or the Internet—both of which he probably did— but if he was the volatile mix of desperation and invincibility Noah Paxton painted him to be, chances were he'd hit the street, as well.

So they spilt up to concentrate on known book-makers in two zones. The Roach Coach got the tour of the Upper West Side in a radius around the Guilford, while Heat and Rook covered Midtown near the Starr Pointe headquarters, roughly Central Park South to Times Square.

"This is exasperating," said Rook after their fourth stop, a street vendor who suddenly decided he didn't speak English when Heat showed him her shield. He was one of several runners for the major bookies whose mobile food carts were a convenient one-stop for bets and kabobs. They were treated to eye-stinging smoke that swirled off his grill and found them wherever they moved, while the vendor furrowed his brow at the photos and ultimately shrugged.

"Welcome to police work, Rook. This is what I call the Street Google. We are the search engine; it's how it gets done."

As they drove to the next address, a discount electronics store on 51st, a front specializing more in bets than boom boxes, Rook said, "Have to tell you, a week ago, if you told me I'd be hitting the shawarma carts looking for Matthew Starr's bookie, I never would have believed it."

"You mean it doesn't fit the image? This is where you and I come from different places. You write these magazine pieces, you're all about selling the image. I'm all about looking behind it. I'm frequently disappointed but seldom wrong. Behind every picture hides the true story. You just have to be willing to look."

"Yeah, but this guy was big. Maybe not elite-elite, but he was at least the bus and truck Donald Trump."

"I always thought Donald Trump was the bus and truck Donald Trump," she said.

"And who's Kimberly Starr, the truckstop Tara Reid? If she's the poor little rich girl, what's she doing blowing ten grand on that face?"

"If I had to guess, she bought it with Barry Gable's money."

"Or she took it in trade with her new doctor boyfriend."

"Trust me, I'll find out. But a woman like Kimberly's not going to start clipping supermarket coupons and eating ramen one night a week. She's all about prepping her face for her next season of *The Bachelor*."

"If they're holding it on *The Island of Doctor Moreau*." She didn't like herself for it but she laughed. It only encouraged him. "Or if she's doing a remake of *Elephant Man*." Rook took guttural breaths and slurred, "I am not a suspect, I am a human being."

The radio call came when they were getting in the car after the discount electronics store dead end. Roach had spotted Miric in front of the Off Track Betting facility on West 72nd and was making a move, calling for back-up.

Heat slapped the gumball on the roof and told Rook to buckle up and hang on.

He beamed and actually said, "Can I work the siren?"

FIVE

There is very little chance of a high-speed pursuit on any street in Midtown Manhattan. Detective Heat accelerated, then braked, eased forward, jerked the wheel hard right, and accelerated again, until she was forced to brake again in a matter of yards. As she continued like that, working the avenue uptown, her face was set in concentration, eyes darting to all mirrors, then to the sidewalk, then to the crosswalk, then to the double-parked delivery guy who swung his van door open and almost became roadkill but for her experience and skill at the wheel. The siren and light meant nothing in this traffic. Maybe to the pedestrians, but the traffic lanes were so packed even the drivers who cared enough to pull aside and make a hole had scant room to maneuver.

"Jeez, c'mon, move it," shouted Rook from the passenger seat, at another taxi trunk sitting there in front of their windshield. His voice was dry from adrenaline, his words punctuated by air squeezed out against his seat belt with each sudden braking, which broke his syllables in two.

Heat maintained her tense composure. This was the live-action video game cops played every day in this borough, a race against the clock through an obstacle course of construction, stalls, jams, daredevils, idiots, sons-of-bitches, and the unaware. She knew Eighth would be all-stop south of

Columbus Circle. Then, for once, gridlock worked in her favor. A stretch Hummer, also heading uptown, was blocking the cross-flow at 55th. Nikki gunned it through the sliver of daylight it created and pulled a sharp left. Taking advantage of the lighter traffic the Hummer block created, she sped crosstown to Tenth with Rook's expletives and Ochoa's radio chatter filling her ears.

Things improved, as she had projected, when she squealed around the corner at Tenth. After a game of dodge 'em through the two-way intersection at West 57th, Tenth became Amsterdam Avenue and grew wider shoulders and a nice emergency lane up the middle that some drivers even respected. She was ripping it north with a little more speed, past the back of Lincoln Center, when the call came from Raley. He had custody of Miric. Ochoa was in pursuit of suspect two, on the run west on 72nd. "That would be Iron Man," she said, her first words since her instructions to Rook back in Times Square, to buckle up and hang on.

Ochoa was gasping into his walkie when she shot through 70th where Amsterdam and Broadway crossed at an X. "Sus . . . pect . . . running . . . west . . . approa . . . Now at Broadway . . ."

"He's heading for the subway station," Heat said to Rook, but more talking out loud.

"Crossing . . ." A loud car horn, and then . . . "Suspect crossing Broadway . . . to subway . . . station."

She keyed her radio. "Suspect description."

"Copy . . . white, male, two-twenty-five . . . red shirt over cammy . . . pants . . . black shoes . . ."

To complicate things there were two station houses at the 72nd and Broadway subway: the old stone historic building on the south side and the newer glass-and-metal atrium station house just across the street to the north. Nikki pulled up to the old stone building. She knew the OTB sat midblock on the north side of 72nd, so a fleeing Iron Man would likely duck into the closest station—the newer one—and Ochoa would be following there. Her idea was to cut off him off from escaping up the tunnel of this one.

"Stay in the car, I mean it," she called over her shoulder to Rook as she bailed out of the driver's side, hanging her shield around her neck. The MTA tunnels ran ten degrees warmer than street temps, and the air that rose up the from underground to greet her as she sprinted past the MetroCard machines toward the turnstiles was a mix of garbage funk and oven blast. Heat vaulted·a turnstile with a sweaty hand that slipped on the stainless steel. She recovered her balance but landed in a low crouch and found herself looking up at the hulk in the red tank top and cammies as he crested the stairs.

"Police, freeze," she said.

Ochoa was coming up the steps behind him. Cut off from retreat, the big man broke around Heat for the turnstiles. She blocked him and he clawed her shoulder. She brought one hand up to break his grip at the wrist and, with the other, grabbed his tricep and pulled his back across the front of her body, so he couldn't reach her to land a punch. Then she grabbed his belt, hooked his ankle with hers, and dropped him on his back. He hit hard. As Heat heard the air come out of him, she scissored a leg over his neck and yanked his wrist toward her in what a certain ex–Navy Seal called an arm bar. He struggled to rise up but found himself staring into her gun.

"Go ahead," she said.

Iron Man laid his head back on the grimy tiles, and that was that.

———

"Not very quotable," said Rook on the drive back to the precinct.

"I told you to wait in the car. You never wait in the car."

"I thought you might need help."

"From you?" she scoffed. "Wouldn't do to reinjure those tender ribs."

"You do need help. Writer help. You take down a character like that, and the best you can you do is 'Go ahead'?"

"What's wrong with that?"

"Sorry, Detective, but I'm left sort of hanging. Like 'shave and a haircut' minus the all-important 'two bits.'" He glanced over his shoulder into the backseat, at the manacled Iron Man staring out the side window at a Flash Dancers ad on a cab top. "Although, plus ten for not saying, 'Make my day.'"

"As long as you're happy, Rook, I've done my job."

———

A column of fluorescent light cut into the dimness of the precinct observation booth as Jameson Rook stepped in to join Heat and her two detectives. "Got one for who wrote 'It's Raining Men.' Ready?" said Ochoa. Spirits were palpably lighter after the afternoon's arrests. One part come-down from the adrenaline, one part feeling this case would clear if their two prisoners did Matthew Starr.

Rook crossed his arms and smirked. "Let me hear it."

"Dolly Parton."

"Oh," moaned Rook, "I knew I should have put money on this."

"Hint," said Raley.

"Living."

"Bigger hint," from Ochoa.

Rook was loving this and announced like a game show host, "This famous cowriter is a he and is on network television every day."

"Al Roker," shouted Raley.

"Excellent guess. No."

"Paul Shaffer," said Heat.

Rook couldn't hide his astonishment. "That's right. Was that a lucky guess, or did you know?"

"Your turn to guess." She flashed a smile that dropped as fast as it appeared. "Oh, and my prize for winning? You wait here in the Ob Room while I do my work."

Detective Heat kept the two suspects separated for their interrogations as a matter of practice. The two had been apart since their arrests, to prevent them from co-formulating stories and alibis. Her first session was with Miric, the bookie, who indeed had ferretlike qualities. He was a small man, five-four, with thin pasty arms that could have gone missing from a Mr. Potato Head. She selected him because he was the known person and, if there were such a thing, the brains of the two.

"Miric," she said, "that's Polish, right?"

"Polish-American," he said with the lightest trace of accent. "I came to this country in 1980 after this thing we called the Gdansk Shipyard strike."

"We, as in you and Lech Walesa?"

"That is right. *Solidarnosc!*, yes?"

"Miric, you were nine."

"No matter, is in the blood, yes?"

Less than a minute and Nikki had this guy down. A time-filler. An amiable who talks and talks but says nothing. If she kept up the ballet, she'd be there hours and come out with a headache and no information. So corral him as best she could, she decided.

"Do you know why we picked you up?"

"Is this like speeding ticket and officer asks you to tell him how fast you are going? I don't think so."

"You've been arrested before."

"Yes, number of times. I think you have a list in there, right?" He nodded his long nose to the file on the metal tabletop in front of her and then looked at her. His eyes were set deep and so close together they almost crossed. Calling him a ferret might be complimentary.

"Why did you go to the Guilford day before yesterday?"

"The Guilford, on West 77th? Very nice building, that. A palace, yes?"

"Why were you there?"

"Was I?"

She slapped the flat of her hand down on the table and he jumped. Good, she thought, let's change the tempo. "Let's cut the bull, Miric. I have eyewitnesses and photographs. You and your goon went to see Matthew Starr and now he's dead."

"And you think I had something to do with this tragedy?"

Miric was a slippery one, a true slimebag, and, from her experience, the ripest type for divide-and-conquer. "I think you can be helpful here, Miric. Maybe whatever happened to Mr. Starr wasn't your doing. Maybe your pal . . . Pochenko . . . got a little more excited than he was supposed to when you went to collect your debt. It happens. Did he get too excited?"

"Whatever you are talking about, I don't know. I had an appointment to see Mr. Matthew Starr, of course. Why else would they allow me in such a wonderful building? But I went to his door and he did not answer."

"So your statement is that you did not see Matthew Starr that day."

"I don't feel I need to repeat when I say so clearly."

This guy had been through the mill too often, she thought. He knew all the moves. And none of his priors, though numerous, involved violence. Scams, cons, and bookmaking only. She shifted back to Iron Man. "This other man, Pochenko, he came with you?"

"The day I did not see Matthew Starr? He did come. You know that already, I bet, so there you go. You have good answer from me."

"Why did you bring Pochenko to meet with Matthew Starr? To show him the wonderful building?"

Miric laughed, showing a tiny row of ocher teeth. "That's a good one, I'll remember that."

"Then why? Why take such a big guy like that?"

"Oh, you know in this economy many people want to rob you on the streets. I sometimes carry sums of money and one can't be too safe, yes?"

"You aren't convincing me. I think you're lying."

Miric shrugged. "Think what you like, is free country. But I say this. You wonder if I killed Matthew Starr and I say, Why would I? Bad for business. Want to know my pet name for Matthew Starr? The ATM. Why would I pull plug on ATM?"

He gave her something to think about. Nonetheless, when she rose, she said, "One more thing. Hold out your hands." He did. They were clean and pale, as if he had spent his days peeling potatoes in a washtub.

Nikki Heat compared notes with her crew while they moved Pochenko from his holding cell to Interrogation. "That Miric's a piece of work," said Ochoa. "You see critters like that covered in sawdust in bitty cages when you raid meth dealers."

"OK, we agree on the ferret profile," said Heat. "What do we come away with that's useful?"

"I think he did it."

"Rook, you say that about everyone we meet on this case. May I remind you of Kimberly Starr?"

"But I hadn't seen this guy before. Or maybe it's his muscle. That is what you guys call them, muscle?"

"Sometimes," said Raley. "There's also goon."

"Or thug," said Ochoa.

"Thug's good," continued Raley. "So's badass."

"Meat," from Ochoa, and the two detectives alternated euphemisms in rapid-fire succession.

"Gangsta."

"G."

"Punk."

"Bitch."

"Gristle."

"Knucks."

"Ballbuster."

"Bang-ah."

"But muscle works," said Ochoa.

"Gets it said," agreed Raley.

Rook had out his Moleskine notebook and a pen. "I gotta get some of these down before I forget."

"You do that," said Heat. "I'll be in with the . . . miscreant."

———

"Vitya Pochenko, you've been a busy boy since you came to this country." Nikki turned pages in his file, silent-reading as if she didn't already know what was on them, and then closed it. His jacket was full of arrests for threats and violent acts, but no convictions. People either shied away from testifying against Iron Man or they left town. "You've gotten away clean. A lot. People either really like you, or they're really afraid of you."

Pochenko sat looking straight ahead with his eyes fixed on the two-way mirror. Not nervously checking himself, not like Barry Gable. No, he was fixed and focused on a point of his choosing. Not looking at her, not like he was even there with her. He seemed deep in his own mind and nowhere else. Detective Heat would have to change that.

"Your pal Miric mustn't be afraid of you." The Russian didn't blink. "Not from what he just told me." Still nothing. "He had some interesting things to say about what you did to Matthew Starr at the Guilford day before yesterday."

Slowly, he unhooked his eyes from the ozone and rotated his head to face her. As he did, his neck twisted, revealing veins and tendons strung deep into bulky shoulders. He stared at her from underneath a thick ginger brow. At this angle in the downcast lighting he had a prizefighter's face with a telltale nose that curved in an unnatural flatness where it had been broken. She decided he had been handsome once before the hardness. With the brush cut, she could picture the boy of him on a soccer field or lofting a stick in a hockey rink. But the hardness was what Pochenko was all about now, and whether it came from doing time in Russia or learning how not to do time, the boy was gone and all she saw in that room was what happens when you get very, very good at surviving very, very bad things.

Something like a smile formed in the deep creases at the corners of his mouth, but it never came. Then he spoke at last. "In the subway station when you were on top of me, I could smell you. Do you know what I'm talking about? Smelling you?"

Nikki Heat had been in all sorts of interrogations

and interviews with every stripe of lowlife in God's creation and those too damaged to make the list. The wiseguys and the crazies thought because she was a woman they could rattle her with some leering porn-movie trash talk. A serial killer once asked her to ride in the van so he could pleasure himself on the way to the penitentiary. Her armor was strong. Nikki had the investigator's greatest gift, distance. Or maybe it was disconnection. But Pochenko's casually spoken words, along with the entitled look he was giving her, the intrusion of his casualness and the threat carried in those amber resin eyes, made her shudder. She held his gaze and tried not to engage.

"I see you do know." And then, most chilling of all, he winked. "I'm going to have that." Then he made wet air kisses at her and laughed.

Then Nikki heard something she had never heard in the Interrogation Room before. Muffled shouting from the observation booth. It was Rook, his voice smothered by soundproofing and double-pane glass, hollering at Pochenko. It sounded like he was shouting through a pillow, but she heard "... animal ... scumbag ... filthy mouth ... ," followed by pounding on the glass. She turned over her shoulder to look. Hard to be nonchalant when the mirror is flexing and rattling. Then came the dampened shouts of Roach and it stopped.

Pochenko glanced from the mirror to her with an unsettled look. Whatever had gotten into Rook's pea brain and made him slip his leash in there, he had succeeded in undercutting the Russian's moment of intimidation. Detective Heat latched onto the opportunity and flipped the subject without comment.

"Let me see your hands," she said.

"What? You want my hands, come closer."

She stood, trying to gain height and distance and, most of all, dominance. "Put your hands flat on the table, Pochenko. Now."

He decided he would choose when it was time, but he didn't wait long. The shackles on one wrist clacked against the table edge, and then the shackles on the other, as he spread his palms on the cold metal. His hands were scuffed and swollen. A few knuckles were plumming into bruises, others were missing skin and wept where they had not yet scabbed over. On the middle finger of his right hand, there was a thick stripe of blanched skin and a cut. The kind a ring would leave.

"What happened here?" she said, relieved to feel in charge again.

"What, this? Is nothing."

"Looks like a cut."

"Yeah, I forgot to take my ring off before."

"Before what?"

"Before my workout."

"What workout at what gym? Tell me."

"Who said anything about a gym?" And then his upper lip curled, and she instinctively took a step back, until she realized he was smiling.

Captain Montrose's office was empty, so Nikki Heat ushered Rook inside and pulled the glass door shut. "Just what the hell was that all about?"

"I know, I know, I lost it."

"In the middle of my interrogation, Rook."

"Did you hear what he was saying to you?"

"No. I couldn't hear him over the pounding on the observation mirror."

He looked away. "Pretty lame, huh?"

"I'd call it a first. If this were Chechnya, right now you'd be riding down the mountain feet-first on a goat."

"Will you knock it off about Chechnya? I get one movie option and you pick, pick, pick at it."

"Tell me you don't have it coming."

"This time, maybe. Can I say something?" He didn't wait for an answer. "I don't know how you can stand doing this."

"You kidding? It's my job."

"But it's so . . . ugly."

"War zones aren't so much fun, either. Or so I've read."

"War, not so good. But that's just one part. In my job I get to move from place to place. It may be a war zone one time or riding in a Jeep with a black hood over my head to visit a drug cartel, but then I get a month in Portofino and Nice with rock stars and their toys, or I shadow a celebrity chef for a week in Sedona or Palm Beach. But you. This is . . . this is a sewer."

"Is this the equivalent of 'what's a nice girl like you doing in a place like this?' Because if it is, I'll kick you in the balls to show you how not nice I can be. I like my job. I do what I do, and deal with the people I deal with, and here's a headline for your article, writer boy: Criminals are scum."

"Especially that G."

She laughed. "Excellent research notes, Rook. You sound so street."

"Oh, and by the way? No goats. Popular misconception. Up in the Caucasus with General Yamadayev, it was all horses. That's how we rolled."

When she watched him leave the room, she was surprised not to feel pissed anymore. How angry could you be at somebody who acted like he cared a little?

A half hour later, she sat with Raley, screening the surveillance video from the Guilford. Detective Heat did not look pleased. "Run it again," she said. "And let's watch every corner of the screen. Maybe we missed a piece of them coming back later."

"What's wrong?" Rook arrived behind them, his breath smelling of contraband espresso.

"It's the damn time code." She tapped her pen on the pale gray digital clock embedded on the bottom of the surveillance video. "It shows Miric and Pochenko arriving at 10:31 A.M. They go up the elevator, right? And come back down to the lobby roughly twenty minutes later."

"Sure puts a big hole in Miric's statement that Starr never answered his door. Unless it was a twenty-minute knock."

"Ask me, the only thing that got knocked was Matthew Starr," said Raley. "This had to be when Pochenko gave him a boxing lesson."

"That's not our problem, guys," said Heat. "According to this, our two Elvises left the building at 10:53 A.M., about two and a half hours before our victim was thrown off his balcony." She tossed her pen onto the desktop in frustration. "So our two primes get cleared by the tape."

"And they've lawyered up," added Ochoa, looking at his BlackBerry. "They're getting sprung now."

From outside the security door, Heat stood with Roach and looked across the processing area as Miric and Pochenko collected their property. Of course Miric was the one who had the attorney on call, and when the lawyer caught Detective Heat's eye, he didn't like what he saw, so he got extra busy with paperwork.

"Guess I should cancel that search warrant for torn blue jeans at their apartments," said Raley.

"No, don't," said Nikki. "I know what the time code says, but what's the harm in checking? Details, gents. You'll never regret being thorough." And as Pochenko spotted her, she added, "In fact, add another item to Iron Man's search warrant. A large ring."

When Ochoa left to get the warrant processed, she gave an assignment to Raley. "I know it's drudgery, but I want you to screen that lobby video again from the moment those jokers left until a half hour after Starr's time of death. And do it in real time so we're sure we don't skip past them at high speed."

Raley left to do his screening. Nikki stayed to watch Miric, his lawyer, and Pochenko head for the exit. The Russian lagged and split off from the other two, crossing to Heat. A uniform shadowed him so he stopped in a safe zone, a good yard away from her. He took his time looking at her head to toe, then said in a low whisper, "Relax. You're gonna like it." Then, with a shrug, "Or not."

And then he left without looking back. Nikki waited until the exit door shut with Pochenko on the other side before she went back to work.

SIX

Nikki stepped into the rooftop bar of the Soho House and wondered what her friend had been thinking when she booked outdoor cocktails during a heat wave. Seven-thirty on a weeknight in summer was too light out to feel cool and too early for any action, especially on this stretch of Ninth Avenue. In the hipper-than-thou meatpacking district, seven-thirty was beyond outré. It was downright early bird.

Lauren Parry, who clearly wasn't bothered by any of that, flagged her from her street-view table where the canopy ended and the pool area began. "Is this too hot?" she said when Nikki arrived.

"No, this is fine." After they hugged, she added, "Who couldn't stand to sweat off a few pounds?"

"Well, sorr-ee. I spend my day in the morgue," said the medical examiner. "I grab all the warm I can get."

They ordered cocktails. Nikki went for a Campari and soda, craving something dry, sparkling, and, most of all, cold. Her friend stuck with her usual, a bloody Mary. When it came, Nikki observed that it was an ironic favorite for a coroner. "Why don't you break out, Lauren? This isn't Sunday brunch. Get one of those sake-tinis or a sex on the beach."

"Hey, you want to talk ironic drinks, that would

be it. In my line of work, sex on the beach is usually what led to body under the pier."

"To life," said Nikki, and they both laughed.

Meeting her friend for a drink after work once a week was more than just cocktails and chill time. The two women had hit it off right away over Lauren's first autopsy, when she started at the M.E.'s office three years ago, but their weekly after-work ritual was really fueled by their professional bond. Despite cultural differences—Lauren came out of the projects in St. Louis and Nikki grew up Manhattan middle-class—they connected on another level, as professional women navigating traditional male fields. Sure, Nikki enjoyed her occasional brew at the precinct-adjacent cop bar, but she was never about being one of the fellas, any more than she was about quilting bees or Goddess book clubs. She and Lauren clung to their camaraderie and the sense of safety they had crafted with each other, to have a time and place to share problems at work, largely political, and, yes, to decompress and let their hair down without having it be in a meat market or at a stitch and bitch.

Nikki asked, "Mind a little shop talk?"

"Hey, sister, on top of being cold all day, the people I hang out with don't do much talking, so whatever the subject, bring it."

Heat wanted to discuss Matthew Starr. She told Lauren she now understood how the victim got those torso bruises. She bullet-pointed her sessions with Miric and Pochenko, concluding by saying she had no doubt the bookie had his muscle man encourage the real estate developer to "prioritize" the repayment of his gambling debt. With experience talking, she added that, thanks to lawyers and stonewalling: Good luck making a case. What she wanted to know was if Lauren recalled any other marks that might be read as a separate event from the Russian's work-over?

Lauren Parry was a marvel. She remembered every autopsy the way Tiger Woods could tell you every golf shot he made in every tournament—as well as his opponent's. She said there were only two relevant indicators. First, a pair of uniquely shaped contusions on the deceased's back, an exact match to the polished brass flip handles on the French doors leading to the balcony, probably where he was pushed outside with great force. Heat recalled Roach's tour of the balcony crime scene and the powdered stone under the spot where the door handles had impacted the wall. And second, Starr had grip marks on both upper arms. The medical examiner air-demoed a thumb in each armpit, hands wrapped around the arms.

"My guess is it wasn't much of a fight," said Lauren. "Whoever did this picked up the victim, slammed him through those doors and then tossed him backwards to the street. I examined his legs and ankles closely and I'm certain Mr. Starr never even touched the railing when he went over."

"No other chafing or cuts, no defensive wounds or marks?"

Lauren shook her head. "Although, there was one irregularity."

"Out with it, girl, next to inconsistency, irregularity is the detective's best friend."

"I was detailing those punch bruises, you know the ones with the probable ring mark? And there was one that was an exact match for the others but no ring mark."

"Maybe he took it off."

"In the middle of a beating?"

Nikki took a long pull on her drink, feeling the carbonation bite her tongue as she stared through the Plexi barrier beside her at the avenue seven floors below. She didn't know what Lauren's information meant, but she got out her notebook and made a note: "One punch, no ring."

They ordered some *arancini* and a plate of olives, and by the time their finger foods arrived they were on to other subjects: Lauren was teaching a seminar at Columbia in the fall; her dachshund, Lola, got picked for a dog food commercial when she took her to the dog run last weekend; Nikki had a week off at the end of August and was thinking of Iceland and did Lauren want to come. "Sounds cold," she said. But she also said she'd think about it.

Nikki's cell phone vibed and she looked at the caller ID.

"What's up, Detective," Laura asked, "are you going to have to deploy or something? Maybe rappel down the face of the building and spring into some two-fisted action?"

"Rook" was all she said and held up the phone.

"Take it. I don't mind."

"It's Rook," she reiterated, as if it required no further explanation. Nikki let his call drop to voice mail.

"Forward him to my phone," said Lauren, stirring her bloody Mary. "You could do worse than Jameson Rook. That man is doable."

"Oh, sure, that's just what I need. The ride-along isn't bad enough without putting that in the mix." When her phone pulsed to indicate voice mail, she pressed the button for a fetch and held the phone to her ear. "Huh. He says he's come upon something big about the Matthew Starr case and needs me to see it . . ." She held up a staying palm to Lauren as she listened to the rest and then hung up.

"What's the development?"

"Didn't say. He said he couldn't talk now but to come to his place right away, and left his address."

"You should go," said Lauren.

"I'm almost afraid to. Knowing him, he's probably made citizen's arrests of anybody who knew Matthew Starr."

———

When the industrial strength elevator reached his loft, Rook was waiting for her on the other side of the accordion mesh doors. "Heat. You actually came."

"Your message said you had something to show me."

"I do," he said and strode from the entry and disappeared around a corner. "This way."

She followed him into his designer kitchen. At the other end of it, in the great room, as the cable designer shows called those open spaces that merged living rooms and dining rooms off an overlooking kitchen, there was a poker table, a real poker table with a felt top. And it was surrounded by . . . poker players. She came to a halt. "Rook, there's nothing you need to show me here about the case at all, is there?"

"Say, you *are* a detective, aren't you?" He shrugged and gave a little impish grin. "Would you have come if I had just plain invited you to play poker?"

Nikki got hit with a major turn-around twinge, but then the poker crowd rose to greet her and there she was.

As Rook escorted her into the room, he said, "If you really, really need a work reason to be here, you can thank the man who got you your warrant for the Guilford. Judge, this is Detective Nikki Heat, NYPD."

Judge Simpson looked a bit different in a yellow polo shirt, hunkered behind tall stacks of poker chips instead of his bench. "I'm winning," he said as he shook her hand. A network news anchor she and the rest of America admired was also there, with her filmmaker husband. The anchorwoman said she was glad a cop was there because she had been robbed. "And by a judge," said her husband. Rook placed Nikki in the empty seat between him and the newswoman, and before Nikki knew it, the anchor's Oscar-winning husband was dealing her a hand.

It was a low-stakes game, she was relieved to discover, and then that turned to worry they had lowered the ante in deference to her pay grade. But it was clear this was more about fun than money. Although winning still mattered, especially to the judge. Seeing him out of his robe for the first time, the overhead light shining on his bald head, the manic obsession he brought to his play, Nikki couldn't shake the comparison to another Simpson. She would have given up a whole pot just to hear the judge say "D'oh!"

After the deal of the third hand, the lights dipped out and came back up. "Here we go," said Nikki. "Mayor said we'd have rolling brownouts."

"How many days is it for this heat wave?" asked the filmmaker.

"This is day four," said his wife. "I interviewed a meteorologist and he said it's not a heat wave unless it's three consecutive days above ninety degrees."

A woman appeared in the kitchen and added, "And if the heat lasts more than four days, consult your doctor immediately." The room burst into laughter, and the woman stepped from behind the counter, taking a deep, theatrical bow, complete with a graceful upward arm sweep. Rook had told her about his mother. Of course, she already knew who Margaret was. You don't win Tony Awards and show up in the *Style* section and *Vanity Fair* party collages as often she did and go unnoticed. In her sixties now, Margaret had gone from the ingénue to the grand dame (although Rook once confided in Nikki that his spelling was grand d-a-m-n). The lady exuded every bit of the joyful diva, from her opening line to the way she entered the great room to take Nikki's hand and fuss about how very much she had heard about her from Jamie.

"And I've heard a lot about you," Nikki replied.

"Believe it all, darling. And if it's not true, when

I get to hell, I'll sort it out there." Then she swept—no, there was no more accurate way to describe it—she swept back into the kitchen.

Rook smiled at Nikki. "As you can see, I believe in truth in advertising."

"So I'm learning." She heard ice plinking in a rocks glass and saw Margaret uncapping a bottle of Jameson. Yes, she thought, I'm learning a lot, Jameson Rook.

The news anchor appealed to Rook's sense of civic responsibility and he killed his air-conditioning. Nikki looked up from her cards, and her eyes followed his shorts and *U-2 3D* T-shirt as he moved barefoot across the oriental rug to the far wall. He bent to open the sash windows that gave onto his penthouse view of Tribeca, and when Nikki's eyes drifted off him, it was to the hulk of a distant building, RiverStarr on the Hudson, backlit by Jersey City. The structure was dark, except for the red aviation lamp atop an idle crane balanced above girders awaiting skin. They'd wait a long time.

Margaret took her son's chair beside Nikki and said, "It is a very good view." And as Rook bent to open the next window, the doyenne leaned in to whisper, "I'm his mother and even I think it's a great view. But that's just me taking credit." And then, just to be clear: "Jamie got my ass. It got a marvelous review in *Oh! Calcutta!*"

Two hours later, after Rook, then the news anchor, and then her husband folded, Nikki won yet another hand against the judge. Simpson said he didn't care, but judging from his expression, she was glad she got the court order out of him before the poker game. "Guess the cards aren't falling my way tonight for some reason." She really wanted him to just say "D'oh!"

"It isn't the cards, Horace," said Rook. "For once, somebody at this table can read your tells." He got up and crossed to the counter to peel a tepid slice of Ray's out of the box and fish another Fat Tire from the ice in the sink. "Now, to me, tonight, anyway, you've got a great poker face. I can't see what's going on behind the taciturn judicial mask. It could be woo-hoo or yay-boo. But this one here, she's gotcha." Rook took his seat again, and Nikki wondered if the whole pizza-and-beer run had been a ruse to move his chair closer to hers.

"My face gives nothing away," said the judge.

"It's not about you giving it away, it's what she's taking," said Rook. He turned to her as he spoke to the judge. "I've been with her weeks now, and I don't think I've ever known someone so adept at reading people." He held that look to her, and although they were nowhere close to breathing each other's exhalations like they had on Starr's balcony that day, she felt a flutter. So she turned away to rake in the pot, wondering what the hell she was playing with here, and she didn't mean the cards. "I think I should call it a night," she said.

———

Rook insisted on walking her down to the sidewalk, but Nikki stalled until they were embedded in the group departure of the other guests, so she could get away clean. A group seemed the perfect place to fulfill that. Because the truth of it, she reflected on the ride down, was that she didn't want so much to be alone as not to be paired up.

Not tonight anyway, she thought.

The news anchor and her husband lived in walking distance and made their exit just as Simpson flagged a cab. The judge was heading uptown near the Guggenheim and asked if Nikki wanted to share the ride. She sorted her feelings about leaving Rook hangdogging on the sidewalk versus staying and having to deal with the awkwardness of the good-night moment, or worse, the comeback-up moment, and answered yes.

Rook said, "Hope you don't mind I sort of Punk'd you into coming over."

"Why would I mind? I'm leaving with money, jokey boy." Then she slid way across the taxi seat to make room for Simpson. Ten minutes later, she was unlocking her lobby door in Gramercy Park, thinking about a bath.

————

Nobody would accuse Nikki Heat of leading a life of indulgence. "Delayed gratification" was a phrase that came to her mind often, usually invoked as a means to talk herself down off some rare flash of anger at what she was doing instead of what she would rather be doing. Or saw other people doing.

So as she ran the tap to revitalize the bubbles in her tub, allowing herself one of her few indulgences, a bubble bath, her mind ran back to thoughts of the road not taken. To Connecticut and a yard and the PTA and a husband who took the train to

Manhattan, and having the time and resources to get a massage once in a while or maybe take a yoga class.

Yoga class instead of close-quarter combat training.

Nikki tried to imagine herself in bed with a ropy tofu advocate with a Johnny Depp beard and a "Random Acts of Kindness" bumper sticker on a rusted-out Saab, instead of sheet grappling with the ex-Seal. She could do worse than Johnny Depp. And had.

A couple of times that evening she had thought about calling Don but didn't. Why not? She wanted to boast about her perfect arm-bar takedown of Pochenko at the subway station. Quick and easy, take a seat, sir. But that wasn't why she wanted to call him, and she knew it.

So why didn't she?

It was an easy arrangement with Don. Her trainer with benefits never asked her where she was or when she'd be back or why she didn't call. His place or hers didn't matter; it was logistical, whichever was closer. He was looking neither to nest nor to get away from anything.

And the sex was good. Once in a while he would get a bit too aggressive, or a bit too into task completion, but she knew how to work with that and get what she needed. And how much different was that from the commuter guys, the Noah Paxtons of the world? The Don thing wasn't the be-all, but it worked fine.

So why didn't she call?

She shut off the tap when the bubbles tickled her chin, and inhaled the scent of her childhood.

Nikki thought about the delays, tried to imagine fulfilling purpose instead of needs, and wondered if this was what it would be like in, say, eleven years, when she hit forty. That used to seem like such a long way off, and yet the last ten years, a full decade of rearranging her life around the end of her mother's, had blipped along like a TiVo on forward. Or was that for the lack of savoring?

She went from convincing her mother she should be a Theater Arts major to transferring to the College of Criminal Justice. She wondered if without realizing it she was getting too tough to be happy. She knew she did less laughing and more judging.

What had Rook said at the poker game? He called her adept at reading people. Not what she wanted on her tombstone.

Rook.

OK, so I was checking out his ass, she thought. Then the flutter came over her, probably embarrassment at being transparent enough to be caught in the act by The Grand Damn. Nikki submerged under the bubbles and held her breath until the pounding of her flutter got lost in the pounding of oxygen debt.

She broke the surface and palmed the suds off her face and hair, and floated, weightless in the cooling water, and let herself wonder what it would be like with Jameson Rook. What would he be like? How would he feel and taste and move?

And then the flutter hit her again. What would she be like with him? It made her nervous. She didn't know.

It was a mystery.

She unstopped the drain and got out.

————

Nikki had her air-conditioning off and walked her apartment naked and wet, not bothering to towel off in the humidity. The die-hard soap bubbles felt good on her skin, and besides, once she dried off, she'd be damp in no time in the soggy air, so why not be damp and smell like lavender?

Only two of her windows gave views to facing neighbors, and since there was no breeze to obstruct anyway, she drew the shades down on them and went to the utility closet off the kitchen. Detective Nikki Heat's miracle time- and money-saver was to press her own clothes the night before. Nothing stopped the crooks in their tracks more than defined pleats and sharp creases. She drew the board down on its hinge and plugged in the iron.

She hadn't overdone the alcohol that night, but what she had drunk had made her thirsty. In the fridge she found her last can of lemon-lime seltzer. It was quite ungreen of her, but she held open the refrigerator door and moved herself close to it, feeling the cool air cascade out against her naked body, chilling her skin into gooseflesh.

A small click turned her away from the open door. The red light had popped on, indicating the iron was ready. She set the can of seltzer on the counter and hurried to her closet to find something relatively clean and, above all, breathable.

Her navy linen blazer only needed a touch-up.

Walking up the hall with it, though, she noticed that a button on the right sleeve was cracked and she paused to look at it, to remember if she had a match.

And then, from the kitchen, Nikki heard the seltzer can open.

SEVEN

Even as she stood frozen in her hallway, Nikki's first thought was that she hadn't really heard it. Too many replays of her mother's murder had embedded that pop-top sound in her head. How many times had that snap-hiss jolted her out of nightmares or made her flinch in the break room? No, she could not have heard it.

That is what she told herself in the eternal seconds she stood there, cotton-mouthed and naked, straining to hear over the damned night noise of New York City, and her own pulse.

Her fingers hurt from digging the broken sleeve button into herself. She relaxed her grip but did not drop the blazer for fear of making noise that would give her away.

To whom?

Give it one minute, she told herself. Stay still, be a statue for a count of sixty and be done with this.

She cursed herself for her nakedness and how vulnerable it made her feel. Indulged in the bubble bath and now look. Stop that and focus, she thought. Just focus and listen to every square inch of the night.

Maybe it was a neighbor. How many times had she heard lovemaking, and coughing, and dishes stacking, come across the air space into her open windows?

The windows. They were all open.

A mere fraction through her minute, she lifted one bare foot off the runner and set it down one step closer to the kitchen. She listened.

Nothing.

Nikki chanced another slo-mo step. In the middle of it, her heart skipped when a shadow moved across the slice of floor she could see in the kitchen. She didn't hesitate or stop to listen again. She bolted.

Racing past the kitchen door to the living room, Nikki hit the light switch, killing the one lamp that was on, and lunged for her desk. Her hand landed inside the large Tuscan bowl that lived there on the back corner. It was empty.

"Looking for this?" Pochenko filled the archway, and he was holding up her off-duty piece. The bright kitchen light behind him cast him in silhouette, but she could see that the Sig Sauer was still in its holster, as if the arrogant bastard wouldn't be needing it, at least not yet.

Confronted by facts, the detective did what she always did, pushed fear aside and got practical. Nikki ran a checklist of options. One: She could scream. The windows were open, but he might start shooting, which, for the moment, he didn't seem inclined to do. Two: Get a weapon. Her backup gun was in her handbag in the kitchen or the bedroom, she wasn't sure which. Either way she would have to get past him. Three: Buy time. She needed it to improvise a weapon, to escape, or to take him out. If she had been confronting a hostage situation, she would have used conversation. Engage, humanize, slow the clock.

"How did you find me?" Good, she thought, to her ear she didn't sound afraid.

"What, you think you're the only ones who know how to tail somebody?"

Nikki took a small step backward to draw him into the room and away from the hall. She retraced the places she had been since she had left the precinct—Soho House, Rook's poker game—and got a chill realizing this man had been watching her each stop.

"It's not hard to follow someone who doesn't know they have a tail. You should know that."

"And how do *you* know that?" She took another step backward. This time he moved with her a step. "Were you a cop in Russia?"

Pochenko laughed. "Sort of. But not for police. Hey, stay there." He took the Sig out and tossed the holster aside like litter. "I don't want to have to shoot you." And then he added, "Not till I'm through."

Game changer, she said to herself, and prepared for the worst option. Nikki had drilled the handgun disarm only a million times. But always on a mat with an instructor or cop partner. Still Heat thought of herself as an athlete, in constant training, and had run it only two weeks ago. As she choreographed the moves in her head, she kept talking. "You've got balls coming here without your own gun."

"I won't need it. Today, you tricked me. Not so tonight, you'll see."

He reached for the light switch when he turned, and this time she took a step toward him. When the lamp came on he looked at her and said, "Daddy like." He made a show of looking her body up and down. Ironically, Nikki had felt more violated by him that afternoon in Interrogation when she had her clothes on. Still she folded her arms over herself.

"Cover all you want. I told you I'd have it, and I will."

Heat took stock. Pochenko was one-handing her gun, a plus since he had strength on her. He also had size, but she knew from his subway takedown that he was big but not quick. But then, he had the gun.

"Come here," he said and took a step to her. The conversation phase was over. She hesitated and took a step toward him. Her heart thudded and she could hear her own pulse. This would all be a blink if it came off. She felt like she was on a high dive about to initiate a plunge, and the thought made her heart race more. She remembered the uniform in the Bronx who'd botched this last year and lost half his face. Nikki decided that wasn't helping and focused herself again, visualizing her moves.

"Bitch, when I say come here, come here." He brought the gun up level with her chest.

She moved the step closer that he wanted and that she needed, and as she did, she raised her hands in submission, quaking them slightly so their small movements would not telegraph the big one when it came. And when it came, it had to be lightning. "Just don't shoot me, OK? Please, don't shoo—"

In one motion, she brought her left hand up and clamped it on top of the gun, wedging her thumb on the hammer while she pushed it away and slipped in and to his right. She hooked her foot between his and threw her shoulder against his arm while she wrenched the gun up and around toward him. As she yanked it to point at him she heard his finger break as it twisted in the trigger guard and he cried out.

Then it got messy. She tried to pull the gun away, but his broken finger was hung up in the guard, and when it finally jerked free the gun had such momentum it slipped out of her hand and across the rug. Pochenko grabbed her by the hair and threw her toward the foyer. Nikki tried to gain her feet and get to the front door, but he lunged for her. He grabbed one of her forearms but it didn't hold. His hands were sweaty and she was slick from the bubble bath. Nikki slid out of his grip and twirled, shooting the heel of her other hand up into his nose. She heard a crack and he swore in Russian. Torquing herself, she raised her foot to chest-kick him back into the living room, but he had his hands up to the twin trails of blood coming from his broken nose, and her kick glanced off his forearm. When he reached for her, she fired two rapid lefts to his nose, and while he dealt with that, she turned to flip the deadbolts on her front door and screamed, "Help, fire! Fire!"— sadly the surest way to motivate citizens to make a 911 call.

The boxer in Pochenko came alive. He landed a hard left to her back that smacked her flat against the door. Her advantage was speed and movement, and Nikki used it, dropping so that his next shot, a left to her head, missed and he smashed his fist into the wood. While she was down, she rolled right through his ankles, sweeping his legs from under him and sending him face-first into the door.

While he was down, she broke for the living room, looking for the fallen gun. It had taken a bounce under the desk, and the time it took her to find it was too much time. Just as Nikki bent for it Pochenko bear hugged her from behind and picked her up off the floor, kicking and punching air. He put his mouth to her ear and said, "You're mine now, bitch."

Pochenko carried her to the hallway leading to the bedroom, but Nikki wasn't done. At the passage to the kitchen, she splayed out her arms and legs and hooked them on the corners. It was like hitting the brakes, and as his head whiplashed forward, she shot hers back and felt a sharp pain when his front teeth broke against the back of her skull.

He cursed again and flung her onto the kitchen floor, where he pounced on top of her, pinning her with his body. This was the nightmare outcome, letting him get his full weight on her. Nikki jerked and twisted, but he had gravity working for him now. He let go her left wrist, but it was only to free the hand without the broken finger to clamp around her throat. With one hand free, she pushed at his chin, but he didn't budge. And his grip tightened on her neck. Blood dripped off his nose and chin onto her face, waterboarding her. She flailed her head side to side and took swipes at him with her right hand, but his choke was sapping her strength.

Fog crept into the edges of her vision. Above her, Pochenko's determined face became dappled by a shower of tiny shooting stars. He was taking his time, watching her lungs slowly lose oxygen, feeling her weaken, seeing her head flails become less rapid.

Nikki rolled her face to the side so she wouldn't have to look at him. She thought of her mother, murdered three feet away on this very floor, calling her name. And as blackness drew over her, Nikki thought how sad that she had no name to call for.

And that is when she saw the cord.

Lungs searing, strength draining, Nikki fumbled for the dangling wire. After two failed swipes, she snagged it and the iron crashed down off the board. If Pochenko cared, he didn't show it, and probably took it as the last thrashing of the bitch.

But then he felt the hot sear of the iron on the side of his face.

His scream was like no animal Nikki had heard. As his hand came off her neck, the air she gulped tasted of his burning flesh. She brought the iron up again, this time in a hard swing. The hot edge of it hit his left eye. He screamed again, and his scream mixed with the sirens pulling up to her building.

Pochenko struggled to his feet and stumbled toward the kitchen door, holding his face, bouncing off the corner of the entryway. He recovered and lumbered out. By the time she pulled herself up and made it to the living room, Nikki could hear his heavy footsteps clanging up the fire escape toward the roof.

Heat grabbed her Sig and climbed the metal steps to the roof, but he was long gone. Emergency lights strobed off the brick fronts on her street, and another approaching siren triple-burped through the intersection at Third Avenue. She remembered she had no clothes on and decided she had better go back down and put something on.

―――――

When Nikki came into her bull pen the next morning, after her meeting with the captain, Rook and Roach were waiting there for her. Ochoa was leaning back in his chair with his ankles crossed on his desk and said, "So. Last night I watched the Yankees win and had sex with the wife. Can anybody top that?"

"Beats my night," said Raley. "What about you, Detective Heat?"

She shrugged, playing along. "Just some poker and a little workout at home. Not as exciting as you, Ochoa. Your wife actually had sex with you?" Cop humor, dark and laced with sideways affection only.

"Oh, I see," said Rook. "This is how you people deal. 'Attempt on my life? No biggie, too cool for school.'"

"No, we pretty much don't give a shit. She's a big girl," Ochoa said. And the cops laughed. "Put that in your research, writer boy."

Rook approached Heat. "I'm surprised you came in this morning."

"Why? This is where I work. Not going to catch any bad guys at home."

"Clearly," said Ochoa.

"Nailed it," Raley said to his partner.

"Thank you for not high-fiving," she said. Even though the precinct, and by now most of the cop shops in five boroughs, knew about her home invasion, Nikki recapped her firsthand highlights for them and they listened intently, with sober expressions.

"Bold," said Rook, "going after a cop. And in her own home. Guy must be psycho. I thought so yesterday."

"Or . . . ," said Heat, deciding to share the feeling she'd been harboring since she saw Pochenko in her living room holding her gun. "Or maybe somebody sent him to get me out of the way. Who knows?"

"We'll bag this bastard," said Raley. "Spoil his day."

"Damn straight," from Ochoa. "On top of the all-points, we've notified hospitals to be on alert for anybody whose face is only half-pressed."

"Cap said you guys already gave Miric an early wake-up call."

Ochoa nodded. "At oh-dark-thirty. Dude sleeps in a nightshirt." He shook his head at the vision, and continued. "Anyway, Miric claims no contact with Pochenko since they got sprung yesterday. We've got surveillance on him and a warrant for his phone records."

"And a tap on his incomings," added Raley. "Plus we have some blue jeans from both Miric's and Pochenko's apartments in the lab now. Your Russian pal had a couple of promising rips on the knees, but it's hard to know what's fashion and what's wear and tear. Forensics will know."

Nikki smiled. "And on the upside, I may have a match for those grip marks on Starr's upper arms." She opened her collar and showed the red marks on her neck.

"I knew it. I knew it was Pochenko who threw him off that balcony."

"For once, Rook, I'd take that guess, but let's not jump there yet. The minute you start closing doors this early in an investigation is the minute you start missing something," said the detective. "Roach, go run a check on overnight retail robberies. If Pochenko's on the run and can't go to his apartment, he'll be improvising. Pay special attention to pharmacies and medical supply stores. He didn't go to an ER, so he might be doing some self-care."

———

After Roach left for their assignment and as Nikki was downloading a report from the forensic accountants, the desk sergeant brought in a package that had been delivered to her, a flat box the size and weight of a hallway mirror.

"I'm not expecting anything," said Nikki.

"Maybe it's from an admirer," said the sergeant. "Maybe it's Russian caviar," he added with a deadpan look and then left.

"Not the most sentimental crowd," said Rook.

"Thank God." She looked at the shipping label.

"It's from the Met Museum Store." She got scissors from her desk, opened the box, and peeked inside. "It's a framed something."

Nikki drew the framed something out of the box and discovered what it was, and when she did, whatever darkness she had carried into that morning-after gave way to soft, golden sunlight, breaking across her face in the reflected glow of two girls in white play dresses lighting Chinese lanterns in the gloaming of *Carnation, Lily, Lily, Rose.*

She stared at the print and then turned herself to Rook, who stood frowning beside her. "There should be a card somewhere. It says, 'Guess who?' By the way, you'd better guess me, or I'll be massively pissed I sprung for next-day delivery."

She looked back at the print. "It's . . . just so . . ."

"I know, I saw it on your face yesterday in Starr's living room. Little did I know when I called in my order it would be a get well gift. . . . Well, actually more like a glad-you-didn't-get-killed-last-night gift."

She laughed so he wouldn't notice the small quiver that had come to her lower lip. Then Nikki turned away from him. "I'm getting a little glare right under this light," she said, and all he saw was her back.

————

At noon she shouldered her bag, and when Rook stood to go with her she told him to get himself some lunch, she needed to go on this one by herself. He told her she should have some protection.

"I'm a cop, I am the protection."

He read her determination to go solo and for once didn't argue. On her drive to Midtown Nikki felt guilty for ditching him. Hadn't he welcomed her to his poker table and given her that gift? Sure he bugged her sometimes on the ride-alongs, but this was different. It could have been the ordeal of her night and the aching fatigue she was carrying, but it wasn't. Whatever the hell Nikki Heat was feeling, what the feeling needed was space.

"Sorry about the mess," said Noah Paxton. He threw the remains of his deli tossed salad into the trash can and wiped off his blotter with a napkin. "I wasn't expecting you."

"I was in the neighborhood," said Detective Heat. She didn't care if he knew she was lying. In her experience, dropping in on witnesses unexpectedly brought unexpected results. People with their guard down were less careful and she learned more. That afternoon she wanted a couple of things out of Noah, the first being his unguarded reaction to seeing the photo array from the Guilford again.

"Are there new pictures in here?"

"No," she said as she dealt the last one in front of him. "You're sure you don't recognize any of them?" Nikki made it sound casual, but asking if he was sure put pressure on. This was about cross-checking Kimberly's reason he hadn't identified Miric. As he had the day before, Paxton gave a slow and methodical pass over each shot and said he still didn't recognize any of them.

She took away all the photos but two: Miric and Pochenko. "What about these. Anything?"

He shrugged and shook no. "Sorry. Who are they?"

"These two are interesting, that's all." Detective Heat was in the business of getting answers, not giving them, unless there was an advantage. "I also wanted to ask you about Matthew's gambling. How did he pay for that?"

"With cash."

"Money you gave him?"

"His money, yes."

"And when he went in the hole to bookmakers, how did that get repaid?"

"Same way, with cash."

"Would they come to you for it, the bookies, I mean?"

"Oh, hell no. I told Matthew, if he chose to deal with that level of person, that's his business. I didn't want them coming here." He shivered for emphasis. "No thanks." She'd back-doored him but had her answer. Kimberly's reason the money man didn't know the bookie checked.

Heat then asked him about Morgan Donnelly, the woman whose name Kimberly had given her. She of the intercepted love letter. Paxton verified Donnelly had worked there and was their top marketing executive. He also verified that the two had a hidden office affair that was hidden to no one and described at great length how the staff would refer to Matthew and Morgan as "Mm . . ." Morgan earned a few nicknames of her own, he said. "The two that won the office pool were Top Performer and Chief Asset."

"One more piece of business and I'll get out of your hair. I got the report this morning from the forensic accountants." She took the file out of her bag and watched his brow fall. "They told me you were no Bernie Madoff, which is, I guess, what we needed to make sure of."

"Makes sense." Quite nonchalant, but the detective knew guilt when she saw it, and it was clinging to his face.

"There was one irregularity in your accounting." She handed him the page with the spreadsheet and summary and watched him tense. "Well?"

He put the page down. "My attorney would advise me not to answer."

"Do you feel you need an attorney to answer my question, Mr. Paxton?"

She could see her squeeze work on him. "It was my only ethical breach," he said. "All these years, the only one." Nikki just looked and waited. Nothing screamed louder than silence. "I hid money. I created a series of transactions to funnel a large sum to a private account. I was hiding a portion of Matthew Starr's private funds for his son's college education. I saw how fast it was going—to gambling and hookers—I'm just a functionary, but I was heartsick about what was happening to that family. For their own good, I hid money so Matty Junior could go to college. Matthew discovered it, same way drunks can find bottles, and raided it. Kimberly is almost as bad as he was. I think you have a good idea how she likes to spend."

"I got that impression."

"The wardrobe, the jewelry, the vacations, the

cars, the surgeries. Plus she was hiding money. Of course, I spotted it. Much like your forensics guys— the numbers talk if you know what you're looking for. Among other things, she had a love nest, a two-bedroom spot on Columbus. I told her to get rid of it, and when she asked why, I told her because they were broke."

"How did she react?"

"Devastated doesn't begin to cover it. I guess you could say she freaked."

"And when did you tell her all this?"

He looked at the calendar under the glass on his desktop. "Ten days ago."

Detective Heat nodded, reflecting. Ten days. A week before her husband was murdered.

EIGHT

When Detective Heat nosed the Crown Vic out of underground parking at the Starr Pointe tower, she heard the low, steady thrum that could only mean helicopters, and rolled her window down. Three of them hovered to her left about a quarter mile west, on the far side of the Time Warner building. The lower one, she knew, would be the police chopper, the two deferential ones at higher altitude would belong to TV stations. "Breaking nyoooz!" she said to her empty car.

She dialed in the tactical band on her radio and before long put together that a steam pipe had blown and geysered, further evidence that the ancient Gotham infrastructure was no match for nature's oven. Almost a week of the big heat, and Manhattan was starting to bubble and blister like a cheese pizza.

Columbus Circle would be impossible, so she took the longer but faster route back to the precinct, entering Central Park across from the Plaza and taking its East Drive north. The city kept the park closed to motor vehicles until three, so without traffic, her ride had a Sunday-in-the-country feel, lovely as long as she blasted the air conditioner. Sawhorses blocked the drive at 71st, but the auxiliary cop recognized her car as an unmarked and slid the barrier with a wave. Nikki pulled to a stop beside her. "Who'd you piss off to get this duty?"

"Must be karma from a past life," said the uniform with a laugh.

Nikki looked at the unopened bottle of cold water sweating in her cup holder and passed it to the woman. "Stay cool, Officer," she said and drove on.

The heat tamped everything down. Aside from a handful of certifiable runners and insane cyclists, the park had been left to the birds and squirrels. Nikki slowed as she passed the back of the Metropolitan Museum, and looking at the sloped glass wall of the mezzanine, she smiled, as she always did, at her classic movie memory of Harry in there with Sally, teaching her how to tell a waiter there was too much pepper on the paprikash. A young couple ambled across the lawn hand in hand, and without deciding to, Nikki stopped the car and watched the two of them, simply together, with all the time in the world. When a ripple of melancholy stirred in her, she pushed it down with a slow press of the gas pedal. Time to get back to work.

———

Rook sprang up from her desk chair when Nikki came into the bull pen. It was clear he was waiting for her to get back and wanted to know where she'd gone, meaning, without saying it, Why didn't you bring me? When she told him it was to follow up with Noah Paxton, Rook didn't get any more relaxed or much less obvious.

"You know, I get it that you aren't the biggest

fan of my ride-along thing, but I'd like to think I'm a pretty useful set of eyes and ears for you on these interviews."

"Can I mention that I am in the middle of an active murder investigation? I needed to see a witness alone because I wanted him to be open to me without any extra eyes and ears, useful though they may be."

"So you're saying they are useful?"

"I'm saying this isn't a time for you to personalize or be needy." She looked at him, just wanting to be with her and, she had to admit, being more cute than needy. Nikki found herself smiling. "And yes—sometimes—they are useful."

"All right."

"Just not every time, OK?"

"We're in a good place, let's not overexamine," he said.

"Got some news about Pochenko," said Ochoa as he and Raley came through the door.

"Tell me he's on Rikers Island and can't get a lawyer, that would be good news," she said. "What have you got?"

"Well, you called it," said Ochoa. "A guy fitting his description shoplifted half the first aid aisle at a Duane Reade in the East Village today."

"Got surveillance vid, too." Raley popped a DVD in his computer.

"Positive ID on Pochenko?" she asked.

"You tell me."

The drugstore video was ghosty and jerky, but there he was, the big Russian, filling a plastic bag with ointments and aloe, then ducking through

the first aid section to help himself to wrapping
tape and finger splints.

"Dude's in bad shape. Remind me never to get
in a fight with you," said Raley.

"Or to have you press my shirts," added Ochoa.

They went back and forth like that. Until somebody came up with a magic pill, gallows humor
was still the best coping mechanism for a cop.
Otherwise the job ate you alive. Normally, Nikki
would have been right there taking shots with
them, but she was too raw to laugh it off just yet.
Maybe if she could see Pochenko shackled in the
back of a van on his way to Ossining for the rest of
his life, then she wouldn't still be smelling him or
feeling his skillet hands on her throat in her own
home. Maybe then she could laugh.

"Whoa, check out the finger, I think I'm gonna
yack," said Ochoa. Raley added, "He can kiss off
that piano scholarship to Juilliard."

Rook's smart mouth was uncharacteristically
silent. Nikki checked him out and caught him
watching her with something like what she'd seen
in his eyes at the poker table the night before, but
magnified. She broke off, feeling the need to get
clear of whatever this was, just like she had after
he gave her the framed print. "All right, so that's
definitely our man," she said and moved away to
contemplate the whiteboard.

"And do I need to point out he's still in the
city?" said Rook.

She chose to ignore him. The fact was obvious
and the worry useless. Instead she turned to Raley.
"Nothing at all on your Guilford tape?"

"I went over that puppy until I was cross-eyed. No way they came back through that lobby after they left. I also screened video of the service entrance. Nothing."

"All right, we gave it a shot."

"Screening that lobby video was totally the worst," said Raley. "Like watching C-SPAN only not as exciting."

"Tell you what, then, I'll get you out in the world. Why don't you and Ochoa drop in on Dr. Van Peldt's office and see if Kimberly Starr's alibi clears? And since it's a safe bet she's tipped off her one true love that we'll be checking—"

"I know," said Ochoa, "verify with his receptionist, nurses, and/or hotel staff, etcet-yadda, etcet-yadda."

"Gosh, Detective," said Heat, "it's almost like you know what you're doing."

Detective Heat stood at the whiteboard and under the heading "Guilford Surveillance Video" wrote two red letters: N.G. It must have been the angle she was writing at that brought on the pinching stiffness from the previous night's brawl. She let her shoulders drop and rolled her head in a slow circle, feeling the delicious edge of discomfort that told her she was still alive. When she was done, she circled "Matthew's Mistress" on the board, capped her marker, and yanked the magazine out of Rook's hands. "Want to take a ride?" she asked.

They took the West Side Highway downtown, and even the river showed symptoms of heat strain.

To their right, the Hudson looked as if it was too hot to move and its surface lay there in surrender, all flat and dozy. The zone west of Columbus Circle was still a mess and would surely lead the five o'clock news. The erupting steam jet had been shut off, but there was a lunar-sized crater that would close West 59th for days. On the scanner, they listened to one of the NYPD quality of life squads report they had busted a man for public urination who admitted he tried to get arrested so he could spend the night in air-conditioning. "So the weather caused two eruptions that required police action," said Rook, which made Heat laugh and feel almost glad he was along.

When she'd set up the meeting with Matthew Starr's former mistress, Morgan Donnelly asked if they could meet her at work, since that's where she spent most of her time. That fit the profile Noah Paxton had sketched of her when Nikki asked him about her in their conversation earlier that day. As was his way, once he opened up, Nikki's pen could hardly keep pace. In addition to revealing choice office nicknames, he'd called their romance the inter-office elephant in the conference room and summed up Starr's not-so-secret mistress by saying, "Morgan was all brains, tits, and drive. She was the Matthew Starr ideal: work like crazy, screw like mad. Sometimes I'd picture them in bed with their BlackBerrys, texting oh-yeah-like-that's to each other between deals."

So, with that in her head, when Nikki Heat parked the car at the business address off Prince Street in SoHo Donnelly had given her, she had to double-check her notes to make sure she had the right place. It was a cupcake bakery. Her sore neck protested when she twisted to read the sign above the door. " 'Fire and Icing'?" she said.

Rook quoted a poem, " 'Some say the world will end in fire,/Some say in ice.' " He opened his car door and the heat rolled in. "Today, I'm going with fire."

"I still can't believe it," said Morgan Donnelly as she sat down with them at a round café table in the corner. She unsnapped the collar flap of her crisp white chef's tunic and offered the stainless sugar caddy to Heat and Rook for their iced Americanos. Nikki tried to reconcile the Morgan the baker before her with the Morgan the marketing power-house Noah Paxton drew. There was a story there and she would get it. The corners of Donnelly's mouth turned down, and she said, "You hear about things like this in the news, but it's never anybody you know."

The girl came from behind the counter and set a sample plate of mini-cupcakes in the center of the table. When she stepped away, Morgan continued, "I know getting involved with a married man doesn't make me look like the best person. Maybe I wasn't. But when it was happening, it seemed so right. Like in the middle of all the pressure of the job there was this passion, this amazing thing that was just ours." Her eyes filled a little and she swiped her cheek once.

Heat studied her for tells. Too much remorse or not enough were red flags. There were others, of course, but those indicators formed the baseline for her. Nikki hated the term, but so far Morgan's reaction was appropriate. But the detective needed to do more than take her temp. As the ex of a murder victim, she had to be checked out, and that meant getting answers to two simple questions: Did she have a strong revenge motive, and did she stand to gain from the man's death? Life would be so much simpler if Heat could just have her check off boxes on a questionnaire and mail it in, but it didn't work that way and now Nikki's job was to make this woman a little uncomfortable. "Where were you when Matthew Starr was killed? Say, between twelve-thirty and two-thirty P.M.?" She started throwing the high heat to catch Morgan off guard.

Morgan took a moment and answered without any defensiveness. "I know exactly where I was. I was with the Tribeca Film people for a tasting. I won a catering contract for one of their after-parties this spring, and I remember because the tasting went well and I was driving back here to celebrate that afternoon when I heard about Matthew."

Nikki made a note and continued. "Did you and Mr. Starr have any contact after the affair ended?"

"Contact. You mean, did we still see each other?"

"That. Or any contact at all."

"No, although I did see him once a few months ago. But he didn't see me and we didn't talk."

"Where was this?"

"Bloomingdale's. At the lunch counter downstairs. I was going to get a tea and he was there."

"Why didn't you speak to him?"

"He was with someone."

Nikki made a note. "Did you know her?"

Morgan smiled at Nikki's perception. "No. I might have said hello to Matthew, but she had her hand on his thigh. They seemed preoccupied."

"Can you describe her?"

"Blond, young, pretty. Young." She thought a moment and added, "Oh, and she had an accent. Scandinavian. Denmark or Sweden, maybe, I don't know."

Nikki and Rook traded glances, and she could sense him looking over her shoulder as she wrote "Nanny?" in her notes. "So otherwise no contact at all then?"

"No. When it was over, it was over. But it was very cordial." She looked down at her espresso and then up at Nikki and said, "Bullshit, it was painful as hell. But we were both grown-ups. We both went our ways. Life goes . . . well . . ." She left that unfinished.

"Let's go back to the end of your relationship. It must have been difficult in the office. Did he fire you when it was over?"

"It was my decision to leave. Working together would be awkward for us, and I sure as hell didn't want to deal with the gossip residue."

"But still, you had a big career there."

"I had a big love there. At least I told myself it was. When that ended, I wasn't focused on my career so much."

"I'd be angry as hell," said the detective. Sometimes the best way to ask a question was not to ask it.

"Hurt and fragile, yes. Angry?" Morgan smiled. "It ended up for the better. A relationship like that, you know, the fun-and-convenient, going-nowhere kind? I realized I was using that relationship to stay out of relationships, just as I was with my work. Do you know what I mean?"

Nikki shifted uncomfortably in her chair and managed a neutral "Uh-huh."

"At best it was a place holder. And I wasn't getting any younger." Nikki shifted again, wondering how she had ended up as the one feeling uncomfortable. "Matthew was good to me, though. He offered me a huge chunk of money."

Nikki snapped out of herself and back to the interview and made a note to check that out with Paxton. "How much did he give you?"

"Nothing. I wouldn't accept it."

"It's not like he would have missed it," said Rook.

"But don't you see?" she said to him, as if he never would. "If I took his money, then that would be what it was all about. It wasn't like people said. It wasn't about rising to the top on my back with my legs in the air."

Rook persisted. "Still, nobody would have to know you took his money."

"I would," she said.

And with those two words, Detective Heat closed her notebook. A carrot cupcake was screaming at her from that plate and it had to be silenced. As Nikki peeled at the ruffles of the bottom wrapper, she nodded her head to the trendy bake shop and asked, "What about all this? Not where I expected to find the infamous M.B.A. on Red Bull."

Morgan laughed. "Oh, that Morgan Donnelly. She's around somewhere. Makes an appearance once in a while and turns my life nuts." She leaned forward over the table, toward Nikki. "The end of that affair three years ago turned out to be an epiphany. Before it came, I was getting hints, but I ignored them. For instance, some nights I'd stand there in my big old corner office up on the penthouse floor of the Starr Pointe, one phone going, two lines on hold, and a dozen e-mails to answer. And I'd look below on the street and say to myself, 'Look at all those people down there. Going home to some-body.'"

Nikki was licking some buttercream frosting from her fingertip and stopped. "But come on, a career woman at the top of your game, that must have been very satisfying, right?"

"After Matthew, all I could think of was, What was I left with? And all the stuff that had passed me by while I was putting on the power suits and doing the career. You know, life? Well, here was the epiphany. One day I'm watching *Good Morning America*, and Emeril's on, and he was making pies, and it got me remembering when I was a kid, how much I loved to bake. So there I was, in my pajamas and Uggs, creeping up on thirty, no job, no relationship, and let's face it, not getting much out of either one when I had them anyway, think-ing, 'Time to reboot.'"

Nikki found her heart racing. She took a sip of her Americano and asked, "So you just took the jump? No net, no regrets, no looking back?"

"At what? I decided to follow my bliss. Of course, the price of bliss is a loan to the eyeballs, but it's working out. I started small . . . hell, look around, I still am small ... but I'm loving it. I'm even engaged." She held out her hand, which had no ring on it.

"It's lovely," said Rook.

Morgan made a whoops face and blushed a little. "I never wear it when I'm baking, but the guy who does my Web site? He and I are tying the knot this fall. I guess you never know where life's taking you, huh?"

Nikki reflected and unfortunately had to agree.

————

As they headed uptown, Rook balanced a huge box of two dozen cupcakes on his lap. Heat brought the car to a gentle stop at a red light so his gift to the precinct break room wouldn't turn into a box of crumbs. "So, Officer Rook," she asked, "I haven't heard you tell me to slap Morgan Donnelly in jail. What gives?"

"Oh, she's got to be off the list."

"Because?"

"Too happy."

Heat nodded. "Agreed."

"But," said Rook, "you'll still check her alibi and whether Paxton cut her a fat good-bye check."

"That's right."

"And we have a surprise mystery guest to check out, the Nordic Nanny."

"You're learning."

"Oh, yeah, learning a lot. Those were very revealing questions." She watched him, knowing something was coming. "Especially when you finished asking about the case and started getting personal."

". . . Yeah? She had an interesting story and I wanted to hear it."

"Huh. You sure didn't look like it." Rook waited until he saw the color come to her cheeks, and then he just stared straight ahead out the windshield with that stupid grin again. All he said was, "Green."

"Hey, man, it's the thought that counts," said Raley. Rook, Roach, and a number of detectives and uniforms were crowded in the precinct break room, around the open Fire and Icing box Rook had lovingly cradled on the drive. The assortment of buttercream icings, whipped creams, and ganache had melted and run together into what would charitably be described as cupcake roadkill.

"No, it's not," from Ochoa. "Man promised cupcakes, I don't want thought, I want a cupcake."

"I tell you these were perfect when they left the bakery," said Rook, but the room was emptying around his good deed. "It's the heat, it's melting everything."

"Leave 'em outside a little longer. I'll come back with a straw," said Ochoa. He and Raley moved on to the bull pen. When they arrived, Detective Heat was updating the whiteboard.

"Filling up," said Raley. It was always a mixed feeling at this point on an open homicide, when the satisfaction of seeing the board becoming populated with data was offset by the most salient fact: Nothing up there had brought a solve. But they all knew it was a process, and every bit they posted was a step closer to clearing the case.

"So," Nikki said to her squad, "Morgan Donnelly's alibi checks with the Tribeca Film commish." As Rook entered the room eating a cupcake out of a paper cup with a spoon, she added, "For the sake of her cupcakes, I hope the heat wave breaks by April. Roach, you saw Kimberly Starr's cosmetic surgeon?"

"Yeah, and I'm thinking of getting something ugly removed that's been bothering me for the past two years." Raley paused and added, "Ochoa."

"See, Detective Heat?" said his partner. "I give and I give, and this is what I put up with all day." Then Ochoa went to his notes. "The widow's alibi checks. She had a last-minute booking for a 'consultation,' and showed up at one-fifteen. That squares with her departure from the ice cream parlor on Amsterdam at one."

Heat said, "Over to the East Side in fifteen minutes? She got there in a hurry."

"Ain't no mountain high enough," said Rook.

"All right," continued Nikki, "Mrs. Starr managed to tell us the truth about cheating on both her husband and Barry Gable with Dr. Boy-tox. But that's just her whereabouts. Check phone records from her or the doc for any calls to Miric or Pochenko just to button it all down."

"Right," said Roach in unison and they laughed.

"See? I can't stay mad at you," said Ochoa.

———

That evening, darkness was trying to push through the soggy air outside the precinct on West 82nd when Nikki Heat stepped out carrying the Met Store box containing her John Singer Sargent print. Rook was standing at the curb. "I've got a car service coming. Why don't you let me give you a lift?"

"That's all right, I'm fine. And thanks again for this, you shouldn't have." She started off toward Columbus, on her way to the subway near the planetarium. "But you'll notice I'm keeping it. Night."

She got to the corner and Rook was beside her. "If you insist on proving how macho you are by walking, at least let me carry that."

"Good night, Mr. Rook."

"Wait." She stopped but didn't mask her impatience. "Come on, Pochenko's still at large. You should have an escort."

"You? Who'll protect you? Not I."

"Jeez, a cop who uses proper grammar as a weapon. I'm rendered helpless."

"Look, if you have any doubt I can take care of myself, I'll be more than happy to give you a demonstration. Is your health insurance current?"

"All right, what if this is just my flimsy excuse to see your apartment? What would you say to that?"

Nikki looked across the street and back at him. She smiled and said, "I'll bring in some pictures tomorrow," and crossed with the light, leaving him there on the corner.

A half hour later, Nikki came up the steps from the R train onto the sidewalk at East 23rd and saw the neighborhood plunge into darkness as Manhattan finally threw in the towel and collapsed into a citywide blackout. At first a strange silence fell as hundreds of window air conditioners up and down the street ground to a stop. It was as if the city were holding its breath. There was some ambient light from headlights on Park Avenue South. But the streetlights and traffic lights were out, and soon came the angry horns as New York drivers competed for asphalt and right of way.

Her arms and shoulders were aching when she turned onto her block. She set the Sargent print down on the sidewalk and leaned it carefully against a neighbor's wrought iron gate while she opened her shoulder bag. The farther she got from the avenue, the darker it had become. Heat fished for her mini-Maglite and adjusted the tiny beam so she wouldn't take a header on uneven pavement or some dog crap.

The eerie silence began to give way to voices. They floated in the darkness from above as apartment windows were thrust open and she could hear over and over again the same words from different buildings: "blackout," and "flashlight," and "batteries." She startled at a nearby cough and shined her light on an old man walking his pug.

"You're blinding me with that damn thing," he said as he passed, and she pointed the beam down at the ground.

"Be safe," she said but got no response. Nikki picked up her box in both hands and moved on toward her building with the mini-Mag wedged between her palm and the carton, shining light a few feet ahead of each step. She was two doors from her building when a foot scraped on a pebble behind her and she stopped. Listened. Listened hard. But heard no footsteps.

Some idiot hollered, "Awooooo!" from the roof-top across the street and dropped some flaming paper that spun a bright orange swirl until it burned itself out halfway down to the sidewalk. These were healthy reminders that this would be a good time to get off the street.

At her front steps, Nikki set down the box again and bent to get her keys. Behind her came quickening footsteps and then a hand touched her back. She whirled and threw a high, backward circle kick that grazed Rook, and by the time she heard his "Hey!" it was too late to do anything but gain her balance and hope he didn't hit his head on the way down.

"Rook?" she said.

"Down here." Nikki shined her light in the direction of his voice and spotlighted him sitting up in the sidewalk planter with his back against a tree trunk, holding his jaw.

She bent down to him. "Are you all right? What the hell were you doing?"

"I couldn't see you, I bumped into you."

"But why are you here?"

"I just wanted to make sure—"

"—that you ignored what I said and followed me."

"Always the savvy detective." He put one of his hands against the tree and the other on the sidewalk. "You might want to turn away. I am about to struggle. Pay no attention to the groaning." She didn't turn away but put a hand under his arm to help him up.

"Did I break anything?" she asked and shined

the flashlight on his face. His jaw was red and chafed from her foot. "Do this," she said and shined the light on herself as she worked her jaw open and closed. She put the light on him and he followed her instructions. "How's that?"

"The humane thing may be just to put me down. You got a bullet on you?"

"You're fine. You're lucky I only grazed you."

"You're lucky I signed that waiver against law-suits when I started my ride-along."

She smiled in the dark. "I guess we're both lucky." Nikki figured he must have heard the smile in her voice because he drew closer to her, until there was only the slightest gap separating them. They stood there like that, not quite touching but sensing each other's closeness in the dark of the hot summer night. Nikki started to sway, and then leaned ever so slightly toward him. She felt her breast brush softly against his upper arm.

Then the bright light hit them.

"Detective Heat?" said the voice from the patrol car.

She took one step back from Rook and shielded her eyes against the spotlight. "I am."

"Everything all right?"

"Fine. He's . . . ," she looked at Rook, who wasn't appreciating her pause while she struggled to define him, "with me."

Nikki knew the score. As they lowered the beam out of her eyes, she pictured the meeting in Captain Montrose's office after she'd left and the call that went out. It was one thing to rib each other and play their game of Too Cool to Care, but the precinct was family, and if you were one of their own and you were threatened, you could bet your badge they'd have your back. The gesture would have been so much more welcome if she hadn't had Jameson Rook on her hip. "Thank you, but you know, this isn't necessary. Really."

"No sweat, we'll be here all night. You want us to show you upstairs?"

"No," Nikki said a little more urgently than she'd intended. She continued more softly, "Thank you. I've got a," she looked at Rook, who smiled until she said, "flashlight."

Rook lowered his voice. "Nice. Think I'll tell James Taylor I have his new song. 'You've Got a Flashlight.'"

"Oh, don't be so— You know James Taylor?"

"Heat?"

"Yeah?"

"Got any ice up there in that apartment?"

Nikki gave it a moment while he rubbed his sore jaw. "Let's go up and find out."

NINE

Nikki Heat's apartment building was not the Guilford. It was not only a fraction of the size, there was no doorman. Rook looped his fingers in the brass handle and held open the front door as she entered the small vestibule. Her keys clacked against the glass of the inner door, and once Nikki unlocked it, she waved to the blue-and-white still double-parked out front. "We're in," she said. "Thank you."

The cops left on the spotlight for them, and thanks to its spill the lobby was dim but not totally dark. "Chair, see?" Nikki shined her light at it briefly. "Stay close." A row of shiny metal-plated mailboxes caught the reflection beside them. She twisted the beam a little wider, and although it was not as intense, it gave them a better sense of the area, revealing the long, narrow lobby, which was a small-scale match for the footprint of the building. A single elevator sat ahead to the left, and on its right, separated by a table holding some UPS deliveries and unclaimed newspapers, was an open passageway to the staircase.

"Hang onto this." She gave him the box and crossed over to the elevator.

"Unless that thing's steam powered, I don't think it's going to be working," said Rook.

"Ya think?" She shined the light up at the deco brass dial indicating which of the five floors the car was on. The arrow pointed to the 1. Heat rapped the heel of her flashlight on the elevator door and a series of loud bongs resonated. She called out, "Anybody in there?" and put her ear to the metal. "Nothing," she said to Rook. Then she dragged the lobby chair to the elevator door and stood on it. "For this to work, you have to do this up top, at the header." Clenching the tiny flashlight in her teeth to free her hands, she used them to pry the doors open a few inches at the center. Nikki angled her head forward and inserted the light into the partition. Satisfied, she released the doors and stepped down, reporting, "All clear."

"Always a cop," said Rook.

"Mm, not always."

———

She learned just how dark it could get when they started climbing the stairs, which were wall-bound and did not get any of the police spotlight bleeding into the lobby. Nikki led with her Maglite; Rook surprised her with a beam of light of his own. At the second floor landing she said, "What the hell is that?"

"iPhone ap. Cool, huh?" The screen of his cell phone radiated a bright flame from a virtual Bic lighter. "These are all the rage at concerts now."

"Did Mick tell you that?"

"No, Mick didn't tell me that." They resumed their climb and he added, "It was Bono."

It was an easy climb to her third-floor apartment, but the stifling air of the staircase had them both palming sweat off their faces. Inside her foyer she flicked the light switch out of habit and chided herself for being so on autopilot. "Do you have service on that thing?"

"Yep, showing all bars."

"Miracle of miracles," she said and flipped open her own phone to speed-dial Captain Montrose. She had to try twice to get a connection, and while it rang, she led Rook into the kitchen and lit up the freezer. "Ice down that jaw, while I—Hello, Captain, thought I'd check in."

Detective Heat knew the city would be on a tactical alert and wanted to see if she should come to the station or go to a staging area. Montrose confirmed that Emergency Management had called the T.A. and that leaves and days off were temporarily suspended. "I might need you to cover a shift, but so far anyway, the city is behaving. Guess we've got this down from the 2003," he said. "Considering the twenty-four hours you've just had, your best use for me would be to get some rest and be fresh tomorrow in case this drags on."

"Uh, Captain, I was surprised to see I've got a little company out front."

"Oh, right. Put in a call to the Thirteenth Precinct. They're treating you right, I hope."

"Swell, very solid. But here's the thing. With this T.A. on, is this the best use of resources?"

"If you mean covering my best investigator to make sure she doesn't get her sleep disturbed, I can't think of a better use. Raley and Ochoa insisted on doing it themselves, but I put a stop to that. Now, that would be a waste of resources."

God, she thought. That would be just what she

needed, having Roach show up and catch her out there brushing buttons in the dark with Rook. As it was, she wasn't keen on the idea of those uniforms knowing what time Rook was leaving, even if it would be soon. "It's sweet, Cap, but I'm a big girl, I'm home safe, the door's locked, the windows are closed, I'm armed, and I think our city will be better off if you kick that car loose."

"All right," he said. "But you double-lock that door. No strange men in that apartment tonight, you hear?"

She watched Rook leaning against the butcher block holding a dish towel of ice cubes to his face and said, "No worries, Captain. And Cap? Thank you." She pressed End and said, "They don't need me tonight."

"So your obvious attempt to cut my visit short didn't pan out."

"Shut up and let me look at that." She stepped over to him and he lowered the towel so she could examine his sore jaw. "Not swelling, that's good. An inch closer to my foot, you'd have been drinking soup through a straw for the next two months."

"Hold on, that was your foot you hit me with?"

She shrugged and said, "Yeah?" then rested her fingertips on his jaw. "Work it again." Rook moved it back and forth. "That hurt?"

"Only my pride."

She smiled and held her fingers there on him, caressing his cheek. The corners of his mouth turned up slightly, and he looked at her in a way that made her heart flutter. Nikki stepped away before the magnet pull gained real force, suddenly worried that deep down she might be some sort of freak who got turned on at crime scenes. First on Matthew Starr's balcony and now here in her own kitchen. Not the worst thing, to be a bit of a freak, she thought, but crime scenes? That was sure the common denominator. Well, that and, um, Rook.

He shook the ice out of the towel and into the sink, and while he was occupied, her mind raced to figure out just what the hell she was thinking, asking him up there. Maybe she was loading too much meaning into this visit, projecting. Sometimes a cigar is just a cigar, right? And sometimes coming up for ice was just coming up for ice. Her breath was still high in her chest, though, from being close to him. And that look. No, she said to herself, and made her decision. The best course was not to force this. He had his ice, she'd kept her promise, yes, the smart thing would be to stop this now and send him on his way. "Would you like to stay for a beer?" she asked.

"I'm not sure," he said with a grave tone. "Is your iron unplugged? Oh wait, there's no electricity so I don't have to worry about my face getting pressed."

"Funny man. Guess what? I don't need no stinking iron. I've got a Bagel Biter over there and you don't want to know what I can do with that."

He took a moment and said, "I'm good with beer."

There was only one Sam Adams in the fridge so they split it. Rook said he was fine with sharing hits off the bottle, but Nikki got them glasses, and while she got them down, she wondered what had made her ask him to stay. She felt a naughty thrill and smiled about how blackouts and hot nights brought on a certain lawlessness. Maybe she did need guarding—from herself.

Rook and his virtual lighter disappeared into the living room with their beers while she scrounged a kitchen drawer for some candles. When she came into the living room, Rook was standing at the wall adjusting the John Singer Sargent print. "This look level to you?"

"Oh . . ."

"I know it's kind of forward. We know about my boundary issues, right? You can hang it somewhere else, or not, I just thought I'd swap it for your Wyeth poster so you could get the effect."

"No, no, it's good. I like it there. Let me get some more light going for a better look. It might have found its home." Nikki struck a wooden match and the flare-up anointed her face with gold. She reached down into the curved glass of the hurricane lamp on the bookcase and touched the flame to the wick.

"Which one are you?" said Rook. When she looked up, he gestured to the print. "The girls, lighting the lanterns. I'm watching you do the same thing and wondering if you see yourself as one of them."

She moved to the coffee table and set out a pair of votives. As she lit them, she said, "Neither, I just like the way it feels. What it captures. The light, the festiveness, their innocence." She sat on the sofa. "I still can't believe you got it for me. It was very thoughtful."

Rook came around the other end of the coffee

table and joined her on the couch, but putting himself at the far end with his back against the armrest. Allowing some space between them. "Have you seen the original?"

"No, it's in London."

"Yes, at the Tate," he said.

"Then you've actually seen it, show off."

"Mick and Bono and I went. In Elton John's Bentley."

"You know, I almost believe you."

"Tony Blair was so pissed we invited Prince Harry instead of him."

"Almost," she chuckled and glanced over at the print. "I used to love to see Sargent's paintings at the Fine Arts in Boston when I was going to Northeastern. He did some murals there, too."

"Were you an art student?" Before she could answer, he raised his glass. "Hey, look at us. Nikki and Jamie, doin' the social."

She clinked his glass and took a sip. The air was so warm, the beer was already hitting room temp. "I was an English major, but I really wanted to transfer to Theater."

"You're going to have to help me with this. How did you go from that to becoming a police detective?"

"Not such a huge leap," said Nikki. "Tell me what I do isn't part acting, part storytelling."

"True. But that's the what. I'm curious about the why."

The murder.

The end of innocence.

The life changer.

She thought it over and said, "It's personal. Maybe when we know each other better."

"Personal. Is that code for 'because of a guy'?"

"Rook, we've been riding together for how many weeks? Knowing what you know about me, do you think I would make a choice like that for a guy?"

"The jury will disregard my question."

"No, this is good, I want to know," she said, and scooted closer to him. "Would you change what you do for a woman?"

"I can't answer that."

"You have to, I'm interrogating your ass. Would you change what you do for a woman?"

"In a vacuum . . . I can't see it."

"All right, then."

"But," he said and paused to form his thought, "for the right woman? . . . I'd like to think I'd do just about anything." He seemed satisfied with what he'd said, even affirmed it to her with a nod, and when he did, he raised his eyebrows, and at that moment, Jamie Rook didn't look like a globe-trotter on the cover of a glossy magazine at all but like a kid in a Norman Rockwell, truthful and absent of guile.

"I think we need better alcohol," she said.

"There's a blackout, I could loot a liquor store. Do you have a stocking I can borrow to pull over my face?"

The exact contents of her liquor cupboard in the kitchen were a quarter bottle of cooking sherry, a bottle of peach Bellini wine cocktail that had no freshness date but years ago had separated and

taken on the look and hue of nuclear fissionable
material . . . Aha! And a half bottle of tequila.

Rook held the light and Nikki rose up from the
crisper drawer of the refrigerator brandishing a
sad little lime as if she'd snagged a Barry Bonds
ball complete with hologram. "Too bad I don't have
any triple sec or Cointreau, we could have margaritas."

"Please," he said. "You're in my area now." They
returned to the couch and he set up shop on the
coffee table with a paring knife, a salt shaker,
the lime, and the tequila. "Today, class, we're making what we call hand margaritas. Observe." He
sliced a lime wedge, poured a shot of tequila, then
licked the web of his hand at the thumb and forefinger and sprinkled salt on it. He licked the salt, tossed
back the shot, then bit the lime. "Whoa-yeah. That's
what I'm talkin' about," he said. "I learned how to
do this from Desmond Tutu," he added and she
laughed. "Now you."

In one fluid move Nikki picked up the knife,
sliced a wedge, salted her hand, and brought it all
home. She saw his expression and said, "Where the
hell you think I've been all these years?"

Rook smiled at her and prepared another, and
as she watched him, she felt herself relaxing her
sore shoulders and, inch by inch, coming unteth-
ered from the state of alertness she had unwit-
tingly adopted as a lifestyle. But when he was ready,
Rook didn't down this shot. Instead, he held out
his hand to her. She looked down at the salt on his
skin and the lime between his thumb and finger.
Nikki didn't look up at him because she was afraid

if she did she would change her mind instead of taking the leap. She bent toward his hand and darted her tongue out, quickly at first, but then, choosing to slow the moment down, she lingered there licking the salt off his skin. He offered her the shot and she fired it back and then, cradling his wrist in her fingers, she guided the lime wedge he was holding to her lips. The burst of lime juice cleansed her palate, and as she swallowed, the warmth from the tequila spread from her stomach to her limbs, filling her with a luxurious buoyancy. She closed her eyes and ran her tongue on her lips again, tasting the citrus and salt. Nikki wasn't at all drunk, it was something else. She was letting go. The simple things people take for granted. For the first time she could remember in a long time, she was flat-out relaxed.

That's when she realized she was still holding Rook's wrist. He didn't seem to mind.

They didn't speak. Nikki licked her own hand and salted it. Held a wedge. Poured a shot. And then she offered her hand to him. Unlike her, he didn't avert his gaze. He brought her hand up to him and put his lips on it and tasted the salt and then the saltiness of her skin around it as they stared at each other. Then he drank the shot and bit the lime she gave to him. They held eye contact like that, neither one moving, the extended-play version of their perfume ad moment on Matthew Starr's balcony. Only this time Nikki didn't break off.

Tentatively, slowly, each drew an inch closer, each still silent, each still holding the other's steady gaze. Whatever worry or uncertainty or conflict she'd felt before, she pushed it aside as too much thinking. At that moment, Nikki Heat didn't want to think. She wanted to be. She reached out and gently touched his jaw where she had struck him earlier. She rose up on one knee and leaned forward to him and, rising above him, lightly kissed his cheek. Nikki hovered there, studying the play of shadows and candlelight on his face. The soft ends of her hair dangled down and brushed him. He reached out, gently smoothing one side back, lightly stroking her temple as he did. Leaning there above him, Nikki could feel the warmth from his chest coming up to meet hers and she inhaled the mild scent of his cologne. The flickering of the candles gave the room a feeling of motion, the way it looked to Nikki when the plane she was in flew through a cloud. She pressed herself down to him and he came to meet her, the two of them not so much moving as drifting weightless toward each other, attracted by some irresistible force in nature that had no name, color, or taste, only heat.

And then what began so gently took on its own life. They flew to each other, locking open mouths together, crossing some line that dared them, and they took it. They tasted deeply and touched each other with a frenzy of eagerness fired by wonder and craving, the two of them released at last to test the edge of their passion.

A votive candle on the coffee table began to sputter and pop. Nikki pulled away from Rook, tearing herself away from him, and sat up. Chest heaving, soaked with perspiration, both his and her own, she watched the candle's glowing ember fade out, and when it had been consumed by the darkness, she stood. She held out her hand to Rook and he took it, rising up to stand with her.

One candle had sparked brightly and died but one was still burning. Nikki picked that one up and used it to light the way for them to her bedroom.

TEN

Nikki led him wordlessly into her bedroom and set the candle on her dresser, in front of the trifold mirror, which multiplied its light. She turned to find Rook there, close to her, magnetic. She folded her arms around his neck and drew his mouth to hers; he wrapped his long arms around her waist and tugged her body to him. Their kisses were deep and urgent, familiar all at once, her tongue finding the depth and sweetness of his open mouth while he explored hers. One of his hands began to reach for her blouse but hesitated. She clutched it and placed it on her breast. The heat of the room was tropical, and as he touched her, Nikki felt his fingers ride the slick of perspiration above the dampness of her bra. She lowered her hand and found him and he moaned softly. Nikki began to sway, then he did, too, both doing a slow dance in some sort of delicious vertigo.

Rook walked her backward toward her bed. When her calves met the edge of it, she let herself do a slow fall back, pulling him with her. As they both floated down, Heat pulled him closer and twisted, surprising Rook by landing on top of him. He looked up at her from the mattress and said, "You're good."

"You have no idea," she said. They dove into each other again, and her tongue picked up the faint acid tang of lime and then salt. Her mouth left his to kiss his face and then his ear. She felt the muscles of his abdomen flex hard against her as he curled his head upward, nibbling the soft flesh where her neck met her collarbone. Nikki stirred and began to unbutton his shirt. Rook was making a project out of her blouse button so she rose up, straddled him on both knees and ripped the blouse open, hearing one of her buttons skitter against the hardwood floor near the baseboard. With one hand, Rook unhooked the front clasp of her bra. Nikki shook her arms out of it and made a frenzied dive onto him. Their wet skin made a slap as her chest landed on his. She reached down and unhooked his belt. Then undid his zipper. Nikki kissed him again and whispered, "I keep protection in the nightstand."

"You won't need a gun," he said. "I'll be a perfect gentleman."

"You'd better not." And she pounced on him, her heart pounding high in her chest with excitement and tension. A wave crashed over Nikki and washed away all the conflicted feelings and misgivings she had been wrestling with, and she was simply, mightily, powerfully swept up. In that instant, Nikki became free. Free of responsibility. Free of control. Free of herself. Swirling, she clung to Rook, needing to feel every part of him she could touch. They held on with a fury, his passion matching hers as they explored each other, moving, biting, hungry, reaching and reaching to satisfy what they ached for.

———

Nikki couldn't believe it was morning already. How could the sun be so bright when her watch alarm hadn't gone off yet? Or did she sleep through it? She squinted her eyes open enough to recognize she was seeing the Nightsun beam from a police helicopter against her window shears. She listened. No sirens, no bullhorns, no heavy Russian footsteps on her fire escape, and soon, the spotlight was extinguished and the drone of the chopper grew silent as it flew on. She smiled. Captain Montrose may have kept his word and pulled the patrol car, but he didn't say anything about air surveillance.

She rolled her head to her alarm clock, but it was flashing 1:03 and that couldn't be right. Her watch said 5:21, so Nikki calculated that the difference was how long the blackout had lasted.

Rook drew a long, slow breath, and Nikki felt his chest expand against her back, followed by the chill of his exhale against the dampness of her neck. Damn, she thought, he's actually spooning me. With the windows closed, the bedroom was stifling, and there was a film of sweat fusing their naked bodies. She considered moving to get some air between them. Instead, Nikki settled herself back against his chest and thighs and liked the fit.

Jameson Rook.

Now, how did this happen?

Since the day she got stuck with him for this research ride-along business, he'd been a daily annoyance to her. And now here she was in bed with him after a night of sex. And great sex at that.

If she had to interrogate herself, Detective Heat

would end up signing a sworn statement that there was a spark of attraction from their first meeting. He, of course, had no qualms about voicing that every chance he had, a trait that may have had something to do with his high annoyance factor. May have? But his certainty was no match for a greater force, her denial. Yeah, there was always something there, and now, in hindsight, she realized that the more she'd felt it, the more she'd denied it.

Nikki wondered what other denials she had been dealing with.

None. Absolutely none.

Bull.

Why else did Matthew Starr's mistress strike such an uncomfortable chord with her, talking about how staying in a going-nowhere relationship was just a way of avoiding relationships, and asking her—asking *her*—if she knew what she meant.

Nikki knew from her therapy after the murder that she wore a lot of armor. Like she needed the shrink to tell her that. Or to warn her about the emotional peril of constantly deferring her needs, and yes, her desires, by packing them too safely inside her no-go zone. Those shrink sessions were long past, but how often lately had Nikki wondered—scratch that—worried, when she threw up her barriers and put herself in full Task Orientation Mode, if there might be this tipping point at which you can lose something of yourself you have been sheltering and never get it back. For instance, what happens when that hard coating you've developed to protect the most vulnerable part of you becomes so impenetrable that that part can't even be reached by you?

The Sargent print Rook gave her came to mind. She thought about those carefree girls lighting paper lanterns and wondered what became of them. Did they keep their innocence even after they stopped wearing play dresses and lost their soft necks and unlined faces? Did they lose the joy of play, of knowing what it was like to romp barefoot on damp grass simply because it felt good? Did they hold onto their innocence or had events invaded their lives to make them wary and vigilant? Did they, a hundred years before Sting wrote it, build a fortress around their hearts?

Did they have sport sex with ex–Navy Seals just to get their heart rates up?

Or with celebrity journalists who hung with Mick and Bono?

Not to compare—oh, why not?—the difference with Rook was that he got her heart rate up first and that's what made her want him. From that initial blood rush her pulse had only beat faster.

What was it that made sex with Jameson Rook so incredible?

Hm, she thought, he was passionate, for sure. Exciting and surprising, uh huh. And tender, too, at the right times, but not too soon—and not too much, thank God. But the big difference with Rook was that he was playful.

And he made her playful.

Rook gave her permission to laugh. Being with him was fun. Sleeping with him was anything but solemn and earnest. His playfulness brought joy into her bed. I still have my armor, she thought, but tonight, anyway, Rook got in. And brought me with him.

Nikki Heat had discovered she could be playful, too. In fact, she rolled toward him and slid down the bed to prove it.

———

Her cell phone startled them awake. She sat up, orienting herself in the blinding sunlight.

Rook lifted his head off the pillow. "What's that, a wake-up call?"

"You had your wake-up call, mister."

He dropped back on the pillow with his eyes closed, smiling at the memory. "And I answered."

She pressed the cell to her ear. "Heat."

"Hi, Nikki, did I wake you?" It was Lauren.

"No, I'm up." She fumbled for her watch on the nightstand. 7:03. Nikki worked to clear her head. When your friend from the medical examiner's office calls at that hour, it's generally not social.

"I waited until after seven."

"Lauren, really, it's fine. I'm already dressed and I've had my exercise," Nikki said, looking at her naked reflection in the mirror. Rook lifted himself up and his smiling face appeared in the mirror with her.

"Well, that's half-true," he said in a hushed voice.

"Oh . . . Sounds like you have company. Nikki Heat, do you have company?"

"No, that was the TV. Those ads come on so loud." She turned to Rook and put a finger to her lips.

"You have man company."

Nikki pressed for a change of subject. "What's going on, Laur?"

"I'm working a crime scene. Let me give you the address."

"Hang on, I need something to write with." Nikki crossed to the dresser and grabbed a pen. She couldn't find a pad or paper, so she flipped over her copy of *First Press* with Rook and Bono on the cover and wrote on the vodka ad on the back. "OK."

"I'm at the impound lot near the Javits."

"I know the impound. That's West, what, 38th?"

"Yes, at 12th," said Lauren. "A tow driver found a body in a car he was hauling. First Precinct's got jurisdiction, but I thought I'd give you a call because you're definitely going to want to come by for this. I found something that might relate to your Matthew Starr case."

"What? Tell me."

Nikki could hear voices in the background. The mouthpiece rustled as Lauren covered it and spoke to someone, then she came back on. "Detectives from the First just got here all hot to trot, so I've got to go. See you when you get here."

Nikki hung up and turned to see Rook was sitting on the edge of the bed. "Are you ashamed of me, Detective Heat?" He said it with a theatrical air. Nikki could hear a bit of the Grand Damn in his posh accent. "You bed me, but you hide me from your high-class friends. I feel so . . . cheap."

"Comes with the territory.' "

Rook thought a moment and said, "You could have told her I was here for security."

"You?"

"Well . . . I did cover you." He took her hand and pulled her closer, so that she stood between his knees.

"I've got an appointment with a corpse."

He looped his legs behind hers and rested his hands on her hips. "Last night was great, don't you think?"

"It was. And you know what else last night was? Last night." And she strode to her closet to get dressed for work.

———

Rook did the cab fishing on Park Avenue South and hooked a northbound whopper, a minivan-cab. He held the door for Nikki, who got in with one last glance over her shoulder, harboring the concern that Captain Montrose had left a blue-and-white on her and she'd be spotted on her morning after with Jameson Rook. "Looking for Pochenko?" asked Rook.

"Not really. Old habit."

She gave the cabbie Rook's address in Tribeca.

"What's going on?" he said. "Aren't we going to the impound lot?"

"One of us is going to the impound lot. The other is going to go home and change his clothes."

"Thanks, but if you can stand me, I'll wear this again today. I'd rather hang with you. Although, checking out a body isn't exactly our best denouement. After a night like that, the New York thing would be to take you to brunch. And pretend to write down your phone number."

"No, you're going to go change. I can't think of

a worse idea than for the two of us to show up in the same cab at my friend's crime scene first thing in the morning with bed hair and one of us in yesterday's clothes."

"We could show up wearing each other's clothes, that would be worse." He laughed and took her hand. She withdrew hers.

"Have you noticed I don't do a lot of hand holding on the job? Slows down my fast draw."

They rode in silence for a while. As the cab cut across Houston Street, he said, "I'm trying to figure out . . . did I bite my own tongue when you kicked me in the face, or did you do it?" That earned a fast check from the driver in the rearview mirror.

Heat said, "I want to lean on Forensics to cough up that report on Pochenko's blue jeans."

"I can't recall getting bitten either time," said Rook.

"Blackout probably set the lab behind schedule, but it's been long enough."

"Things were happening fast and, dare I say, furious."

"I'm betting those fibers match," she said.

"But still, you'd think I'd remember a bite."

"Surveillance video be damned, somehow he got in there, I'd bet on it. I know he likes his fire escapes."

"Am I talking too much?" Rook asked.

"Yes."

Two blessedly chatter-free minutes later, Rook was out of the cab, standing in front of his building.

"When you're done, go to the precinct and wait for me. I'll meet you there after I finish at the impound." He sulked like a rejected puppy and started to close the door. She held it open and said, "By the way? Yes. I did bite your tongue." Then she slid the door closed. Nikki watched him grinning on the sidewalk through the back window as her cab drove on.

———————

Detective Heat badged herself through the gate of the city impound, and after she signed in, the guard stepped out of his tiny office into the hot sun to point out the medical examiner van on the far end of the lot. Nikki turned to thank him but he was already inside filling his shirtsleeves with air from the window AC.

The sun was still low in the sky, just clearing the top of the Javits Convention Center, and Heat could feel its bite on her back as she paused to take her long, deep breath, her ritual remembering breath. When she was ready to meet the victim, she walked the long row of dusty parked cars with grease-penciled windshields to the investigation scene. The M.E. van and another from Forensics were parked close to a tow truck still hooked up to a newish, green metallic Volvo wagon. Technicians in white coveralls were dusting the outside of the Volvo. As Nikki got closer, she could see the body of a woman slumped in the driver's seat, the top of her head pointed out the open car door.

"Sorry to interrupt your morning workout, Detective." Lauren Parry stepped around the rear of the M.E. van.

"Not much gets by you, does it?"

"I told you Jameson Rook was doable." Nikki smiled and shook her head, she was so busted. "Well, was he doable?"

"And doable."

"Good. Glad to see you enjoying life. Detectives just told me you had a close call the other night."

"Yeah, after SoHo House it was all downhill."

Lauren stepped to her. "You all right?"

"Better than the bad guy."

"My girl." Then Lauren frowned and tugged aside the collar of her friend's blouse to look at the bruising she saw on her neck. "I'd say it was a very close call. Let's take it easy, all right? I have enough customers, I don't need you, too."

"I'll see what I can do," said Nikki. "Now, you dragged me out of bed for this, it better be worth it. What are you working here?"

"Jane Doe. Like I said, found in her car by the tow truck driver when he dropped it off here this morning. He thought it was heat asphyxiation."

"A Doe? In a car?"

"I hear you, but no driver's license. No purse. No plates. No registration."

"You said you found something connected to my Matthew Starr case."

"Give a girl a little sex and she gets very impatient."

Nikki cocked an eyebrow. "A little?"

"And boastful." The M.E. handed Nikki a pair of gloves. While she put them on, Lauren turned to the back of her van and came out with a clear plastic bag. She pinched it at the corner and held it up so that it dangled in front of Nikki's eyes.

Inside was a ring.

A ring shaped like a hexagon.

A ring that was a good match for those bruises on Matthew Starr's torso.

A ring that could have put that cut on Vitya Pochenko's finger.

"Worth the drive?" said Lauren.

"Where did you find this?"

"I'll show you." Lauren took the ring back to her evidence locker and led Heat to the open door of the Volvo. "It was there. On the floor under the front seat."

Nikki looked at the woman's body. "It is a man's ring, isn't it?"

The medical examiner gave her a long, sober look. "I want you to see something." The two leaned in through the open car door. Inside it was humming with blowflies. "OK, we have a female, aged fifty to fifty-five. Hard to get an accurate postmortem interval without labbing the rate test because she's been in that car so long in this heat. My guess—"

"Which is always damn close."

"Thank you—based on the state of putrefaction is four, four and a half days."

"And cause?"

"Even with the discoloration that's taken place over the last few days, it's pretty clear to see what happened here." The woman had a thick curtain of hair across her face. Lauren used her small metal ruler to pull the hair aside and reveal her neck.

When she saw the bruising, Nikki swallowed

dryness and relived her own choking. "Strangulation" was all she said, though.

"Looks like from someone in the backseat. See where the fingers would have laced together?"

"Looks like she put up a hell of a fight," said the detective. One of the victim's shoes was off and her ankles and shins were mottled by scrapes and bruises where she had kicked the underside of the dash.

"And look," said Lauren, "heel marks on the inside of the windshield over there." The missing shoe rested broken on the dash above the glove compartment.

"I think that ring belongs to whoever strangled her. It probably came off in the struggle."

Nikki thought of the woman's desperate last moments and her brave fight. Whether she had been an innocent victim, a criminal getting a payback, or something in between, she was a person. And had she ever battled to live. Nikki made herself look at the woman's face, if for no other reason than to honor that struggle.

And when Nikki looked at her, she saw something. Something death plus time couldn't obscure. Images played hazily in the detective's mind. Grocery clerks, and bank loan officers, and photos of women from society pages, an old schoolteacher, a bartender in Boston. Nothing came to her. "Could you . . ." Nikki pointed at the woman's hair and waved her forefinger. Lauren used her ruler to gently draw all the hair off the face. "I think I've seen her before," said the detective.

Heat shifted her weight on her heels, leaned back from the woman about a foot, and tilted her own head to match the angle of hers. And pondered. And then she knew. The grainy photo, at a three-quarters angle with the expensive furniture in the background and the framed lithograph of a pineapple on the wall. She would have to look it up to be sure, but damn it, she knew. She looked at Lauren. "I think I've seen this woman on the surveillance tape from the Guilford. The morning Matthew Starr was killed."

Her cell phone rang and she jumped.

"Heat," she said.

"Guess where I'm standing."

"Rook, I'm not up for this right now."

"I'll give you a clue. Roach got a call about a burglary last night. Guess where."

A cloud of dread gathered around her. "Starr's apartment."

"I'm standing in the living room. Guess what else. Every single painting in the room is gone."

ELEVEN

Thirty minutes later, Detective Heat stepped off the Guilford's elevator on six and strode the hall to where Raley stood with a uniform outside the open door to the Starr apartment. The door frame bore a crime scene posting and the requisite yellow tape. Stacked on the luxurious hallway carpet by the door were plastic snap-lid tubs labeled "Forensics."

Raley nodded hello and held up the police line tape for her. She ducked under and entered the apartment. "Holy shit," said Nikki, turning a circle in the middle of the living room. She craned her neck upward to the take in the full height of the cathedral ceiling, believing what she was seeing, yet stunned at the sight. The walls were stripped bare, and all that was left were the nails and mountings.

That living room had been Matthew Starr's self-proclaimed Versailles. And even if it hadn't been an actual palace, as a single room it most certainly qualified as a museum chamber with its two stories of wall space graced by some valuable, if not cohesively collected, works of art. "Amazing what happens to the size of a room when you strip everything off the walls."

Rook stepped over beside her. "I know. It looks bigger."

"Really?" she said. "I was going to say smaller."

He flicked his eyebrows. "Guess size is a matter of personal experience."

She shot Rook a furtive cool-it look and turned her back on him. When she did, Nikki was certain she caught a fast glance darting between Raley and Ochoa. Well, she thought she was certain, anyway.

She made a forceful show of getting down to business. "Ochoa. We're absolutely sure Kimberly Starr and her son weren't here when this went down?" The detective needed to know if a kidnapping was rolled into this.

"Daytime doorman said she left yesterday morning with the kid." He flipped back through his spiral pad. "Here it is. Doorman got a call to help her out with a rolling suitcase. That was about ten A.M. Her son was with her."

"Did she say where they were going?"

"He hailed her a cab to Grand Central. From there, he didn't know."

"Raley, I know we have her cell phone number. Dig it out and see if she picks up. And go easy when you break the news, she's had a hell of a week."

"On it," said Raley, who then head-nodded to the pair of detectives on the balcony. "Just to be clear, are we working this, or is Burglary?"

"Heaven forbid, but we may actually have to cooperate. Sure it's a twenty-one, but we can't rule it out as part of our homicide investigation. Not yet, anyway." Especially with the discovery of the Jane Doe from the surveillance tape and the ring at her death scene likely belonging to Pochenko, even a rookie's cop sense would tie it all together.

What remained was to uncover how. "I expect you to play nice with them. Just don't give away our secret handshake, OK?"

———

The pair from Burglary, Detectives Gunther and Francis, were cooperative but didn't have much information to share. There were clear signs of forced entry; they used power tools, obviously battery-operated, to compromise the front door of the apartment. "Beyond, that," said Detective Gunther, "it's all pretty much neatsy tidy. Maybe the lab rats will pick up something."

"Something's not lining up for me," Nikki said. "Moving this haul would take time and manpower. Blackout or not, somebody had to see or hear something."

"Agreed," said Gunther. "I had a thought we should split off now and knock on a few doors, find out if anyone heard anything go bump in the night."

Heat nodded. "Good thought."

"Is there anything else missing?" asked Rook. Nikki liked his question. Not only was it smart, but she felt relieved he had dropped the seventh-grade innuendos.

"Still checking," said Francis. "Obviously we'll know more when the resident, Mrs. Starr, gives it a once-over, but so far, it appears to be just the art."

Then Ochoa did what they all kept doing, looking at the blank walls. "Man, how much did they say this collection was worth?"

Nikki answered, "Fifty to sixty mil, give or take."

"Looks definitely more like take," said Rook.

While Forensics examined the apartment and the Burglary detectives peeled off to canvass residents, Nikki went downstairs to talk with the only eyewitness, the night-shift doorman.

Henry was waiting quietly with a patrol officer on one of the sofas in the lobby. She sat beside him and asked him if he was all right, and he said yes, like he would have said it no matter how bad he felt. The poor old guy had answered these same questions for the first responders, and then again for the Burglary cops, but he was patient and cooperative with Detective Heat, glad to tell someone his story.

The blackout came during his shift, at about nine-fifteen. Henry was supposed to get off at midnight, but his relief called in about eleven and said he couldn't make it on account of the power outage. Nikki asked the man's name, made a note, and Henry continued. It was mostly quiet at the door because with the elevator out and all the heat, people who were in were staying in, and many of those who were out were stuck someplace. The stairwell and halls were equipped with low-level emergency lighting, but the building didn't have a backup generator.

At about three-thirty in the morning, a big van pulled up out front and he thought it was ConEd, because it was big like one of theirs. Four men in coveralls got out all together and jumped him. He didn't see any guns, but they had big five-cell flashlights and one of the men gave him a punch in the solar plexus with his when Henry challenged them. They got him off the street and into the lobby then used plastic zip cords to bind his hands behind his back and hold his feet together. Nikki could still see some flecks of pale gray adhesive on his deep brown skin where they had duct taped his mouth. Then they took his cell phone and carried him into the tiny mail room and closed the door. He couldn't give very good descriptions because it was dark and they all wore baseball hats. Nikki asked if he heard any names or could pick out anything unusual in their voices, like if they were high, or low, or perhaps had accents. He said no, because he never heard their voices, not one of them ever spoke. Not even a word. Professionals, she thought.

Henry said he heard them all walk out later and take off in the truck. That's when he struggled to get free and kick at the door. He was bound too tight, so he had to stay like that until the assistant super came in and found him.

"And do you know about what time they left?"

"I couldn't tell the time, but it felt like it was about fifteen, twenty minutes before the lights came back on."

She wrote, "Left before end of blackout. 4 A.M., approx."

"Think a moment. Is it possible you're confused about these times you've given me, Henry?"

"No, Detective. I know it was three-thirty when

they got there because when I saw that truck pull up out front, I checked my watch."

"Sure, sure. That's good, very helpful to us. But the part that puzzles me is their time of departure. The blackout ended at four-fifteen. If you say they left about fifteen minutes before that, that means they were only here a half hour." He processed what she was saying and then nodded agreement. "Is it possible you fell asleep or were unconscious during that time? Maybe they left later than four A.M.?"

"Oh, believe you me, I was awake the whole time. Trying to think of a way to get out." The old doorman paused and his eyes began to rim with tears.

"Sir, are you all right?" Her eyes darted to the patrolman standing behind him. "Are you sure you don't want medical help?"

"No, no, please, I'm not hurt, it's not that." He turned his face from hers and said in a low voice, "I have been a doorman at this building for over thirty years. I have never seen a week like this one. Mr. Starr and his poor family. Your detective talked with William, you know, the day-shift doorman, about that day. He's still afraid he'll be fired for letting those fellows slip in that morning. And now here I am. I know it's not the fanciest work, but this job means something to me. We've got some characters living here, but most folks are very good to me. And even if they aren't, I'm always proud of my service." He said nothing for a moment and then looked up to Nikki and his lip was quivering. "I'm the gatekeeper. More than anything else I do, it's my responsibility to make sure bad people don't get in here."

Nikki rested a hand on his shoulder and spoke gently. "Henry, this is not your fault."

"How is it not my fault? It was my watch."

"You were overpowered, you're not responsible, can you see that? You were the victim. You did everything you could." She knew he was only half-buying it, knew he was replaying the night, wondering what else he could have done. "Henry?" And when she had his attention again, Nikki said, "We all try. And try as we might to control things, sometimes bad things get in and it's not our fault." He nodded and managed a smile. At least the words Nikki's therapist had once used with her made someone feel better.

She arranged for a patrol car to drive him home.

————

Back in the precinct, Detective Heat drew a vertical red line on the whiteboard to create a separate but parallel case track for the burglary. Then she sketched in the timeline of events beginning with the departure of Kimberly Starr and her son, the time of the blackout, the phone call from the relief doorman, the arrival of the van and its crew, and their departure just before the end of the blackout.

She then drew another red vertical to delineate a new space for the Jane Doe murder. "You're starting to run out of whiteboard," said Rook.

"I hear you. The crimes are getting ahead of the solves." Then she added, "For now, anyway." Nikki taped up the lobby surveillance photo of the Doe.

Beside it, she taped the impound lot death shot Lauren had taken of her an hour before. "But this one is leading us to something."

"Too weird she was in the lobby the same morning Starr got killed," said Ochoa.

Rook rolled a chair over and sat. "Quite a coincidence."

"Weird, yes. Coincidence, no," said Detective Heat. "You still taking notes for your article about Homicide? Get this one down. Coincidences break cases. You know why? Because they don't exist. Find the reason it's not a coincidence, and you can pretty much get out your handcuffs, because you're going to be slapping them on somebody damn soon."

"Any ID yet on the Doe?" said Ochoa.

"Nope. All her personal effects were gone, car registration, license plates. A squad from the Three-Two is Dumpster diving for her purse in a radius around West 142nd and Lenox, where they towed her car from. When we break here, see how they're doing on the VIN."

"Got it," said Ochoa. "What's keeping our fiber test?"

"It's the blackout. But I asked the captain to roll an M-80 under somebody's lab stool at Forensics." Nikki posted on the board a photo of the hexagonal ring Lauren found. She taped it beside the matching bruise pictures of Matthew Starr's body and wondered if it was Pochenko's. "I want those results like yesterday."

Raley joined the circle. "I made contact with Kimberly Starr on her cell phone up in Connecticut.

She said the city was suffocating so she and her son spent the night at a friend's summer cottage in Westport. Some place called Compo Beach."

"Alibi that, OK?" said Heat. "In fact, we're going to split the list of everyone we've interviewed for the homicide and alibi-check all of them. And be sure to include that relief doorman who missed his shift last night." Nikki crossed that item off her pad and turned back to Raley. "How did she react to the burglary?"

"Freaked. I'm still waiting for the hearing to return to this ear. But like you told me, I didn't say what got taken, just that there was a break-in during the blackout." He said Mrs. Starr was hiring a car service to bring her to the Guilford and that she would call when she was near so they could meet her there.

"Good going, Rales," said Heat. "I want one of us to be there when she sees it."

"Whoever it is, take earplugs," he said.

"Maybe she won't be so upset," said Rook. "I assume the collection was insured."

"I have a call in to Noah Paxton right now," said Nikki.

"Well, assuming it was, she might be happy about this. Although, with all her face work, I don't know how you'll be able to tell."

Ochoa confirmed what they suspected, that there was no security video of the burglary because of the blackout. But, he said, Gunther, Francis, and their team from Burglary were still knocking on doors at the Guilford. "Hopefully, it won't be an infringement on anybody's privacy issues to ask a few questions, what with bodies flying by their windows and sixty million bucks' worth of art getting hauled out of their building."

———

Detective Heat didn't want to take a chance Kimberly Starr would get to her apartment before she did, so she and Rook went there to wait at the perennial crime scene. "You know," said Rook as they entered the living room again, "she should just keep a supply of yellow tape on hand in the hall closet."

Nikki had another reason for arriving early. The detective wanted to have some face time with the Forensics geeks, who never seemed to mind conversation with actual people. Even if they always stared at her chest. She found the one she wanted to talk to on his knees, tweezing something usable off the living room rug. "Find your contact lens?" she said.

He turned to look up at her. "I wear glasses."

"That was a joke."

"Oh." He stood up and stared at her chest.

"I noticed you worked the homicide here a few days ago."

"You did?"

"I did . . . Tim." The techie's face pinked around his freckles. "And I've been wondering something maybe you can answer for me."

"Sure."

"It's about access to the apartment. Specifically, could someone have gained entry by the fire escape?"

"On that, I can answer empirically. No."

"You sound so certain."

"Because I am." Tim led Nikki and Rook to the bedroom hall, where the fire escape met a pair of windows. "It's standard to examine all possible points of entry. See here? It's a code violation, but these windows are painted shut, and have been for years. I can tell you how many years if you want me to run it in the lab, but for our purposes, say during the past week, there's no way these have been opened."

Nikki leaned in to the window frame, just to check for herself. "You're right."

"I like to think science isn't about right, it's about thorough."

"Well said." Nikki nodded. "And did you dust for prints?"

"No, it seemed unproductive given that it couldn't be opened."

"I mean on the outside. In case somebody trying to get in didn't know that."

The technician's jaw fell and he looked at the window glass. Whatever pink was in his cheeks bled out, and Tim, with his face of freckles, looked positively lunar.

Nikki's cell phone vibrated, and she stepped away to take the call. It was Noah Paxton. "Thanks for getting back to me."

"I was beginning to wonder if I upset you. It's been how long since we last spoke?"

She laughed. "Yesterday when I interrupted your take-out lunch." Rook must have heard her laughter, and he appeared from the hallway to hover. She turned and took a few steps away from him, not needing that layer of scrutiny, but she could see him hanging close by in her periphery.

"See? Almost a full twenty-two hours. A guy could get paranoid. What's the occasion this time?"

Heat told him about the theft of the art collection. Her news was followed by a long, long silence. She said, "Are you still there?"

"Yeah, I—You wouldn't joke. I mean, not about something like this."

"Noah, I'm standing in the living room now. The walls are absolutely bare."

Another long silence and she heard him clear his throat. "Detective Heat, can I get personal?"

"Go on."

"Did you ever get hit with a big shock, and then, when you think you can't deal with it, you work through it, and then—ahem, excuse me." She heard him sip something. "And so you man-up and work through it, and just when you do, out of nowhere comes another crushing blow, and then another, and then you reach a point where you just say, What the hell am I doing? And then you fantasize about chucking it all. Not just the job but the life. Be one of those guys down on the Jersey Shore who make sub sandwiches in a hut or rent hula hoops and bikes. Just. Chuck. It."

"Do you?"

"All the time. Especially this minute." He sighed and swore under his breath. "So where are you with this? Do you have any leads?"

"We'll see," she said, adhering to her policy of being the sole interrogator in an interview. "I assume you can account for your whereabouts last night?"

"Jeez, you cut right to it, don't you?"

"And now I'd like you to." Nikki waited, knowing his dance steps by now: resist then cave to pressure.

"I shouldn't be pissed, I know it's your job, Detective, but come on." She let her cold silence push him and he surrendered. "Last night I was teaching my weekly night course at Westchester Community College up in Valhalla."

"And that can be verified?"

"I was lecturing twenty-five continuing ed students. If they run true to form, one or two may have noticed me."

"And after that?"

"Home to Tarrytown for a big night of beer and Yankees-Angels at my local hang."

She asked the name of the bar and wrote it down. "One more question, and I'll be out of your life."

"I doubt that."

"Were the paintings insured?"

"No. They had been, of course, but when the vultures started circling, Matthew canceled the policy. He said he didn't want to keep shelling out a small fortune to protect something that would just go to the bankruptcy creditors." Now it was Nikki's turn to be silent. "Are you still there, Detective?"

"Yes. I was just thinking Kimberly Starr is going to be here any minute. Did she know the insurance was canceled on the art collection?"

"She did. Kimberly found out the same night Matthew told her he canceled his life insurance." Then he added, "I don't envy you the next few minutes. Good luck."

———

Raley wasn't kidding about the earplugs. When Kimberly Starr came into the apartment, she flat-out screamed. She already looked ragged getting off the elevator and began a low moan when she saw the door hardware on the hallway rug. Nikki tried to take her arm when she entered her home, but she shook the detective off and her moan revved up into a full-blown 1950s horror film shriek.

Nikki's gut twisted for the woman as Kimberly dropped her purse and screamed again. She wanted no part of anybody's help and held up a straight arm when Nikki tried to approach her. When her screaming subsided, she sat hard on the sofa moaning, "No, no, no." Her head rose up and swiveled to take in the entire room, all two stories of it. "How much am I supposed to take? Will somebody tell me how much I am supposed to take? Who goes through this? Who?" Her voice raspy from screaming, she went on like that, moaning the rhetoricals that any sane or compassionate person in the room would have been foolish to answer. So they waited her out.

Rook left the room and returned with a glass of water, which Kimberly took and gulped. She had gotten half of the water down when she started to choke on it and gagged it onto the rug, coughing and wheezing for air until her cough became weeping. Nikki sat with her but didn't reach for her. After a moment, Kimberly pivoted away and buried her face in her hands, shaking with deep sobs.

Ten long minutes later, without acknowledging them, Kimberly reached across the floor to her bag, took out a prescription bottle, and downed a pill with the remains of her water. She blew her nose to no effect and sat kneading the tissue as she had just days before when she was digesting the news of her husband's murder.

"Mrs. Starr?" Heat spoke just above a whisper, but Kimberly jumped. "At some point I'll want to ask you some questions, but that can wait."

She nodded and whispered, "Thank you."

"When you feel up to it, hopefully sometime today, would you mind looking around to see if anything else was taken?"

Another nod. Another whisper. "I will."

———

In the car on their short drive back to the precinct, Rook said, "I was only half kidding this morning about taking you to brunch. What would you say if I asked you about having dinner?"

"I'd say you're pushing it."

"Come on, didn't you have a good time last night?"

"No, I didn't. I had a great time."

"Then what's the problem?"

"There is no problem. So let's not create one by letting it creep into the job, OK? Or haven't you noticed, I'm working not one, but two open homicides, and now a multimillion-dollar art theft."

Nikki double-parked the Crown Victoria between two double-parked blue-and-whites in front
of the precinct on 82nd Street. They got out and
Rook spoke to her over the hot metal roof. "How
do you ever have a relationship in this job?"

"I don't. Pay attention."

Then they heard Ochoa call out, "Don't lock it
up, Detective." Raley and Ochoa were hustling from
the precinct lot to the street. Four uniforms were
playing catch-up.

"What have you got?" said Heat.

Roach arrived at her open door. Ochoa said,
"Burglary squad got a score on their door knock at
the Guilford."

"Eyewitness coming in from a business trip saw
a bunch of guys leaving the building about four this
morning," continued Raley. "He thought it was
weird so he made a note of the plate on the truck."

"And he didn't call it in?" said Rook.

"Man, you are new at this, aren't you?" said
Ochoa. "Anyway, we ran it and the truck's registered to an address over in Long Island City." He
held up the note and Heat plucked it from his hand.

"Pile in," she said. But Raley and Ochoa knew
this was big and each already had a leg in a door.
Nikki fired the ignition, lit the gum ball, and floored
it. Rook was still closing his backseat door when
she reached Columbus and hit the siren.

TWELVE

The three detectives and Rook maintained a tense silence as Nikki gas 'n' gunned through crosstown traffic to the bridge at 59th Street. She had Ochoa radio ahead, and when they rolled up to the approach under the Roosevelt Island sky tram, Traffic Control had blocked feeder lanes for her and she roared onward. The bridge belonged to her and the two patrol cars running convoy with her.

They killed their sirens to avoid advertisement after they blew out of Queensboro Plaza and turned off Northern Boulevard. The address was an auto body shop in an industrial section not far from the LIRR switching yard. Under the elevated subway line at Thirty-eighth Avenue, they located the small group of patrol cars from the Long Island City precinct that were already waiting a block south of the building.

Nikki got out and greeted Lieutenant Marr from the 108th. Marr had a military bearing, precise and relaxed. He told Detective Heat this was her show, but he seemed eager to describe the logistics he had put in place for her. They gathered around the hood of his car and he spread out a plan of the neighborhood. The body shop was already circled in red marker, and the lieutenant marked blue Xs at intersections in the surrounding blocks to indicate where other patrol cars were staged, effectively choking off any exit the suspects might attempt from the location once they rolled.

"Nobody's getting out of there unless they sprout wings," he said. "And even then I've got a couple of avid duck hunters on my team."

"What about the building itself?"

"Standard issue for this neck of the woods." He laid out an architect's blueprint from the NYFD database. "Single-story, double-height brick box, basically. Office up front here. Machine shop and lavs in the back here. Storage here. Don't need to tell you storage can be tricky, nooks and crannies, bad lighting, so we'll just have to keep our heads on a swivel, right? Door here in front. Another off the machine shop. Three steel roll-downs, two jumbos off the car park, one leading to the yard in the back."

"Fence?" she asked.

"Chain-link with vinyl cover. Razor wire all around, including the roof."

Nikki ran her finger along a boundary line on his neighborhood plan. "What's over this back fence?"

The lieutenant smiled. "Duck hunters."

They fixed five minutes as the time for the raid, suited up in their body armor, and got back in their cars. Two minutes before go, Marr appeared at Heat's window. "My spotter says the near rolling door is up. I assume you want in first?"

"Thanks, yeah, I do."

"I'll have your back then." He checked his watch as casually as if he were waiting for a bus and added, "Spotter also tells me the truck with your plate is in the yard."

Nikki felt her heart pick up a few BPMs. "That's a break."

"Those paintings pretty valuable?"

"Probably enough to pay a day's interest on the Wall Street bailout."

The lieutenant said, "Then let's hope nobody puts any holes in them today," and got in his car.

Ochoa popped his knuckles in the seat beside her. "Don't worry. If the Russian's in there, we'll get him."

"Not worried." In her rearview mirror, Raley's eyelids were half-closed, and she wondered, as she always did with Rales, if he was that relaxed or was, perhaps, praying. She turned around to Rook, who was sitting beside him back there. "Rook."

"I know, I know, stay in the car."

"Actually, no. Out of the car."

"Aw, come on, you want to leave me standing here?"

"Don't make me count three, mister, or you're grounded."

Ochoa checked his watch. "Rolling in fifteen."

Heat gave Rook an insistent glare. He got out and slammed his door. Nikki glanced into the car beside her as Lieutenant Marr brought his microphone up. On her TAC frequency she heard his relaxed "All units green light."

"Let's go to an art show," she said and hit the gas.

Nikki felt her diaphragm cinch when she turned the corner and sped up the block. Long ago she had learned that you could calm-talk your brain all you want, your adrenal glands pretty much had charge of the control panel. One conscious deep breath compensated for the shallow ones she had been taking, and after she took it, Nikki found that sweet spot between nerves and focus.

Ahead, a formation of cop cars rolled down the street toward her, Marr's pincer movement in action. Coming up fast on her right, the auto body shop. Its nearest rolling garage door was still wide open. Heat braked and cranked the wheel. The Crown Vic took a hard bounce on the steep slope of the driveway and was still rocking on its suspension when she roared into the middle of the garage and screeched to a stop. The flashing of her gum ball reflected on the startled faces of the handful of men in the shop.

Nikki had already done her count by the time she was yanking the door handle. "Clock five," she said.

"Roger five," answered Roach in tandem.

"Police, nobody move, hands where I can see them," she shouted, coming around her car door. She heard the backup arriving behind her but didn't turn.

On her right, two laborers in dusty coveralls and white painter's masks dropped the belt sanders they were using on an old LeBaron and raised their hands. Across the garage to her left, at a patio table just outside the storage room, three men rose from a card game. They looked anything but submissive.

"Watch the card players," she said low to Roach. Then loudly, to the group, "I said hands. Now."

It was as if her "Now" were a starting pistol. All three men scattered in different directions. In her periphery, Heat could see uniforms already patting down the two sanders. Free of that pair, she started off toward the biker dude who was running along the wall toward the front office. As she took off after him, Nikki called out, "Ochoa," and pointed to the one breaking for the exit to the rear yard.

"On the green shirt," said Raley, chasing the man booking it for the side door. By the time Raley finished his sentence, the guy had pulled the side door open. Heat was past the point where she could see it, but she heard a ragged chorus of "Police, freeze!" from the uniforms in Marr's flank group who were waiting in the alley.

The biker she was chasing was all muscle and beer gut. Fast as Nikki was, he had the clear path; she had to dodge rolling tool lockers and a crushed fender. Ten feet from the office his swaying gray ponytail was the last thing she saw before the door slammed. She tried the knob but it wouldn't turn. She heard a deadbolt thrown.

"Stand aside, Detective." Marr, cool as can be, was behind her with two uniforms in helmets and goggles holding a battering ram.

The detective slid out of their way and the two cops swung the head of the Stinger into the lock. The ram hit with the shudder of a small explosion and the door popped wide.

"Cover," said Heat. She started into the office with her piece drawn. Two gunshots cracked the air in the small room and a bullet embedded low in the door frame opposite her. She rotated out again, putting her back prone against the brick wall.

"You hit?" asked Marr. She shook no and closed her eyes to study her eidetic image of that brief instant. Muzzle flashes from high up. Window along the wall. But biker dude was standing on the desk. Reaching up high with his other arm. Dark square in the ceiling above him.

"He's going for the roof," she said and ran through the garage to the rear yard, where Ochoa had his man down and cuffed. "Eyes high, Detective," she said. "We've got a monkey."

Heat walked the perimeter of the building, her head tilted up as she went. In the gap between the body shop and the auto glass place next door, she stopped. A small piece of torn cloth waved from the razor wire on the rooftop. Nikki stood on the concrete directly under the flag of cloth and looked down. Between her shoes were two bright red spatters of blood.

She turned and caught Raley's eye from the yard, then hand signaled the arc of the biker's jump to the next-door roof before she trotted out the gate to the corner of the building. Heat peeked around it and pulled back. The sidewalk was clear. She figured her dude would not exit down the front but would stay up there as far as he could get before coming down.

As she ran along the façade of the auto glass shop, she told herself to be grateful that this was an industrial area and that there was a heat wave, both of which made it so she didn't have to deal with pedestrians. The end of the building marked the corner of the side street. She flattened her back against the concrete and felt it warm the back of her neck above her vest. Nikki peeked around the building's edge. Halfway up the block, the biker was climbing down a gutter drain. Her backup was coming but was a building's length away. Biker dude was using both hands to shimmy. If she waited, he'd be on the sidewalk with a free gun hand.

Heat pivoted around the corner, gun up. "Police, freeze!" She couldn't believe it. Rook was strolling up the sidewalk between her and the biker.

"Whoa, it's me," he said.

"Move," she yelled, and waved him to the side. Rook turned behind him. For the first time, he saw the man climbing down the pipe and dashed out of the way behind a parked oil delivery truck. But by then the biker was holding onto the pipe with only one hand and drew. Heat pivoted behind the wall and his shot went wide, punching into a stack of wooden pallets at the curb.

Then she heard boots landing hard on pavement, a loud curse, and the clatter of something metal on concrete. The gun.

Heat fast-peeked again. The biker was standing on the sidewalk, ass to her, bending to pick up his fallen gun. She stepped out, Sig braced. "Freeze!"

And that was when Rook flew in from the side and blind-tackled him. Nikki lost her clear shot as the two struggled on the ground. She ran to them with Raley and the rest of her backup following close behind. Just as she arrived, Rook flipped on top of the guy and held the gun to his face.

"Go ahead," he said. "I need the practice."

————

After they loaded the biker into the rear of a patrol car for transport to the precinct in Manhattan, Heat, Raley,

Rook, and the backup officers herded around the corner toward the auto body shop. On the walk, Rook tried to speak to Nikki, but she was still fuming about his interference and strode to the head of the group, showing him her back.

Lieutenant Marr was making notes for his report when they entered the garage. "Hope you don't mind me using your vehicle as a desk," he said.

"It's been used for lots worse. Everybody tucked in?" she asked.

"You bet. Our two rabbits are cuffed and loaded. These other two," he said with a side nod to the pair who had been working on the LeBaron, "they seem all right. I think their biggest problem is no job here tomorrow. Congrats on nailing your biker."

"Thanks. And thanks for the setup. I owe you one."

He shrugged it off. "What makes me happy is the good guys are all going home safe for supper tonight." He set his clipboard on the car hood. "Now, Detective, I don't know about you, but I want a look inside that truck."

Marr and Heat led the others out to the side yard, where the sun-bounce off the truck came at them like a pizza oven. The lieutenant gave the word, and one of his patrol officers mounted the rear bumper and opened the double doors. When the doors parted, Nikki's heart sank.

Except for a pile of quilted mover's blankets, there was nothing in the truck.

THIRTEEN

In the precinct interrogation room, the biker, Brian Daniels, seemed more interested in the gauze on the back of his upper arm than in Detective Heat. "I'm waiting," she said. But he ignored her, contorting himself by hooking his chin on his shoulder and twisting himself to see the bandage under the ripped sleeve on the back of his T-shirt.

"This sucker still bleeding?" he asked. He shifted his angle to get a look at it in the mirror, but it was too far away to work for him and he gave up, flopping back in the plastic chair.

"What happened to the paintings, Brian?"

"Doc." He shook his iron gray hair. When they processed him, they'd taken the elastic off of his ponytail, and his hair hung like a polluted waterfall down his back. "Brian's for the IRS and the DMV, call me Doc."

She wondered when the last time was this piece of shit paid any taxes or a driver's license fee. But Nikki held the thought and stayed on message. "After you left the Guilford last night, where did you move that art collection?"

"I have no idea what the hell you are talking about, lady."

"I'm talking about what was in that truck."

"What, blankets? All yours." He snorted a laugh

and pretzeled his body to look at his razor-wire cut again.

"Where were you last night between midnight and four?"

"Damn, this was my favorite shirt."

"Know something, Doc? You're not only a lousy shot, you're stupid, too. After your little circus act this morning, you have enough charges against you to make your stretch up in Sing Sing feel like a weekend at the Four Seasons."

"And?"

"And . . . you want to see this prosecuted to the max? Keep acting like an asshole." The detective rose. "I'll give you some time to think about that." She hefted his file. "Judging from this, you know what time is." Then she left the room so he could sit there and contemplate his future.

———

Rook was alone in the bull pen when she came in, and he wasn't happy. "Hey, thanks for ditching me in picturesque Long Island City."

"Not now, Rook." She brushed past him to her desk.

"I had to ride all the way over here sitting in the backseat of a blue-and-white. Do you know what that's like? People in other cars kept looking in at me like I was in custody. A couple of times I waved just to show I wasn't in handcuffs."

"I did it for your own protection."

"From what?"

"From me."

"Why?"

"Let's start with not listening."

"I got tired of standing around by myself. I figured you'd be done, so I came to see how it was going."

"And interfered with my suspect."

"You bet your ass I interfered. That guy was trying to shoot you."

"I'm the police. People shoot at us." She found the file she was looking for and slammed the drawer. "You're lucky you didn't get shot."

"I had a vest. And by the way, how can you stand those things? Very confining, especially in this humidity."

Ochoa came in, tapping his notebook on his upper lip. "We're not catching a single break anywhere. I ran alibis on our majors. They're all checking out."

"Kimberly Starr, too?" asked Heat.

"That was a two-fer. She was in Connecticut with her doctor of love at his beach cottage, so they both clear." He closed his notebook and turned to Rook. "Hey, man, Raley told me what you said when you got the drop on that biker."

Rook eyed Nikki and said, "We don't need to talk about that."

But Ochoa continued in a hoarse whisper, " 'Go ahead. I need the practice.' Is that cool, or what?"

"Oh yeah," said Heat. "Rook is like our very own Dirty Jamie." Her desk phone rang and she picked up. "Heat."

"It's me, Raley. He's here."

"On my way," she said.

———

The old doorman stood with Nikki, Rook, and Roach in the observation booth, looking through the glass at the men in the lineup. "Take your time, Henry," said Nikki.

He walked a step closer to the window and took off his glasses to clean them. "It's hard. Like I said, it was dark and they wore hats." In the next room, six men stood facing a mirror. Among them, Brian "Doc" Daniels, plus the two other men from that morning's body shop raid.

"No hurry. Just let us know if anyone clicks for you. Or doesn't."

Henry slid his glasses back on. Moments passed. "I think I recognize one of them."

"You think, or you know for sure?" Nikki had seen it many times where the urge to help or to take revenge forced good people to make bad choices. She cautioned Henry again. "Be certain."

"Uh-huh, yes."

"Which one?"

"You see the scruffy guy with the arm bandage and the long gray hair?"

"Yes?"

"It's the one to the right of him."

Behind him, the detectives shook their heads. He had identified one of the three cops who were shills in the lineup.

"Thank you, Henry," said Heat. "Appreciate you coming down."

———

Back in the bull pen, the detectives and Rook sat with their backs to their desks, tossing a Koosh Ball around the horn at a lazy pace. This is what they did when they were stuck.

"It's not as if this biker is going to go anywhere," said Rook. "Can't you hold him for assault on Detective Heat alone?"

Raley put his hand up and Ochoa lobbed the Koosh into his palm. "It's not about holding the biker."

"It's getting him to give up the paintings." Ochoa held up his hand and Raley returned the Koosh to it. They had this down so well, Ochoa didn't have to move.

"And who hired him," added Heat.

Rook held his hand up and Ochoa tossed it to him. "So how do you get a guy like that to talk when he doesn't want to?"

Heat held up her hand and Rook lobbed it over for an easy catch. "That's always the question. It's finding the spot where can you apply pressure." She jostled the Koosh in her palm. "I may have an idea."

"Never fails. It's the power of Koosh," said Raley.

Ochoa echoed that, "Power of Koosh," and held up his hand. Nikki threw the ball and it smacked Rook in the face.

"Huh," she said. "Never did that before."

————

Nikki Heat had a new customer in the interrogation room, Gerald Buckley. "Mr. Buckley, do you know why we asked you to come in to talk with us?"

Buckley's hands were folded together in a tight lace on the table in front of him. "No idea at all," he said with a look of hard study. Heat noticed he dyed his eyebrows black.

"Did you know there was a burglary at the Guilford last night?"

"No shit." He licked his lips and ran a knuckle backhand across his drinker's nose. "Probably the blackout, huh?"

"What do you mean?"

"Well, I dunno. You know. Not politically correct to say it, so I'll just say 'certain types' like to run wild the minute the fences come down." He felt her eyes on him and couldn't come up with a safe place to look, so he concentrated on picking at an old scab in the back of his hand.

"How come you called in off your shift at the Guilford last night?"

His eyes rose slowly and met hers. "I don't understand the question."

"It's a simple question. You're a doorman at the Guilford, right?"

"Yeah?"

"Last night you called in to the doorman on duty, Henry, and said you wouldn't be in for your overnight shift. Why did you do that?"

"What do you mean why?"

"I mean just that. Why?"

"I already told you, there was a blackout. You know how this city turns into a friggin' insane asylum when the lights go out. You think I was going out in that? No way. So I called in off my shift. Why are you making such big deal?"

"Because there was a major burglary, and whenever things happen out of the ordinary like routines getting broken, like employees who work on the inside not showing up, I get very interested. That, Gerald, is the big deal." She stared at him and waited. "Prove your whereabouts last night and I'll shake your hand and open that door for you."

Gerald Buckley pinched his nostrils twice and snapped in air the way she had seen so many coke users do it. He closed his eyes a full five seconds, and when he opened them he said, "I want my lawyer."

"Of course." She had an obligation to acknowledge his request, but she wanted him to talk some more. "Do you have something you feel you need a lawyer for?" This guy was stupid and a cokehead. If he would just keep talking, she knew she could get him to box himself in. "Why did you beg off the shift? Were you on the truck with the burglary crew, or were you too scared that if it came down on your shift you couldn't playact your innocence the next morning?"

"I'm not saying anything more." Damn, so close. "I want my attorney." At that, he crossed his arms and sat back.

But Nikki Heat had a Plan B. Ah, the power of Koosh.

———

Five minutes later she was in the observation booth with Ochoa. "Where did you and Raley put him?" she asked.

"You know the bench by the Community Affairs desk near the staircase?"

"Perfect," she said. "I'll do this in two minutes."

Ochoa left the booth to take his position while Nikki returned to Gerald Buckley inside Interrogation.

"You get me my lawyer?"

"You're free to go." He looked at her suspiciously. "Really," she said.

He got up and she held the door for him.

When Nikki emerged with Buckley into the outer office of the precinct, she didn't look at the Community Affairs desk but could make out the forms of Ochoa and Raley blocking Gerald Buckley's view of Doc the biker, who was sitting on the bench there. The idea was for Doc to see Buckley, not the other way around. At the head of the stairs, Nikki positioned the doorman so that his back was to Doc and then stopped. "Thank you for coming in, Mr. Buckley," she said, just loudly enough. Over Buckley's shoulder came the parting of the Roach. She pretended not to notice the biker's head crane to see if she was talking to *the* Gerald Buckley.

As soon as Heat saw alarm on the biker's face, she took Buckley by the elbow and led him down the steps out of sight. As he continued on to the bottom of the stairs, Nikki stepped back up onto the landing and called off to him, "And thank you for your cooperation. I know it's difficult, but you did the right thing."

Buckley looked up at her like she was nuts and left in a hurry.

————

Things were quite a bit different with Brian "Doc" Daniels when he returned to the Interrogation Room. Nikki made sure she was already seated when Roach brought him in, and the Iron Ponytail was scoping her out, trying to read some sign off her face before he sat down. "What's going on, what did that guy say to you?"

Heat didn't answer. She gave a nod to Raley and Ochoa and they left the room. It was a very silent place when they went.

"Come on, what did he say?"

Nikki made a show of opening a file and scanning the top page. She looked up over the top of the file at Doc and said, "So just to be clear, you consider Gerald Buckley to be a friend of yours?" She shook her head and closed the file.

"Friend? Hah. He's a liar, is what he is."

"Is he?"

"Buckley'll say anything to save his ass."

"That's kind of what happens when things start going bad, Doc. People start shoving friends and family off the lifeboat." When she was good and ready, Nikki crossed her arms and leaned back in her chair. "Question I guess is, Which one of you is going to be treading water with the sharks?"

The biker was running odds in his head. "Tell me what he said, and I'll tell you if it's bull."

"Like I'm going to do that."

"Well, what am I supposed to do? Confess?"

She shrugged. "Let's call it cooperate."

"Yuh, right."

"Hey, your call, Doc. But the smart man would get out ahead of this. Prosecutors are going to want a head on a pole. Whose is it going to be, yours or Buckley's?" She picked up the file. "Maybe Buckley's the smart man today." Then Nikki stood. "See you at the arraignment."

The biker thought that one over but not for very long. He shook his mane of hair and said, "All right, here's the God's truth. We didn't steal any paintings. When we broke into that apartment, they were already gone."

———

"I believe the dude," said Raley. He was slouched back in his chair with his feet up on a two-drawer filing cabinet in the middle of the bull pen.

Heat was standing at the whiteboard tossing a marker from hand to hand. "Me, too." She uncapped it and circled the arrival of the truck and its departure on the burglary timeline. "No way they could move out all that art in a half hour. Let's suppose Henry is off in his timing and it's an hour. Still no way." She tossed the marker into the aluminum sill on the bottom of the board. "And not be seen or heard doing it in a building full of people? Un-uh."

From his seat, Rook raised his hand. "May I ask a question?"

Heat shrugged. "Go ahead."

"I need the practice," added Raley, chuckling. Nikki suppressed her own smile and nodded for Rook to continue.

"Do Penn and Teller have a burglary crew? Because somebody sure as hell took all those paintings."

Across the bull pen Detective Ochoa hung up his phone and said, *"Madre de Dios."* Then he shoved off his desk with his foot, launching himself the length of the room on his chair rollers, coming to a stop at the group. "This is big. Got back the VIN result off that Volvo from the impound." He looked down and read from his notes, which is what Ochoa did when he had news and wanted to get it right. "The vehicle was registered to a Barbara Deerfield. I made some calls including Missing Persons. Barbara Deerfield was reported missing by her employer four days ago."

"Who was her employer?" said Heat.

"Sotheby's"

Nikki cursed. "The art auction house . . ."

"That's right," said Ochoa. "Our dead woman was an art appraiser."

FOURTEEN

aley came back into the bullpen dangling his sport coat on one finger. His powder blue shirt was two-tone from sweat. "Brought you a present from Sotheby's."

Nikki rose from her desk. "I do love presents. What is it, a Winslow Homer? The Magna Carta?"

"Better." He handed her a folded sheet of paper. "They let me print out a page from Barbara Deerfield's Outlook calendar. Sorry it's all buckled and everything. Humidity's a bear out there."

Nikki held the page like she would catch something from it. "It's damp."

"It's only perspiration."

While she unfolded the sheet and read it, Ochoa swiveled in his desk chair and covered his phone. "Never saw a dude sweat like you, man. Shaking your hand is like squeezing Sponge Bob's ass."

"Ochoa, I believe that's a think, not a say." Rook stepped over to surf the page over Nikki's shoulder.

"All right, we have our . . ." Nikki seemed to feel that Rook was standing a little too close, so she handed him the page and created some distance. "We have our confirmation that Barbara Deerfield had an art appraisal booked at Matthew Starr's apartment the morning he was killed."

"And the morning she was killed," added Rook.

"Likely. We still need confirmation on time of

death from the M.E., but let's call it a safe assumption." Nikki used the fine tip of the marker to squeeze Barbara Deerfield's appraisal appointment with Starr into the timeline on the whiteboard, then capped the pen.

Rook said, "Aren't you going to put her death on the board, too?"

"No. Safe or not, it's still an assumption."

"Right." And then he added, "For you, maybe."

Raley filled her in on what he had learned about the victim from her coworkers. The whole Sotheby's office was distraught and shocked by the news. After someone goes missing, you hope for the best, but this was confirmation of their worst fears. Barbara Deerfield had a good relationship with her colleagues, was by all appearances stable, loved her work, seemed to enjoy a happy home life, with kids in college, and was excited about planning a vacation to New Zealand with her husband. "Sounds good to me," said Raley. "It's winter there. No unsightly perspiration."

"Well, check out the family and friends and lovers angles to cover the bases, but my instincts aren't taking me there, how about you?"

Raley agreed and said so.

Ochoa hung up his phone. "That was Forensics. Do you want the news or the news?" He read Detective Heat's look and wisely decided this wasn't the time for screwing around. "Got two sets of results for you. First, the fiber on the balcony is a match for a pair of Pochenko's jeans."

"I knew it," said Rook. "Scumbag."

Nikki ignored his outburst. Her heart was

gaining speed, but she acted as if she was merely sitting through the day's Tokyo Stock Exchange average while waiting for the traffic report on news radio. She had learned over the years that every case had a life. This one was not near a solve yet, but it was entering the phase where she finally had hard data to sift through. Each piece needed to be listened to, and excitement, especially her own, just made noise.

"And second, you were right. There was a set of prints outside those windows off the fire escape. And we know whose."

"*Duh*," said Rook.

The detective sat and reflected a moment. "OK. So we have one piece of evidence that points to Pochenko tossing Matthew Starr over that balcony, and we have another piece that tells us at some point he tried unsuccessfully to get in a window." She went back to the whiteboard and wrote Pochenko's name beside "fibers." In a blank space, she printed "access?" and circled it.

While she stood there, tossing the marker hand to hand, a new habit she noticed, her gaze went to the photo of the hexagonal ring and then to the bruises on Matthew Starr's torso. "Detective Raley, how sick are you of screening surveillance video from the Guilford?"

"Like totally?"

She rested a hand on his shoulder. "Then you are going to hate your next assignment." Then she removed her hand and discreetly wiped it on her thigh.

Ochoa chuckled to himself and hummed the SpongeBob theme.

————

While Raley dug out and loaded the surveillance video, Heat made her usual phone and computer rounds to check petty thefts, assaults, and ATM robberies to see if the latest reports lit up any Pochenko radar for her. There had been no sign of him since his drugstore grab. A friend of Nikki's, an undercover vice cop who was tapped into the Russian neighborhoods in Brighton Beach, had come up with nothing, either. Heat told herself these compulsive checks were good detective work, so much of success was just donkey-level diligence. But in her true heart she just didn't like the idea that there was a dangerous man out there who'd made it personal with her and slipped off the grid. This challenged Detective Heat's cherished ability to separate herself from the emotional aspects of her work on a case. After all, she was supposed to be the cop, not the victim. Nikki allowed herself her momentary trespass onto the turf of the fully human and then got back on the path.

Where did he go? A man like that, big and obvious, injured, on the run, cut off from his apartment, would have to convert into scavenger mode at some point. Unless he had a support system and/ or money stashed, his presence should be felt somewhere. Maybe he had those things. Maybe. It didn't feel right. She hung up her last call and stared out of focus at nothing.

"Maybe he got on one of those reality shows where they sequester the competitors on some desert island to eat bugs and berate each other," said Rook. "You know, like *I'm a Mouth-Breathing Killer, Get Me Outta Here.*"

———

"Black with one Equal, right?" Nikki set a coffee down on Raley's desk.

"Oh . . . thanks, yeah, appreciate it." Raley scanned forward in the surveillance video of the Guilford lobby. "Unless that means I'm pulling another all-nighter on this."

"No, this won't take long. Roll up to Miric and Pochenko and slow it down for me." Raley had plenty of experience with this section and found the exact spot where they came in from the street. "OK, when you hit just Pochenko, stop there."

Raley froze the picture and manipulated it to zoom in on the Russian's face. "What are we looking for?"

"Not that," she said.

"But you wanted to stop on this frame."

"That's right. And what have we been doing? Focusing only on his face for the ID array, right?"

Raley looked at her and smiled. "Ah, I getcha." He pulled out from the zoom of Pochenko's face and reconfigured the shot.

Nikki liked what he was going for. "Exactly, there you go. Rales, you catch on quick. Keep this up, I'm going to let you screen all the surveillance vid from now on."

"You've seen through my plan to become the

precinct video czar." He moused over to the other part of the freeze frame and worked a drag and zoom. When he had what he wanted, he sat back and said, "How's that?"

"No more calls, please. We have a winner."

Filling the computer screen was Pochenko's hand. And on it, a not-bad shot of his hexagonal ring, the same one Lauren had shown her at the impound. "Do a save and print that for me, Czar Raley."

Minutes later, Heat added the shot of Pochenko's ring to the gallery that was growing on the whiteboard. Rook stood leaning against the wall, taking it in, and raised his hand. "Am I allowed to ask a question?"

"Rook, I'll take a question over one of your open-mic-night comedy attempts any day."

"I'll mark that down as a yes." He stepped up to the board and pointed to the autopsy shots of Matthew Starr's torso. "What exactly was it your M.E. ghoul friend said about the punch bruises and the ring?"

"She has a name, it's Lauren, and she said all of the bruises on the torso had the telltale ring mark except one. Have a look." She indicated each. "Bruises with the ring: Here, here, here, and here."

Rook pointed to one of the bruises. "But this one here, one punch, same hand, no ring mark."

"Maybe he took it off," said Nikki.

"Pardon me, ah, Detective, who's the speculator here?" Nikki shook her head. She hated it that he was so cute. Sort of hated it. He continued. "Pochenko had the ring on when he and Miric came

by to 'encourage' Starr to pay up his debt, right?"
Rook shadowboxed. "Boom, boom, and boom. Get
Raley to rack up that video again and I'll bet you
anything Pochenko's still wearing the ring on his
way out."

Heat called across the room. "Raley?"

Raley answered, "I hate you," and reloaded the
video to check.

"After they go, the art appraiser comes for her
meeting and leaves. My speculation is this," said
Rook. "This bruise here, the one without the mark,
came later, when Pochenko returned in the afternoon to kill Matthew Starr. Pochenko didn't have
the ring on then because he lost it in the car fight
when he was strangling Barbara Deerfield."

Heat sucked in her lips, thinking. "That's all
fine, very likely in fact."

"So don't you think I've made my case for the
time of death for Barbara Deerfield?"

"Oh, I'm already with you there. But you're
missing an even bigger point, Mr. Reporter."

"Which is?"

"Which is a big why," said the detective. "If there
is a connection between these two murders, why
did Pochenko kill Barbara Deerfield first? That's a
motive question. Work backwards from the motive and you usually find a killer."

Rook looked at the board and then back to her.
"You know, Mick Jagger never made me work this
hard."

But she didn't seem to hear him. Heat was
focused on Ochoa, who was coming into the room.

"Did it come in?" she asked. Ochoa held up some folded papers. "Excellent."

"What's going on?" said Rook.

"Some people wait for ships to come in, I wait for warrants." Heat stepped to her desk and picked up her shoulder bag. "If you promise to be a good boy this time, I'll let you come watch me arrest someone."

———

Heat and Rook walked up the stairs of the dingy apartment building and turned onto the second floor at the landing. It was an old brownstone gone duplex in Hell's Kitchen that somebody must have thought could use some paint because everything was painted instead of repaired. At this hour of the day, the air was ripe with a combo of disinfectant and cooking odors. The stifling heat only made it a more tactile experience.

"Are you sure he's here?" said Rook in a whisper. Even then, his voice echoed like a cathedral rotunda.

"Positive," she said. "We've had him under surveillance all day."

Nikki stopped at apartment 27. The brass numerals had long ago, and many times, been painted over. A fossilized drip of pale green enamel formed a tear off the 7. Rook was standing right in front of the door. Nikki put her hands on his waist and placed him to the side. "In case he shoots. Don't you ever watch *Cops*?" She stood to the opposite side. "Now, you stay out in the hall until I give the all clear."

"I could have waited in the car for this."

"You still can."

He weighed that and took a half step back and leaned against the wall with his arms crossed. Heat knocked.

"Who is it?" came the muffled voice inside.

"NYPD, Gerald Buckley, open the door, we have a warrant." Nikki made a short count of two, pivoted, and kicked the door down. She drew and entered the apartment, catching the door on the rebound and giving it her shoulder as she went through. "Freeze, now!"

She caught a glimpse of Buckley disappearing into the hall. She made sure the living room was clear before she followed, and in the brief lag before she entered the bedroom, he had time to get a leg out the window. Through the curtains she could see Ochoa waiting on the fire escape for him. Buckley stopped and started to come back inside. Nikki gave him a surprise assist, holstering her gun and yanking him backward by the collar.

"Whoa," said Rook with awe.

Nikki turned to see him standing in the bedroom behind her. "I thought I told you to wait outside."

"It smells out there."

Turning her attention back on Buckley, who was facedown on the floor, Heat pulled his hands behind him.

———

Gerald Buckley, dishonored Guilford doorman, sat a few minutes later with his hands cuffed at his own dinette. Nikki and Rook sat on either side of him while Roach searched his place.

"I don't know why you're bugging me," he said. "This what you do every time there's a rip-off somewhere, hassle the guys who happen to work there?"

"I'm not hassling you, Gerald," said Heat, "I'm arresting you."

"I want a lawyer."

"And so you shall have one. You're going to need one, too. Your biker pal, Doc? He . . . I don't want to say 'dropped the dime,' that's so Starsky and Hutch." Nikki's digressions were pissing him off, which made her want to do them all the more. Get him rattled, loosen his tongue. "Let's be more civilized, let's say he implicated you in a sworn statement."

"I don't know any bikers."

"Interesting. Because Doc, a biker, by the way, says you were the one who hired him to pull the art theft at the Guilford. He says you made a rush call to him when the blackout hit. You asked him to get a crew together to break into the Starr apartment and steal all the artwork."

"Bullshit."

"It's tough to put a crew together for a big job like that on short notice, Gerald. Doc says he came up short and asked you to be his fourth on the job. Which, I guess is why you had to call in and tell Henry you couldn't make your shift. I love the irony. You had to call in and say you couldn't work so you could come in and pull a job. Do you appreciate irony, Gerald?"

"Why are you tearing my place up? What are you looking for?"

"Anything that can make your life difficult," Heat said. Raley appeared in the doorway, held up a handgun, and continued his search. "That might do. Hope that's got a permit, or this could be a troublesome visit."

"Bitch."

"You know it," she said with a smile. He turned his head away and just sat there. "So much to talk about."

Ochoa spoke from the living room. "Detective Heat?" Raley came in to take her place with the prisoner as Nikki excused herself.

Buckley looked at Rook and said, "What are you staring at?"

"A man in deep doo-doo."

Ochoa stood at the far end of the couch, where the liquor cabinet door was open. He pointed inside and said, "I found this stashed in here behind the peppermint schnapps and gin bottles." With his gloved hand, he held up a camera. An expensive, high-quality digital SLR.

"Check it out." He turned the camera body upside down so she could read the tiny rectangular inventory label with the bar code and serial number on the bottom. And the print above the code read, "Property of Sotheby's."

FIFTEEN

ameson Rook stood in the precinct Observation Room staring in at Interrogation, where Gerald Buckley waited, fully involved in picking his nose. The door opened and closed behind Rook. Nikki Heat glided up to his elbow and looked through the window with him. "Charming," she said.

"Know what's worse? I can't look away." Indeed, Rook kept watching as he said, "Don't they know people are watching them on the other side of that mirror? And the guy's got to want it, manacled like that."

"Are you quite done?"

"Yes."

"Sotheby's confirms the serial number as Barbara Deerfield's camera. The memory chip is full of shots she took of Starr's art collection."

"Taken that morning?" he asked. "The shots will be time stamped."

"Ooo, scary good. Somebody's catching on." He took a small bow and she continued. "Yes, from the morning of. Raley's copying all the photos to his hard drive."

"Raley, the new king of all media."

"I believe that would be czar."

"So that means Buckley was either there when she was killed, or he got her camera from Pochenko after." He turned to her. "Or am I offending your methodical ways with my reckless speculation?"

"No, actually, I'm right there with you this time, writer boy. Either way, that camera connects Buckley and Pochenko." She moved toward the door to Interrogation. "Let's see if I can get him to say how."

She was just reaching for the door when Ochoa came in from the hall. "His lawyer just got here."

"You know, I thought I heard the garbage truck."

"You may have a little time. Somehow her briefcase got lost when she was coming through security."

"Ochoa, you dog."

"Woof."

Buckley sat upright when Detective Heat came in, a sign he knew this wasn't the foreplay interview he'd had in that very room earlier. He tried to wear a look of defiance, but his concentration on her, trying to get a reading of how deep this shit was, told Nikki he could be had at some point. Maybe not in this meeting, but he'd fall. Once she saw that look, they all toppled, eventually.

"The bitch is back," she said and then eased into her chair. Nikki was in a hurry. The lawyer would be there too soon, she knew that. But she had to play the poker game. Buckley's tell gave him away; she wasn't about to level the playing field by letting her impatience show. So she sat back with her arms crossed like she had all the time in the world. He did his nervous mouth lick. Soon as she saw the dry tongue squeegee across the gums, she began.

"Would you be offended if I said you don't

strike me as the art thief type? I could see you doing a lot of things, dealing drugs, stealing a car, dine-and-dash. But masterminding a multimillion-dollar art heist? Sorry, I'm just not seeing it." The detective sat up and leaned toward him. "You put out the call for Doc the Biker to get a crew up for the burglary, but somebody had to call you first, and I want to know who that was."

"Where's my lawyer?"

"Gerald. You ever watch those infomercials where they say special limited time offer, so act now? With the shit storm you're facing, we're in that zone now, you and I." His eyes were flicking but he wasn't budging yet. She pressed him from another angle. "Of course, you don't see a lot of those infomercials. Mostly, they're on late at night and that's your usual door shift."

He shrugged. "You know that, everybody knows that."

"But it leads me to wonder. As we went over the surveillance video from the Guilford the day of Matthew Starr's murder, we saw you were there in the early afternoon."

"So, I work there."

"That's what I thought when I saw you on video the other day. But recent events have me looking at your presence in a whole new light."

"Hey, I did not kill Mr. Starr."

"I'll make a note of that." She flashed a smile and dropped it. "I'm wondering about something else, and you're just the guy to ask. You didn't by any chance help anybody into the building during your off-the-clock visit, did you? I know there's a locked access door on the roof. Is it possible you opened it up for somebody when you were hanging around at about 12:39 P.M.?"

There were two light knocks on the door. Damn, Ochoa signaling the attorney.

"Gerald? Limited time offer."

A woman's muffled rant seeped through from the Ob Room. "Sounds like my lawyer," said Buckley.

Sounds like a dental drill, thought Nikki. "Well? Did you let someone in from the roof?"

There was an air suck as the door opened. Ochoa came in with a brittle woman in a mud-colored suit. She reminded Nikki of someone who would hold up the grocery line insisting on a price check for parsley. The woman said, "This is not appropriate."

Nikki ignored her and pressed on. "Where did you get the camera?"

"Don't answer that."

"I'm not."

With the attorney as room monitor, Heat shifted to a new tack. She stopped looking for answers and started planting seeds. "Did Pochenko give it to you as a gift in exchange for the favor?"

"My client has nothing to say."

"Or did you rip the camera off from him? Pochenko's not the kind of guy you rip off, Gerald."

"Detective, this interview is over."

Nikki smiled and stood up. "There'll be others." And she stepped out.

———

Shortly after Roach clocked out for the day, Nikki heard Rook amble up behind her chair and watch her computer slide show of the pictures from Barbara Deerfield's camera. The photography was not the best. Straight-on flat shots of every painting snapped in pairs, one in natural light followed by a twin but using flash.

"Clearly these were for internal reference only. You wouldn't put them in a brochure or on the Web site," she said.

"So these were like her notes from the meeting with Matthew Starr."

"Right. And Lauren, my, what did you call her—my ghoul friend—called and confirmed her time of death as sometime around noon that same day." Nikki continued to click through each of the shots.

Rook must have read her mood, because instead of a victory gloat, he watched silently for a while. But only a while, before he said, "Are you free tonight?"

She continued to click the mouse, maintaining a cadence, enjoying her private art show, or looking for clues, or both. "I'm going to be working tonight."

"This is work. How would you like to meet New York's greatest art thief? Well, retired art thief."

A tiny thrill buzz hit Nikki and she spun around to face him. "Casper?"

"You know him?"

"I know of him. I read the profile you did on him for *Vanity Fair* a few years ago." She regretted it the moment she said it. But it was out there now.

"You read my article?"

"Rook, I read. I read a lot of stuff. Don't get

yourself in a lather." She was trying to downplay it, but she'd shown her hand.

"Anyway," he said, "I was thinking if someone's trying to move art in this city, Casper would know."

"And you can arrange for me to meet him?"

Rook hit her with a faceful of mock disdain.

"Right," she said, "what was I thinking? You're Mr. First-name-basis."

He got out his cell phone and scrolled through the contacts. Without looking up at Nikki, he said, "That *Vanity Fair* piece was five years ago. And yet you remembered it?"

"It was good. Informative."

"And you remembered I wrote it?"

". . . Yes."

Then he looked up at her. "Informative."

————

In the ghetto of antiques galleries south of Union Square, a dictionary's toss from the Strand Bookstore, Heat and Rook approached a single glass door between a Shaker furniture house and a rare maps shop. An eye-level door sign in 1940s style gold leaf read, "C. B. Phillips—Fine Acquisitions." Nikki reached to press the buzzer embedded in the metal frame. "I wouldn't do that," said Rook.

"Why not?"

"Don't insult the man." He held up a forefinger to say, Wait a sec. It was actually two seconds before the buzzer sounded. Rook said, "He's Casper. He knew, he always knows," and pushed the door open.

They climbed a flight of polished blond hardwood stairs through a mellow downdraft, the ghost scent of an old public library. At the landing, Nikki took in the room and was reminded of one of the Truths of New York City: You can never tell from the door what's behind a door.

The hushed showroom of C. B. Phillips Fine Acquisitions sat one flight of stairs from Broadway but was a time journey across latitudes, to a vast drawing room empty of people and teeming with dark, heavy furniture in velvets, and needle-points lit low below the tasseled maroon shades of small table lamps and muted ochre wall sconces. Clubby artworks of maritime scenes, bulldogs in military dress, and cherub architects adorned walls and carved mahogany easels. Nikki looked up and was staring at the pattern of the vintage stamped tin ceiling, when the soft voice right beside her made her jump.

"It's been too long, Jameson." His words were whiskey soft, carried on candle smoke. In it, there was a hint of Euro-somewhere she couldn't pinpoint but found pleasant. The dapper old man turned to her. "I apologize if I startled you."

"You came out of nowhere," she said.

"A knack that has served me well. Leaving as quietly, that's a diminishing talent, I'm sorry to say. It has led to a comfortable retirement, though." He gestured to his showroom. "Please, after you." As they crossed the thick oriental rug, he added, "You didn't tell me you were bringing a police detective."

Nikki paused. "I never said I was a detective." The old man simply smiled.

Rook said, "Wasn't sure you'd see me if I told you that, Casper."

"I probably wouldn't have. And it would have been my loss." From anyone else it would have been a laughable bar pickup line. Instead, the dashing little man made her blush. "Have a seat."

Casper waited until she and Rook took places on a navy corduroy sofa before he folded into his green leather wing chair. She could see the outline of a sharp kneecap through his linen trousers when he crossed his legs. He wore no socks and his slippers looked custom-made. "I have to say, you're every bit what I pictured."

"She thinks my article made you sound debonair," said Rook.

"Oh, please, that old label." Casper turned to her. "It's nothing, trust me. When you reach my age, the definition of debonair is that you shaved this morning." She noticed that his cheeks gleamed in the lamplight. "But one of New York's finest doesn't have time to come here simply to visit. And since I'm not wearing bracelets and being read my rights, I can safely assume my past hasn't caught up with me."

"No, it's nothing like that," she said. "And I do know you're retired." He answered with a little shrug and opened a palm, perhaps hoping she'd believe he was still an art thief and cat burglar. And, in fact, he convinced her at least to wonder.

"Detective Heat is investigating an art theft," Rook said.

"Rook tells me you're the one to talk to about

major art sales in the city. On or off the books."
Again, he answered with the shrug and hand wave.
Nikki decided the man was right, she didn't have
the inclination to sit and visit, and dove in. "During the blackout someone burglarized the Guilford and stole the entire Matthew Starr collection."

"Ho, I love it. Calling that glorified hodgepodge
a collection." He shifted and recrossed his bony
knees.

"Good, then you are familiar with it," she said.

"From what I know, it's not a collection at all so
much as a Cobb salad of vulgarity."

Heat nodded. "Similar comments have been
made." She handed him an envelope. "These are
copies of photos of the collection made by an appraiser."

Casper shuffled through the prints with undis-
guised disdain. "Who collects Dufy together with
Severini? Why not add a toreador or a clown on
black velvet?"

"You can keep those. I was hoping you could
look them over or show them around, and if you
hear of anyone trying to sell any of the pieces, let
me know."

"That's a complex request," said Casper. "One
side of that equation or another could involve friends
of mine."

"I understand. The buyer doesn't interest me so
much."

"Of course. You want the thief." He turned his
attention to Rook. "Times haven't changed, Jameson. They still want the one who took all the risk."

Rook said, "Difference here is that whoever did this probably did more than steal art. There's a possibility of a murder, maybe two."

"We don't know that for a fact," Heat said. "Just to be honest."

"My, my. A straight shooter." The elegant old thief gave Nikki a long look of appraisal. "Very well. I know an unorthodox art merchant or two who might be of service. I'll make some inquiries as a favor to Jameson. Plus it never hurts to pay forward a bit of goodwill with the gendarmerie."

Nikki bent over to pick up her bag and started to thank him, but when she looked up he was gone.

"What's he talking about?" said Rook. "I think he still makes a great exit."

———

Nikki stood in the precinct break room staring through the observation window of the microwave at the spinning carton of barbecued pork fried rice. Not for the first time, she reflected on how much time she spent in that building observing through windows, waiting for results. If it wasn't into interrogation rooms at suspects, it was into microwave ovens at leftovers.

The chirp sounded and she took out the steaming red carton with Detective Raley's name Sharpied on two sides, triple exclamation points included. If he really meant it, he would have taken it home with him. And then she thought about the glamour of the cop's life. Finishing off the workday with more work, eating a dinner of leftovers that aren't even your own.

Of course, Rook had tried to press for an evening. The obvious advantage of his generous offer to engage Casper was that the meeting ended at dinnertime, and even on a humid, uncomfortable night, there was nothing like sitting outdoors at the Boat Basin Café with some baskets of char-grilled burgers, a galvanized bucket of Coronas planted in shaved ice, and a view of the sailboats on the Hudson.

She told Rook she had a date. When his face started to rearrange, she told him it was in the bull pen with the whiteboard. Nikki didn't want to torture him. Yes, she did, just not like that.

In the after-hours quiet of the bull pen, without phones or visits to interrupt her, Detective Heat once again contemplated the facts laid out before her on the landscape of the jumbo porcelain enamel board. Just half a week ago she had sat in this very chair with the same late night view. There was more information for her to look at this time. The board was filled with names, timelines, and photographs. Since her previous night of silent deliberation two more crimes had gone down. Three, if you counted the assault on her by Pochenko.

"Pochenko," she said. "Where did you Po-chenk-go?"

Nikki went meditative. She was anything but mystical, but she did believe in the power of the subconscious. Well, at least hers. She pictured her mind as a whiteboard and erased it. Clearing herself, she became open to what sat before her and whatever patterns formed in the evidence so far. Her thoughts floated. She batted stray ones away and stuck to the case. She wanted an impression. She wanted to know what spoke to her. And she wanted to know what she'd missed.

She let herself travel, gliding above the days and nights of the case using the big board as her Fodor's. She saw Matthew Starr's body on the sidewalk and revisited Kimberly surrounded by art and opulence in her faux-preppie grief, saw herself interviewing the people in Starr's life: rivals, advisors, his bookie and Russian enforcer, his mistress, doormen. The mistress. Something the mistress said pulled her back. A nagging detail. Nikki paid attention to nags because they were the voices God gave to clues. She stood and went to the board and faced the mistress info she had posted there.

Office romance, love letter intercepted, top performer, left the company, muffin shop, happy, no motive. And then she looked to the side. Nanny affair?

The former mistress had seen Matthew Starr in Bloomingdale's with a new mistress. Scandinavian. Nikki found Agda personally inconsequential and, more importantly, properly alibied for the murder. Yet what was that nag?

She put the empty Chinese take-out carton on Raley's desk and slapped a Post-it note to it, thanking "Raley!!!" and taking perverse glee in her triple exclamations. Underneath, she wrote another note to bring in Agda for a 9 A.M. chat.

———

There was a blue-and-white from the One-Three parked outside her apartment when she got there. Detective

Heat said hi to the officers inside it and went upstairs. She didn't call her captain to wave it off that
night. Barbara Deerfield's neck bruises were fresh
in her mind. Nikki was exhausted and ached for
sleep.

No indulgence for her. She showered instead of
bathing.

Nikki got into her bed and smelled Rook on the
pillow beside her. She pulled it to her and breathed
deeply, wondering if she should have called him to
come over. Before she could answer, she was asleep.

―――――

It was still dark when her phone rang. The sound reached
her through a depth of slumber she had to claw her
way up from. She reached for her cell phone on the
nightstand with sleep-dead hands and it fell to the
floor. By the time she got to it, the ringing had
stopped.

She recognized the number and did a voice-
mail fetch. "Hey, it's Ochoa. Call me right away,
all right? Soon as you get this." He vibed a breathless urgency not like him. The sweat on Nikki's
naked skin chilled when his message continued,
"We found Pochenko."

SIXTEEN

Nikki was tucking in her blouse as she sailed down her front steps, raced to the cruiser, and asked the cops for a lift. They were glad to have their monotony broken and roared off with her in back.

At 5 A.M. the northbound traffic was light on the West Side Highway and they hauled ass. "I know the area, there's no vehicle access from this direction," Nikki told the driver. "Instead of killing time looping back from 96th, hop off at the next exit. When you get to the bottom of the ramp, I'll get out and hoof it the rest of the way."

The officer was still braking at the bottom of the 79th Street off-ramp when Heat told him she was good to go. She called over her shoulder to say thanks for the ride. Soon Nikki was running under the highway, scuffing over dried pigeon droppings on her way to the river and the police lights in the distance.

Lauren Parry was working Pochenko's body when Nikki jogged up, panting and sweaty from her sprint. "Catch your breath, Nik, he's not going anywhere," said the M.E. "I was ready to call about our man here, but Ochoa beat me to it."

Detective Ochoa joined them. "Looks like this guy won't be bothering you anymore."

Heat circled around to look at the corpse. The big Russian was slumped to one side on a park bench facing the Hudson. It was one of those picturesque rest stops on the slope of grass between the bike path and the bank of the river. Now it was Pochenko's final rest stop.

He had changed clothes since the night he tried to kill her. His cargo shorts and white T-shirt looked brand-new, which was how criminals on the run dressed, using stores as their closets. Pochenko's outfit was right off the shelf, except it was covered in blood.

"The homeless outreach patrol found him," said Ochoa. "They've been making rounds trying to get guys into the cooling shelters." He couldn't resist adding, "Looks like he's gonna stay nice and cool."

Nikki understood Ochoa's dark humor, but seeing the body didn't put her in a sporting mood. Whatever he had been, Vitya Pochenko was a dead human now. Any personal relief she felt about the end of his threat was just that, personal. He was now in the category of crime victim and was owed justice like anyone else. One of Nikki Heat's talents for The Job was her ability to put her own feelings in a box and be a professional. She looked at Pochenko again and realized she was going to need a bigger box.

"What do we have?" she asked Lauren Parry.

The M.E. beckoned Nikki around behind the bench. "Single gunshot to the back of the head."

The sky was starting to brighten, and the buttermilk light gave Nikki a clearer view of the bullet hole in Pochenko's brush cut. "There's muzzle burn," she said.

"Right. So it was extremely close range. And look at his body position. Big bench, he had the whole damn thing to himself, but he's all the way on one end."

Heat nodded. "Someone was sitting with him. No sign of struggle?"

"None," said the M.E.

"So it's most likely a friend or associate to get that close."

"Close enough for a sneak attack," said Ochoa. "Bring it up behind, and pop." He gestured behind them at the West Side Highway, which was already filling with morning commuters. "No witnesses, traffic noise covered the shot. Don't see a D.O.T. cam aimed this way, either."

"What about the gun?" Nikki asked the M.E.

"Small-caliber. I'd call it a twenty-five if you put a gun to my head."

"Lauren, honey, you need to get out more."

"I would, but business is too good." Then she pointed at the dead Russian. "This facial burn and the broken finger. Your work?" Heat nodded. "Anything else I should know about?"

"Yeah," said Ochoa. "Don't mess with Nikki Heat."

————

Rook was waiting back at the precinct when she and Ochoa came in. "I heard about Pochenko." He bowed his head grandly. "I'm sorry for your loss."

Ochoa laughed. "Hey, writer monkey's catching on."

Again, Nikki ignored the gallows humor.

"Ochoa, double-check the tail we have on Miric. He's Pochenko's known associate. I want to know where his bookie pal was when he was shot."

Detective Ochoa hit the phones. Rook brought a Dean & DeLuca cup to Heat's desk. "Here, I got you your usual. A nonfat, no-foam, double-pump vanilla latte."

"You know how I feel about frou-frou coffees."

"And yet you have one every morning. Such a complex woman."

She took it from him and sipped. "Thanks. Very thoughtful." Her phone rang. "And next time remember the chocolate shavings."

"So complex," he said.

Nikki picked up. It was Raley. "Two things," he said. "I've got Agda waiting in the outer."

"Thanks, I'll be right there. And the other?"

"Before I went home last night, I hocked one in that Chinese."

———

Agda Larsson had dressed up for her interview. She wore vintage wear from the East Village accessorized with a pink and white Swatch Beach Volleyball watch on one wrist and a knotted twine bracelet on the other. She pinch-rolled one of the knots between her thumb and finger and said, "Am I in some sort of trouble?"

"No, this is just a formality." That was only partially true. Nikki was basically crossing Ts with this interview; however, she did want to satisfy one question, the nagging one. She would work it in at the right time. "How are you coping with all this?

Between the murder and the burglary, you must be ready to go right back to Sweden."

Agda wagged her head in disbelief at it all. "Oh, it is quite upsetting, yes? But we have murder in my country, too. Almost two hundred last year, they say."

"In the entire country?"

"Yes, isn't that terrible? It is everywhere."

"Agda, I want to ask you some questions about life inside the Starr family."

She nodded slowly. "Mrs. Kimberly said you would want to do that when I told her I was coming here."

Nikki's antenna went up. "Did she caution you against talking about those things?"

"No, she said to say what I wanted."

"She said that?"

The nanny chuckled and shook her blond hair so it fell straight. "Actually, she said it did not matter because the police are incompetent and they could eat it." Agda read Nikki's lack of amusement and frowned, a futile attempt to look serious. "She says what she likes, Mrs. Starr."

And gets what she wants, thought Heat. "How long have you worked for her?"

"Two years."

"How is your relationship with her?"

"Oh, she can be tough. Out of nowhere, she'll snap at me, 'Agda get Matthew out of here to the park,' or she knocks on my bedroom door in middle of the night, 'Agda, Matthew got sick and threw up, come clean it.'"

"Day before yesterday Mrs. Starr and her son went out of town."

"That's right, they went to Dr. Van Peldt's beach cottage in Westport. In Connecticut."

"You didn't leave with them. Did you meet them up there, or possibly at Grand Central?"

Agda shook no. "I did not go with them."

"What did you do?"

"I stayed the night with a friend at NYU."

Heat jotted "NYU" in her notebook. "Is that unusual? I mean, if Mrs. Starr is knocking on your door at night with child care issues, I'm betting she takes you along on her out-of-town trips."

"This is true. Usually, I go on vacations and trips so she can enjoy herself and not be bothered with her son."

"But not that day." Nikki got to what was nagging her. "Was there a reason she didn't want you to be with her?" The detective eyed her keenly and continued, "Like some reason Mrs. Starr didn't want you around?"

"No, I only stayed behind so I could handle the piano delivery. She wanted Matty to get off the computer and get some culture, so she bought him a grand piano. It is gorgeous. When they took it out of the crate I almost fainted. Must have cost a fortune."

Grief takes many forms, thought Nikki. "Tell me about your relationship with Matthew Starr."

"Oh, much what you would expect. He likes me but calls me names when I tell him to go to bed or to turn off *The Suite Life of Zack and Cody* for dinner." She raised questioning eyebrows to Nikki. "You mean like that?"

Detective Heat made a mental note that she was not sitting across the table from the poet laureate of Sweden. "Thank you, now let me ask you about Matthew Starr, Sr. What kind of relationship did you have with him?"

"Oh, that was a very good one."

"In what way?"

"Well, he was very kind to me. Mrs. Starr, she snaps her fingers and she's all like, 'Agda do this,' or 'Agda keep him quiet, I am having my yoga time.'"

"Agda? About Mr. Starr?"

"Mister was always sweet. He would comfort me after she yelled at me. Mr. Starr would give me some extra money and treat me to a dinner out on my night off. Or take me shopping for clothes or . . . See, he gave me this Swatch."

"Was Mrs. Starr aware of this?"

"Oh, *tvärtom,* no. Matthew said to keep it only to us."

Nikki was amazed by her guileless sharing, and decided to keep that ball rolling. "Was your relationship with Mr. Starr ever physical?"

"Of course."

"To what extent?"

"He would rub my shoulders to comfort me after I got yelled at. Sometimes he would hug me or stroke my hair. It was very soothing. He was so gentle."

"How old are you, Agda?"

"Twenty-one."

"Did you and Matthew Starr ever sleep to-gether?"

"You mean have sex? *Skit nej!* That would not be appropriate."

———

There had obviously been some raucous laughter and jock snapping going on in the Observation Room during her interview with the nanny to the Starrs. It carried back to the bull pen when Roach and Rook followed her there.

"What's your take on Agda?" asked Raley.

Rook considered and said, "She's like Swedish furniture. Beautiful to look at but pieces missing."

"My favorite part," added Ochoa, "was hearing how this guy was basically horndogging her under his wife's nose and she says she didn't have sex with him because it would be inappropriate."

"That's called *horndogus interruptus,*" said Raley from over at the coffeepot. "I think Agda's just one of the deals Matthew Starr never got a chance to close before he was killed."

Rook turned to Nikki. "Hard to believe she's from the same land that brought us the Nobel Prize. Did she tell you anything useful?"

"You never know until you know," said Heat.

The theme from *Ghostbusters* by Ray Parker, Jr., started to play. "Rook, please tell me that's not coming from your pants," she said.

"Custom ringtone. Like it?" He held up his cell phone. The caller ID read "Casper." "Ghostbusters, get it? Excuse me, Detective Heat, my source may have information related to this case." Rook strode off to take his call with an air of smugness.

In less than a minute, he returned, still on the phone but stripped of arrogance. "But I was the one who introduced you to her. . . . Can't you just tell me?" He closed his eyes and sighed. "Fine." Rook extended his phone to Nikki. "He says he'll only share this with you."

"This is Nikki Heat."

"A pleasure, Detective. First, assure me that Jameson Rook is in anguish."

She looked at Rook, chewing his lower lip, straining to eavesdrop. "Quite."

"Good. If ever anyone needed a swift dismount from a high horse, it is he." The old man's soft, smoky tone warmed her ear. Hearing Casper without seeing him isolated his voice and she heard David Bowie with notes of Michael Caine's mellowness.

"To business," he said. "After your visit, I burnt some midnight oil because I could tell time was pressing on you."

"Never had a case where it wasn't," said the detective.

"And although you downplayed it, you do believe there is a murder connected to this art theft."

"Yes, I downplayed it, and yes I believe it. Perhaps two murders."

"A wonderful art appraiser, a fine woman who knew her business, was killed this week."

Nikki jumped to her feet. "Do you know anything about that?"

"No, I only knew Barbara from occasional meetings years ago. But she was among the best. Let's say knowing her death might be part of this only engages me more in your investigation."

"Thanks for that. Please call me with anything you find out."

"Detective, I have information right now. Trust me, I wouldn't have wasted either of our time unless I could provide substance."

Nikki flipped open her pad. "Has someone already tried to fence the paintings?"

"Yes and no," answered Casper. "Someone did sell just one of the paintings, the Jacques-Louis David. But that sale took place two years ago."

Nikki began to pace. "What? And you're absolutely sure of this?"

There was a pause and a half before the dapper art thief replied. "My dear, think of what you know about me and consider if you truly require an answer to that question."

"Point made," said Nikki. "I'm not doubting you, I'm just confused. How can a painting be in Matthew Starr's collection if it was sold two years ago?"

"Detective, you're smart. How good are you at math?"

"Pretty good."

"Then your answer is to do some."

And then Casper hung up.

SEVENTEEN

The receptionist at Starr Real Estate Development popped back on and told Detective Heat that Paxton would be right with her. Nikki felt like she was straining at a leash. Even hearing Anita Baker on the hold music didn't soothe her. It wasn't the first time in her life she seemed to be moving at a different pace than the rest of the world. Hell, it wasn't even the first time that day.

At last, a ring-through. "Hi, sorry about the wait. I'm buttoning up a lot of Matthew's affairs."

That could have so many meanings, she thought. "Last call, I promise."

"It's no bother, honest." Then he laughed and said, "Although . . ."

"Although what?"

"I wonder if it would be easier if I just set up my office over there at your precinct."

Nikki laughed, too. "You could. You have the better view, but we have nicer furniture. How sad is that?"

"I'll stick with the view. So tell me how I can help you, Detective."

"I was hoping you could look up the name of the company that insured Matthew's art collection."

"Sure thing." He paused. "But you recall I told you he had me cancel that policy."

"Yes, I know. I just want to ask them if they kept documentary photos of the collection I can use to hunt it down."

"Oh, oh, pictures, right. Never thought of that. Good idea. Got a pen?"

"Ready."

"It's GothAmerican Insurance here in Manhattan." She heard sharp keystrokes and he continued, "Ready for the phone number?"

After she took it down, Nikki said, "May I ask you one more question? It will save me a call later."

She could hear the smile in his voice when Noah answered, "I doubt that, but go ahead."

"Did you cut a check for Kimberly Starr to buy a piano recently?"

"A piano?" And then he repeated, "A piano? No."

"Well she bought one." Heat looked at the CSI photo in her hand of the Starr living room. "It's a beaut. A Steinway Karl Lagerfeld edition."

"Kimberly, Kimberly, Kimberly."

"These list for eighty thousand. How could she afford that?"

"Welcome to my world, Detective. Not the craziest thing she's done. Want to hear about the speedboat she bought last fall in the Hamptons?"

"But where did she get the money?"

"Not from me."

Nikki checked her watch. She might be able to get to the insurance folks before lunch. "Thanks, Noah, that's all I need."

"Until next time, you mean."

"Sure you don't want to set up a desk over

here?" she said. They were both laughing when they hung up.

————

Heat punctuated her "Yesss!" with a fist-pump when Raley finished his call to the archives manager at Go-thAmerican. They not only routinely maintained photographic documentation of insured art collections, they held them for seven years following the cancellation of a policy. "How soon can we get them?"

"Faster than you can microwave my leftovers," said Raley.

She pressed her detective. "Exactly how soon?"

"The archive manager is e-mailing them to me as an attachment now."

"Forward it to Forensics as soon as it comes."

"Already had GothAmerican do a cc to them," he said.

"Raley, you are the czar of all media." Heat clapped him on the shoulder. She grabbed her bag and hurried out to Forensics, brushing past Rook on his way in without seeming to notice him.

The world still hadn't caught up to Heat speed. When Nikki was closing in, it had little chance.

————

Detective Heat returned to the bull pen from Forensics an hour and a half later wearing the game face Rook had seen when she was staging for the body shop raid.

"What did you learn?" he asked.

"Oh, just that Matthew Starr's art collection was all forgeries."

He sprang to his feet. "The whole collection?"

"Fakes." She slung her bag on the back of her chair. "The ones in the insurance pictures are real. The ones in Barbara Deerfield's camera? Not so much."

"That's big."

"It sure provides a motive for someone to murder an art appraiser."

He gestured, punctuating with his forefinger. "I was thinking the same thing."

"Oh, you were, were you?"

"I am a trained journalist. I'm capable of reading clues, too, you know."

He was getting cocky and she decided to have some fun with him. "Great. Then tell me who had the motive."

"You mean who murdered Barbara Deerfield? Pochenko."

"On his own initiative? Doubt that."

He pondered and said, "What do you think?"

"I'll tell you what I think. I think it's too early to go shooting my mouth off." She went to the board and put a check mark beside her notation to screen the insurance photos. He followed her like a puppy and she smiled to herself.

"But you're on to something, aren't you?" he said. She just shrugged. "Do you have a suspect in mind?" Nikki flashed a grin and walked back to her desk. He trailed her and said, "You do. Who is it?"

"Rook, aren't you doing this whole ride-along so you can get into the mind of a homicide detective?"

"Yeah?"

"Just telling you wouldn't be helping you. Know what would help you? For you to think like a homicide detective and see what you come up with on your own." Nikki picked up her desk phone and pushed a speed-dial button.

Rook said, "That sounds like a lot of work."

She held up a staying palm while she listened to a ring at the other end of the line. He brought his knuckle up and pushed it to his lips, agonized. She loved driving Rook crazy like this. It was fun, and besides, if she was wrong, she didn't want him to know.

Finally, someone picked up. "Hi, it's Detective Heat at the Two-Oh. I want to arrange for transport of a prisoner you're holding. His name's Buckley, Gerald Buckley. . . . Yeah, I'll hold."

While she was waiting, Rook said, "Aren't you beating a dead horse? That guy's not going to tell you anything. Especially with that ambulance chaser of his."

Nikki beamed a smug grin. "Ah, but that was yesterday in Interrogation. Today, we're going to stage a little theater."

"What kind of theater?"

"A play. As in," she switched to an Elizabethan accent, " 'The play's the thing, Wherein I'll catch the conscience of the king.' " Then she added, "That would be Buckley."

"You really wanted to be an actress, didn't you?"

"Maybe I am," said Nikki. "Come along and see."

———————

Heat, Roach, and Rook were waiting in the hallway at the Office of the Chief Medical Examiner in Kips Bay when the corrections officers delivered Gerald Buckley with his attorney in tow.

Nikki looked him up and down. "Coveralls flatter you, Mr. Buckley. Rikers all it's cracked up to be?"

Buckley turned his head away from Heat the way dogs do when they're pretending they didn't deliver the nearby turd to the new carpet. His lawyer stepped between them. "I've advised my client not to answer any further questions. If you have a case, bring it. But no more interviews unless you have lots of time to waste."

"Thanks, Counselor. This isn't going to be an interview."

"No interview?"

"That's right." The detective waited as his lawyer and Buckley traded confused looks, then she said, "Step this way."

Nikki led the entourage, Buckley, his lawyer, Roach, and Rook, into the autopsy room where Lauren Parry stood beside a stainless table with a sheet over it.

"Hey, what are we doing in here?" said Buckley.

"Gerald," said the lawyer, and he pursed his lips. Then she turned to Nikki. "What are we doing in here?"

"They pay you to do that? Repeat what he says?"

"I demand to know why you dragged my client down here to this place."

Nikki smiled. "We have a body that needs identification. I believe Mr. Buckley may be able to provide it."

Buckley leaned toward his attorney's ear and got as far as muttering, "I don't wanna see any—" when Heat signaled Lauren Parry, who whipped the sheet off the table and revealed the corpse.

Vitya Pochenko's body was still clothed as they had found him. Nikki had phoned ahead to debate the subject with her friend, who felt that naked-for-the-autopsy was an impactful display that was tough to beat. Heat managed to persuade her that the Great Lake of dried blood on his white T-shirt told a better story, and so that was the presentation the M.E. made.

The Russian lay on his back, eyes left open to make the maximum impression, the irises fully dilated, leaving only pupil, the effect exhibiting the darkest window to his soul. All color was gone from his face except for blotches of deep empurplement near one jaw, where gravity had pooled blood in the direction of his bench slump. Then there was that gruesome butterscotch and salmon burn welt covering one side of his face.

Nikki watched the color drain from Gerald Buckley's cheeks and lips until he was only about two hardware-store paint chips from matching Pochenko.

"Detective Heat, if I may interrupt," said Lauren, "I may have a determination on the caliber of the weapon."

"Excuse us just one moment," Nikki said to Buckley. He took a hopeful half step to the door, his disbelieving eyes still riveted on the body. Ochoa stepped to corral him and he stopped without contact.

Gerald Buckley stayed put, staring. His lawyer had found a chair and was sitting sideways, at a right angle to the play. Nikki snapped on a pair of gloves and joined the M.E. at her table. Lauren placed expert fingertips on Pochenko's skull and gently rotated it to expose the bullet hole behind his ear. A small puddle of brain fluid pooled on the gleaming stainless steel under the wound, and Buckley moaned when he saw it. "I did critical measurements and ballistics comparisons after our on-site angle-of-entry reconstruction."

"Twenty-five?" asked Nikki.

"Twenty-five."

"Mighty small caliber to bring down such a big man."

The medical examiner nodded. "But a small-caliber round delivered to the brain can be remarkably effective. In fact, one of the highest one-shot-stop ratings is the Winchester X25." In the metal pan of the hanging scale, Heat could see Buckley's reflection, craning to hear every bit as Lauren continued. "That round is fabricated like a hollow point, but the hollow is filled with a steel BB to aid expansion inside the body once the slug is delivered."

"Whoa. When that puppy hit his brains, it must have been like taking a hammer to a plate of scrambled eggs," said Raley. Buckley was regarding him with fearful eyes, so the detective added for good measure, "Like the front row of a Gallagher concert in there."

"Quite," said Lauren. "We'll know more once we cut open his brain for the treasure hunt, but one of those slugs would be my guess."

"But such a small gun would mean whoever did this knew they'd get a chance to work close."

"Sure," said Lauren. "Definitely knew what they were doing. Small-caliber mouse gun. Easy to conceal. Victim never sees it coming. Could be anytime, anywhere."

"Pop," said Ochoa.

Buckley yipped and flinched.

Heat crossed over to him, making sure to leave an unobstructed view of the dead Russian. The doorman was a fish on a dock. His lips opened and closed but no sound came. "Can you positively identify this man?"

Buckley belched and Nikki was afraid he'd ralph on her, but he didn't, and it seemed to help him locate his voice. "How could somebody . . . get to Pochenko?"

"People involved in this case are dying, Gerald. Are you sure you don't want to give me a name to help stop this before you join them?"

Buckley was incredulous. "He was a wild animal. He laughed when I called him Da Terminator. Nobody could kill him."

"Somebody did. Single shot to the head. Bet you know who." She waited a three count and said, "Who hired you to steal that art collection?"

The lawyer got to her feet. "Don't answer that."

"Maybe you don't know who," Heat said. Her tone was all the more intimidating because she was so casual. Instead of shouting or grilling him, she was washing her hands of him. "I'm thinking we're chasing our tails. We should spring you. Bail you out on your own recognizance. Let you think things over out there. See how long you last."

"Is that a *bona fide* offer, Detective?" asked the attorney.

"Ochoa? Get the keys to unlock his handcuffs."

Behind him, Ochoa rattled a set of keys and Buckley recoiled, hunching his shoulders at the sound as if it was a bullwhip cracking.

"Isn't that what you want, Gerald?"

The man was swaying where he stood. White saliva strings connected the roof of his mouth to his tongue.

"What . . ." Buckley swallowed. "What's happened to his . . . ?" He gestured up and down his own face to indicate the burn area on Pochenko.

"Oh, I did that," said Nikki, sounding casual. "Burned his face with a hot iron."

He looked to Lauren, who nodded affirmation. Then he looked at Heat and then Pochenko and back to Heat. "All right."

"Gerald," the lawyer said, "shut up."

He turned to her. "You shut up." Gerald Buckley then looked at Nikki and spoke gently, resigned. "I'll tell you who hired me to steal that art."

Nikki turned to Rook. "You'll excuse us, won't you? I need you to wait outside while Mr. Buckley and I talk."

EIGHTEEN

On their drive back from the M.E.'s office, Nikki didn't need to turn around to know Rook was pissed off in the backseat. She was dying to, though, because seeing his torment would have added to her wicked pleasure.

Ochoa was sitting back there with him and said, "Hey, homes, you carsick or something?"

"No," said Rook. "Unless I caught a chill when I got sent out in the hall when Buckley was going to talk."

Heat wanted to turn around so bad.

"Some play. You kicked me out during the last scene."

Raley braked at the light on Seventh Avenue and said, "Hey, when a subject's about to open up, the fewer the better. You especially don't want a reporter there."

Nikki leaned back on the headrest and scoped the digital temperature on the JumboTron outside Madison Square Garden. Ninety-nine degrees. "You probably know who Buckley named anyway, right, Rook?"

"Tell me and I'll let you know."

That brought a round of chuckles inside the Crown Vic.

Rook snorted. "When did this become a hazing?"

"It's not a hazing," she said. "You want to be all

with the detectives, right? Do what we do and think like one."

"Except Raley," said Ochoa. "He doesn't think right."

"I'll even help you out," said Heat. "What do we know? We know the paintings were fake. We know they were gone when Buckley's crew got there. Shall I go on, or do you have it figured?"

The light changed and Raley drove on. "I'm developing a theory," Rook said.

At last, she hooked her elbow over the seat to face him. "That doesn't sound exactly like naming a name."

"All right, fine." He paused and blurted, "Agda." Rook waited for a response and just got stares, so he filled the silence. "She had full access to that apartment that day. And I've been thinking about her interview. I don't buy the naïve nanny pose and the innocent shoulder rubs. That girl was doing Matthew Starr. And I think he dumped her like he did all his mistresses, only she got pissed enough to want some payback."

Heat said, "So Agda had him killed?"

"Yes. And stole the paintings."

"Interesting." She thought a moment. "And I guess you also figured out why Agda killed the art appraiser. And how she got the paintings out."

Rook's eyes lost contact with hers and fell to his shoes. "I haven't plugged every hole, this is still a theory."

She looked around to poll her colleagues. "It's a process. We get it."

"But am I right?"

"I don't know, are you?" Then she turned all the way around so he wouldn't see her smile.

————

Rook and Detectives Raley and Ochoa had to hustle to keep stride with Heat when they got back to the precinct. As soon as she entered the bull pen, Nikki beelined for her desk and pulled open the file drawer.

"All right, now I've got it," said Rook as he arrived in her wake. "When did Agda start working for the Starr family?"

"Two years ago." Heat didn't bother to face him. She was occupied sorting through pictures in a file.

"And when did Casper say that painting was fenced? That's right, two years ago." Rook waited, but she just kept shuffling her deck of pictures. "And Agda got the paintings out of the Guilford because she doesn't work alone. I think our Swede could be part of some art theft ring. An international art theft and forgery ring."

"Uh-huh . . ."

"She's young, she's pretty, she gets into the homes of wealthy people and has access to their artwork. She's their inside man. Woman. Nanny."

"And why would an international forgery ring be dumb enough to steal a bunch of fakes?"

"They weren't fakes when she stole them." He crossed his arms, quite satisfied with himself.

"I see," said the detective. "And you don't think they'd notice their nanny going out of the apartment with a painting? Or the space gaping on the wall?"

He reflected then shut down. "You have a question for everything, don't you?"

"Rook, if we don't poke holes, the defense attorneys will. That's why I need to build a case."

"Didn't I just do that for you?"

"Notice I'm still building." She found the picture she was looking for and slipped it into an envelope. "Roach."

Raley and Ochoa stepped over to her desk. "You're taking the Roach Coach on a short drive out of town with this photo of Gerald Buckley. Go to that place he mentioned back at the M.E.'s. Shouldn't be hard to find. Show the picture, see if you get any hits, and then I want you back here, pronto."

"Going out of the city, how'd I miss that? Oh, right, Buckley freeze-out again," said Rook. "Let me guess. You're going to see if Agda lied about NYU and was really somewhere else with the paintings?"

"Raley, do you have a map?"

"I don't need a map."

"No, but Rook does," said Heat. "He's been all over his."

After Raley and Ochoa left, she put the file away in her desk. Rook was still lurking. "What are we going to do?"

Nikki indicated a chair. "We? We, which is to say you, are going to park your Pulitzer Prize–winning butt and stay out of my way while I scare up some warrants."

Rook took a seat. "Arrest warrants? Plural?"

"Search warrants, plural. I need two of them plus a warrant for a wiretap." She looked at her watch and whispered a curse. "Day's half-shot and I need them like now."

"Um, I believe I can be of service if you're in a hurry."

"No, Rook."

"It's cake."

"I said no. Stay out of this."

"I did it before."

"Ignoring my instructions."

"And getting you your warrant." He glanced around to make sure the bull pen was empty and lowered his voice. "After the other night, aren't we past this?"

"Don't. Even."

"Let me help you."

"No. Do not call Judge Simpson."

"Give me one good reason."

"Because now that the judge and I are poker buddies," she grinned and picked up her phone, "I can call him myself."

"You sleep with me, then you make fun of my theories and steal all my friends." Rook leaned back and crossed his arms. "Just for that, you're not meeting Bono."

––––––

Horace Simpson came through with the warrants, accompanied by a judicial warning that Heat had better get her heinie back to Rook's poker table so he could win back his losses. And to think all these years the detective had been going through channels to reach judges.

Getting the search warrants in hand turned out

to be the easy part. Her wiretap required time to set up, meaning several hours of waiting. Not Nikki Heat. She strode into the bull pen from Captain Montrose's office and grabbed her bag.

"What now?" asked Rook.

"Cap sprung a team off patrol for me. We're rolling to execute my search warrants." When he stood up to join her, she said, "Sorry, Rook, we're at a critical phase. This is police-only."

"Come on, I'll stay in the car, I promise. It's hot, but just leave the window open a crack for me. They say that's dangerous, but I'm tough, I'll bring water."

"You're better off right here reviewing your evidence. You've got the whiteboard to study, you've got air-conditioning, and you'll have time, lots of time." As she crossed the room with her back to him, she said, "Remember, think like a detective."

"You might as well take me, I know where you're going." That stopped her. When she turned to face him from the doorway, he said, "The Guilford and to a personal storage place on Varick."

She looked down at her bag. "You snooped my warrants, didn't you?"

His turn to grin. "Just thinking like a journalist."

———

Two hours later, Heat returned to find Rook staring at the whiteboard. "Come up with any more theories while I was out?"

"In fact, yes."

She went to her desk and checked her voice mail. Her mailbox was empty. Nikki tossed the handset onto the cradle in frustration and looked at her watch.

"You all right? Trouble with your search warrants?"

"*Au contraire*," she said. "I'm just stressing my wiretap. The other stuff went great. Better than great."

"What did you find?"

"You first. What's your new theory?"

"Well. I've been thinking it all over and now I know who it is."

"Not Agda?"

"Why? Is it Agda?"

"Rook."

"Sorry, sorry. OK. This is off-the-wall. I'm off Agda. But I'm thinking about something she said about the new piano." This piqued Nikki's interest. She sat against the edge of her desk with her arms folded. "Am I getting warmer?" he asked.

"I know I'm not getting younger. Get to it."

"When you interviewed her, Agda said something like the new piano was so gorgeous, she almost fainted when it came out of the crate." He paused. "Who delivers pianos in crates anymore? Nobody."

"Interesting, go on." In fact, these were waters she was fishing in, and Nikki was curious to hear his take.

"We know the piano came in because we saw it there after the theft. So I got to wondering, why bring in a crate unless something is going to go out in it after you remove the piano from it?"

"And so now you are saying it's who?"

"Obviously. The piano company is a front for art thieves."

"Is that your final answer?" The flat expression she showed him made Rook backpedal so fast, Nikki wanted to burst out laughing. But she held her poker face.

"Or . . . ," he said, "let me finish. You served a warrant at the Guilford and at a personal storage place. I'm sticking with my piano crate scenario, but I say it's . . . Kimberly Starr." Although her face remained neutral, Rook became animated. "I'm right, I know it. I can see it all over you. Tell me I'm wrong, then."

"I'm not telling you squat." Raley and Ochoa came into the bull pen. Heat started over to them. "Why spoil the fun?"

"Raley and I showed around Buckley's picture," said Ochoa. "We scored two positive hits. That doesn't suck."

"Doesn't suck at all." Nikki dared to let herself feel the thrill of gathering momentum on the case. "And they'll testify?"

"Affirm," said Raley.

Nikki's desk phone rang and she lunged for it. "Detective Heat." She kept nodding as if the caller could see her, and said, "Excellent. Great. Excellent. Thanks much." When she hung up, she turned to her team. "Wiretap's up. We're going to the dance." For once things were moving at Heat speed.

———

Nikki and Rook sat wedged into a corner of the tiny room, knee-to-knee on metal folding chairs behind the police technician who was recording the calls. The AC vent whistled, so Heat had had the air turned off to let her hear without that distraction, and it was suffocating in there.

A blue LED meter spiked on the console. "Picking up," said the technician.

Heat put on her headphones. The ring purred on the line. Her breathing became shallow the way it had on the raid in Long Island City, only this time she couldn't calm herself. Her heart thunked at a disco cadence until Nikki heard the click of the answer and one of the beats skipped.

"Hello?"

"I'm using your direct line because I don't want the receptionist knowing I'm calling you," said Kimberly Starr.

"OK . . ." Noah Paxton sounded wary of her. "I don't understand why not."

Nikki hand-signaled the technician to ensure he was recording. He nodded.

Kimberly continued, "You're about to understand, Noah."

"Is something wrong? You sound strange."

Nikki closed her eyes into a tight squint of concentration, wanting only to hear. With headphones on, the fidelity was iPod-quality. She clocked every nuance. The air hiss of the office chair Noah was sitting in. The hard swallow that came from Kimberly.

Now Nikki waited. Now she wanted words.

"I need your help with something. I know you always did things for Matthew, and now I want you to do the same for me."

"Things?" His tone was still guarded.

"Come on, Noah, cut the shit. We both know Matt pulled a lot of crap that was shady and you handled it. I need some of that from you now."

"I'm listening," he said.

"I have the paintings."

Nikki caught herself making tension fists and loosened her grip.

Paxton's office chair creaked. "Excuse me?"

"Am I not speaking English? Noah, the art collection. It wasn't stolen. I took it. I hid it."

"You?"

"Not me personally. I had some guys do it while I went out of town. Forget all that. The thing is, I have them and I want you to help me sell them."

"Kimberly, are you nuts?"

"They're mine. I didn't get insurance. I deserve something out of all those years with that son of a bitch."

Now it was Heat's turn to swallow hard. It was starting to come together. Her heart was punching to get out.

"What makes you think I'd know how to sell them?"

"Noah, I need help. You were Matthew's fixer, now I want you to be mine. And if you're not going to help me, I'll find someone who will."

"Whoa, whoa, Kimberly, slow down." Another pneumatic hiss, and Heat pictured Noah Paxton rising up behind his horseshoe-shaped desk. "Don't call anybody. Are you listening to me?"

"I'm listening," she said.

"We should talk this out. There's a solution to

all this, you just need to keep your head." He paused and asked, "Where are these paintings?"

A swell of anticipation gathered up Nikki and carried her until she felt suddenly weightless at its crest. A trickle of sweat curved around the vinyl ear seal of one of her headphones.

"The paintings are here," said Kimberly.

"And where's here?"

Say it, thought Nikki, say it.

"At the Guilford. Pretty cool, huh? All the searching they've been doing and they never left the building."

"All right, listen to me. Don't call anybody, just relax. We need to work this out face-to-face, OK?"

"OK."

"Good. Stay there. I'll be right over." And then he hung up.

Nikki took off her headphones. When Rook removed his, he said, "I called it. I was right. It was Kimberly. Ha-ha, where's my five?" He held up his palm to her.

"Uh, we don't do fives."

Rook stood. "Listen, we'd better get over there before Noah. If this woman killed her husband, who knows what she'll do next."

Nikki rose. "Thanks for the pointer, Detective Rook." He held the door for her and they strode out.

NINETEEN

Heat, Raley, Ochoa, and Rook crossed through the lobby of the Guilford to the elevators. When the doors opened, Nikki put the palm of her hand on Rook's chest. "Whoa, whoa, where do you think you're going?"

"With you."

She shook her head. "No way. You stay down here."

The automatic doors kept trying to close. Ochoa braced them open with his shoulder to keep them from bouncing.

"Come on, I did what you said. I thought like a detective and I deserve to be there when you take her down. I've earned that." When all three of the detectives broke into laughter, Rook walked it back a hair. "How about I just wait in the hall?"

"You told me you'd wait in the hall when I arrested Buckley."

"OK, I got impatient once."

"And on our raid in Long Island City, what did you do after I told you to stay behind?"

Rook kicked the toe of his shoe against the lip of the rug. "Look, this is starting to sound more like an intervention than an arrest."

"I promise, we won't make you wait long. After all," she said with mock solemnity, "you've earned that." She got in the elevator with Roach.

"Just for that I may do my whole article about someone else."

"Break my heart," she said as the doors shut on him.

When Detective Heat entered through the front door of the apartment, she found Noah Paxton by himself in the living room. "Where's Kimberly?"

"She's not here."

Raley and Ochoa stepped in behind Nikki. "Check all the rooms," she said. Ochoa disappeared with Raley down the hallway.

"Kimberly's not back there," said Paxton. "I already checked."

Heat said, "We're do-it-yourselfers. We're funny that way." Her gaze went to the room full of artwork, hanging as it always had been, floor to ceiling. Nikki marveled at the sight. "The paintings. They're back."

Noah seemed to share her bewilderment. "I don't understand it, either. I'm just trying to figure out where the hell they came from."

"Relax, you don't have to playact anymore, Noah." She watched the furrows crease his brow. "They never left the Guilford, right? We tapped her phone call to you not twenty minutes ago."

"I see." He thought a few seconds, no doubt sorting through his side of the conversation, wondering if he could be an accessory after the fact. "I told her she was nuts," he said.

"Now, that's a good citizen."

He opened his palms to her. "I apologize, Detective. I knew I should have called you. Guess I still have my protective instinct for the family. I came over here to talk sense into her. Too late now." Nikki just shrugged. "When did you find out she stole them? During that phone call?"

"No. The alarm bells sounded for me when I heard our widow-in-mourning bought a piano and left town for the delivery. Does Kimberly strike you as someone who'd leave rearranging her precious antiques to a work crew and a dimwit nanny?" Nikki ambled to the Steinway and tinkled one key. "We checked with the building super. He confirmed the piano movers came here in the morning with a huge crate, but didn't recall them leaving with one. It fell off his radar, I guess, after all the confusion around the blackout."

Noah smiled and shook his head. "Wow."

"I know, pretty sneaky, huh? They never left the building."

"Ingenious," said Paxton. "And not a word I associate with Kimberly Starr."

"Well, she wasn't as smart as she thought."

"What do you mean?"

Nikki had run this over and over in her head so that it was crystal clear to her. Now she would bring Noah along on the ride. "Did you know Matthew had changed his mind about selling his collection?"

"No, I didn't know anything about that."

"Well, he had. The same day he was killed, a woman from Sotheby's named Barbara Deerfield came over here to appraise it. She was murdered before she got back to her office."

"That's horrible."

"I believe her murder was connected to Matthew's."

His brow darkened. "It's tragic, but I don't understand the connection."

"Neither did I. I kept wondering, Why would anyone kill an art appraiser? Then I discovered that Starr's entire art collection was made up of forgeries." Nikki watched a pallor wash out Noah Paxton's face.

"Forgeries?" He let his gaze wander the walls. Nikki saw his eye fall upon a piece of art near the archway. The one covered by a shroud.

"Fakes, Noah." His attention snapped back to her. "The whole collection."

"How can that be? Matthew paid top dollar for these paintings, and from reputable dealers." Paxton's color was coming back and then some as he grew more agitated. "I can assure you when we bought these they were not fakes."

"I know," said the detective. "The insurance documentation pictures bore that out."

"Then how could they now be fakes?"

Nikki sat on the arm of a sofa that cost more than most people's cars. "The appraiser took her own set of photos of the collection as notes. We found her camera and her pictures didn't match the insurance shots. She had documented a roomful of forgeries." Heat paused to let that sink in. "Sometime between the purchase and her appraisal, someone switched the art."

"That's unbelievable. You're sure of this?"

"Absolutely. And Barbara Deerfield would have come to the same conclusion if she had lived to study her pictures. In fact," said Nikki, "I'd say that the reason Barbara Deerfield was killed was because somebody didn't want it to get out that the sixty-million-dollar Starr Collection was bogus."

"Are you saying Matthew was trying to palm off fakes?"

Heat shook her head no. "Matthew never would have hired an appraiser if he knew they were fakes. And after all the money and ego he invested in his Little Versailles? He'd have had a meltdown if he ever found out."

Noah's eyes widened in revelation. "Oh my God. Kimberly . . ."

Nikki rose and strolled over to the John Singer Sargent oil of the two innocents, enjoyed it for just a glance, and said, "Kimberly beat someone else to stealing that art collection. I arrested a second crew that broke in here later, during the blackout, and they found nothing but empty walls."

"Everyone went to a lot of trouble just to steal something that's worthless."

"Kimberly didn't know the paintings were worthless. The grieving Mrs. Starr thought she was scoring her multimillion-dollar Lotto hit for a shitty marriage."

"Obviously the other burglars thought it was valuable, too." Paxton gestured to the art. "Otherwise why would they try to steal it?"

Nikki stepped away from the painting and faced him. "I don't know, Noah. Why don't you tell me?"

He took his time before he answered, looking at her to gauge if she was asking a rhetorical question or something with more stink on it. He couldn't have liked the way her eyes were boring into him, but he went for rhetorical. "I could only guess."

If her session at the medical examiner's that morning was theater, for Nikki this was Brazilian jujitsu and she was done boxing. On to the grappling. "Do you know a Gerald Buckley?"

Paxton squeezed his mouth into an upside-down U. "Doesn't sound familiar."

"Curious, Noah. Gerald Buckley knows you. He's the overnight doorman here." She watched him work his earnest face. Nikki found him almost convincing; he wasn't bad. She was better. "Here's a refresher. Buckley's the man you hired to set up the second burglary during the blackout."

"That's a lie. I don't even know him."

"Now that is truly weird," said Ochoa from the archway. Paxton was edgy. He hadn't seen the other two detectives return, and he flinched when Ochoa spoke. "Me and my partner took a drive up to Tarrytown this afternoon. To a bar there."

Raley said, "Place called the, uh, Sleepy Swallow?"

"Whatever," said Ochoa. "Guess that's your regular hang, right? Everybody knows you. And the bartender and a waitress both ID'd Mr. Buckley sitting at your table for a very long time a few nights ago."

"During the blackout," added Raley. "About the time Buckley should have been in for that shift he canceled."

"Buckley is not your strongest point man," said Heat. Noah's eyes were getting less focused and he whipped his head from detective to detective as each spoke, like he was following the ball at a tennis match.

"Dude caved like a sandcastle," added Ochoa.

"Buckley also says you called him up and told him to hurry over here to the Guilford and let Pochenko in the rooftop door. That was just before Matthew Starr was murdered," said Nikki.

"Pochenko? Who's Pochenko?"

"Smooth. Not going to trip you up, am I?" said Heat. "Pochenko's somebody whose picture you didn't recognize in my photo array. Even though I showed his picture to you twice. Once here, once at your office."

"You're fishing. This is all speculation. You're putting everything on hearsay from a liar. An alcoholic who's desperate for money." Paxton was standing in a direct sun ray from one of the high windows, and his forehead glistened in the light. "Yes, I'll admit I met this Buckley guy at the Swallow. But only because he was shaking me down. I used him a couple of times to arrange hookers for Matthew and he was trying to extort hush money out of me." Paxton raised his chin and thrust his hands in his pockets, body English for that's my story and I'm sticking to it, thought Nikki.

"Let's talk about money, Noah. Remember that little transgression of yours my forensic accountants uncovered? That time when you fudged the books to hide a few hundred grand from Matthew?"

"I already told you that was for his kid's college."

"Let's pretend that's the truth for now." Nikki didn't believe him but was applying another rule of jujitsu: When you're closing in for a takedown, don't get faked into a sucker hold. "Whatever your reason, you managed to cover your tracks by putting that money back two years ago, right after one of the paintings from this collection, a Jacques-Louis David, got fenced for that exact amount. A coincidence? I don't believe in coincidences."

Ochoa shook his head. "No way."

"The detective is definitely not coincidence-friendly," said Raley.

"Is that how you started, Noah? You needed a few grand so you had one of his paintings forged and then swapped it for the real one, which you sold? You said yourself that Matthew Starr was a philistine. The man never had a clue the painting you put on his wall was a fake, did he?"

"That's bold," said Ochoa.

"And you got bolder. After you saw how easy it was to get away with that, you tried it with another painting, and another, and then started flipping the whole collection like that, piece by piece, over time. Do you know Alfred Hitchcock?"

"Why, is he accusing me of the Great Train Robbery?"

"Somebody asked him once if the perfect crime had ever been committed. He said yes. And when the interviewer asked him what it was, Hitchcock said, 'We don't know, that's what makes it perfect.'"

Nikki joined Ochoa and Raley near the archway. "I have to hand it to you, swapping the real paintings for the fakes was the perfect crime. Until Matthew suddenly decided to sell. Then your crime no longer would be secret. The appraiser had to be silenced first, so you had Pochenko kill her. And then you had Pochenko come here and throw Matthew over that balcony railing."

"Who is this Pochenko? You keep talking about this guy like I'm supposed to know who he is."

Nikki beckoned him to her. "Come here."

Paxton hesitated, eyeing the front door, but he came over to stand near the archway with the detectives.

"Take a look at these paintings. Any one you like, Noah, take a good long look." He leaned closer to one, gave it a cursory examination, then turned to her.

"OK, so?" he said.

"When Gerald Buckley gave you up, he also gave up the address of the storage facility where you instructed him to deliver the stolen paintings. Today, I got a search warrant for it. And guess what I found there." She gestured to the collection hanging there in the glow of the orange light of the setting sun. "The original Starr Collection."

Paxton tried to keep his cool, but his jaw dropped. He twirled to look again at the painting. And then the one beside it.

"That's right, Noah. These are the originals you stole. The forgeries are still in the piano crate in the basement."

Paxton was coming unglued. He stepped from painting to painting, shaken, his breath rasping.

Detective Heat continued, "I must say that storage facility you rented is first-rate. Climate-controlled, state-of-the-art fire technology, and very secure. They have the highest definition surveillance cameras I've seen. Look at one of the freeze-frames I got off it. It's a small picture but quite sharp."

Paxton held out an unsteady hand. Nikki gave him a still-frame print from the storage security camera. He became even more ashen.

"We're still going over their archives. So far, they have video of you bringing one piece of Matthew Starr's art into your storage unit about every eight weeks. This particular shot of you was taken a month ago, carrying a very big painting." She pointed across the room to a large-format canvas. "It's that one over there." Paxton didn't even bother to turn; he just gaped at the photo in his hands. "But that's not my favorite picture. This is my favorite."

She nodded to Ochoa, who yanked the shroud off the frame on the wall beside him, revealing a blow-up of another security still. "Time code says it was taken one-point-six seconds after the picture in your hands. That is one jumbo canvas, Mr. Paxton. Too unwieldy and too valuable for one man to risk carrying it by himself. And look who that is coming around the corner helping you by holding the back end."

Paxton forgot all about the photo in his hands and let it flutter to the floor. He stared in disbelief at the framed surveillance picture on the wall of him carrying the painting, assisted by Vitya Pochenko.

He dropped his head and his body sagged. He fumbled to brace himself on the back of a sofa.

"Noah Paxton, you're under arrest for the mur-

ders of Matthew Starr and Barbara Deerfield."
Nikki turned away from him to Raley and Ochoa.
"Cuff hi—"

"Gun," shouted Roach in tandem. Raley and
Ochoa went for their hips. Nikki already had her
hand on her Sig in its holster. But when she whirled
back to Paxton, he was holding his gun on her.

"He got it from the couch cushion," said Raley.

"Drop it, Paxton," said Heat. She didn't draw
but took a step closer, trying to position herself for
a disarm. He took two steps back, well out of reach.

"Don't," he said. "I'll do it, I will." His hand was
quaking and Nikki worried he'd fire by accident,
so she stayed put. Plus Raley and Ochoa were behind her. If she went for him, she would take the
risk that a wild shot might hit one of them.

Her plan was to buy time by keeping Paxton
talking. "This isn't going to work, Noah. It never
does."

"It's only gonna be ugly," said Ochoa.

"Don't be stupid," added Raley.

"Quiet." Paxton took another backward step
toward the front door.

"I know what you're doing, you're trying to
think of a way out, but there isn't one." Behind
her, Nikki could hear the soft rug steps of her two
detectives slowly spreading out to flank Paxton.
She engaged him to give them time. "You should
know there's a cruiser out front and cops in the
lobby. It's the same detail that's been tailing you
since this morning when Buckley tagged you."

"You two. Stop. I swear if you move, I'll start
shooting."

"Do what he says." Heat turned around to face them and said, "You guys hear me? I mean it." Nikki used her rotation to block Paxton from seeing her unholster her Sig. She let her hand drop to her side and held the gun tight against the back of her thigh when she faced Paxton again.

Meanwhile, he had retreated another step. His free hand rested on the doorknob. "Everybody back up."

They held their positions. Nikki continued trying to talk him down, even as she gripped her weapon behind her. "You're the expert with numbers, right? What do you think your odds are of making the street?"

"Shut up, I'm thinking."

"No, you're not thinking."

His hand started to shake even more. "What's it matter? I'm screwed."

"But you're not dead. Would you rather leave this to your lawyer or your undertaker?"

He pondered a brief moment, moving his lips in some silent inner dialogue. And just when Nikki thought he might have come to his senses, he threw the front door open. She brought her piece up, but Paxton had already lunged behind the door and run out into the hallway.

Everything that happened next happened fast. The door slammed hard as Nikki scrambled for it. Behind her she heard guns clearing holsters, footfalls, and Raley on his walkie-talkie. "Suspect is ten-thirty-two. Suspect is armed, repeat armed, with handgun on sixth floor. Detectives in pursuit."

Heat slammed her back flat to the wall, shoulder even with the door frame, and her Sig Sauer up in an isosceles stance. "Cover," she said. Ochoa performed like clockwork. He went low, crouching on one knee, fisting his Smith & Wesson in his right hand and grabbing the knob with his left. "On yours," he said.

Without pause, Detective Heat calmly said, "Go."

Ochoa pulled the door and held it open for her. Nikki pivoted around the jamb, squaring her aim up the hall. She stopped, still holding her combat stance, shook her head, and mumbled, "Mother . . ."

Ochoa and Raley rolled out behind her and stopped, too. Raley spoke quietly into his radio, "All units, we have a hostage."

Rook was standing halfway up the hall with Paxton snugged behind him holding the gun to his head. He looked at Nikki sheepishly and said, "So, I'm gonna guess it's Noah."

TWENTY

"Stop squirming," said Noah Paxton. Rook started to turn his head to say something to his assailant, but Paxton jammed the muzzle of the gun hard into his skull.

"Ow. Hey."

"I said hold still, damn it."

"Do as he says, Rook." Nikki still had her Sig Sauer up, keeping a bead on the small sliver of Noah Paxton that was showing behind his human shield. She didn't need to turn to know that Raley and Ochoa were doing the same thing with their weapons behind her.

Rook raised his eyebrows contritely and looked at her like a kid who'd broken a living room lamp with a baseball. "I am really sorry about this."

"Rook, be quiet," said Nikki.

"From now on, I'll do what I'm told."

"Start now by shutting up."

"OK." Then he realized he was not shutting up. "Oops, sorry."

"I want you to drop your guns," said Paxton. "All of you."

Heat didn't say no because a direct verbal confrontation could heighten tensions. Instead she maintained her isosceles stance and let that be her answer. She spoke in a calm tone. "You're smart enough to know you're not getting out, Noah, so why don't you let him go and end this peacefully."

"You know, she makes sense," said Rook. Heat and Paxton told him to shut up at the same time.

Paxton's left hand held a handful of the back of Rook's shirt in a bunch to keep him close. He gave it a tug. "Back up." When he didn't move, Noah gave a sharp pull. "I said move. That's right, go with me, easy, easy." He led Rook backward, taking baby steps to the elevator. When he saw that the three detectives were moving forward, matching his pace, he stopped. "Hey, stay back."

Heat and Roach stopped but didn't retreat.

"I'm not afraid to use this," Paxton warned.

"Nobody said you were." She was calm but sounded in command. "But you don't want to."

Paxton moved the gun away slightly to adjust his grip, and Rook slid forward, only to get jerked back. "Don't be stupid." Noah again pushed the muzzle hard against the soft bone behind Rook's ear. "All it takes is one. Do you have any idea what this will do to you?"

Rook nodded as much as he dared. "Scrambled eggs."

"What?"

"Like a hammer hitting a plate of—Never mind, I don't want to talk about it."

Paxton tugged his shirt again and they continued to back toward the elevator. And again the detectives advanced with them. As they all drew closer to the elevator, Nikki looked at the panel above the door. It indicated that the car was waiting there on six.

Heat spoke in a barely audible voice. "Rales."

"Yo."

"Lose that car."

Behind her, Raley keyed his mic and spoke quietly. "Lobby, call elevator down from six immediately."

Paxton heard the elevator softly kick into motion right behind him. "What the hell do you think you're doing?" He turned quickly over his shoulder, in time to see the 6 digit go dark and the 5 light up. He didn't move enough for Nikki to get a clear shot, but while he was distracted, she took two steps closer.

He turned back and saw her. "Stop right there."

Heat stopped. She had closed the gap and he was ten feet away. Not close enough yet, but closer. She couldn't see Paxton's face, just his eye, looking wild peeking out from the gap between the gun barrel and Rook's head. His voice was building to a rage. "Now you boxed me in."

"You're not leaving. I told you that." She worked to keep the calm in her tone to counter his fury.

"I'm going to shoot."

"It's time to put your gun down, Noah."

"His blood will be on you."

Rook made eye contact with her and mouthed, Shoot. Him.

She had no shot and said so with the smallest head shake.

"You screwed up everything, Detective, you know that? I wish Pochenko had finished the job on you."

Nikki's eyes fluttered and a weight sank in her gut.

"You did that?" said Rook.

"Let it go, Rook," said Nikki, struggling to let go of it herself. Behind her she heard F-bombs muttered by Raley and Ochoa.

"You sent that animal to her apartment?" Rook's nostrils flared. "You sent him to her home?" His chest expanded with each breath as his outrage grew more heated. "You son of a . . . bitch." He spun his body away from the pistol, hurling himself. A loud gunshot echoed in the hall as Rook dropped hard to the floor.

Paxton fell to one knee beside him, moaning, with blood streaming from his shoulder onto Rook. His gun was on the rug beside them and Noah grabbed for it.

Nikki lunged and body-tackled him. She slammed Paxton onto his back and pinned him down with her knees on his chest. He had the gun in his hand, but he hadn't had time to raise it. She held her Sig Sauer inches from his face. His eyes flitted to his gun hand, calculating.

"Go ahead," said Detective Heat. "I need a new blouse anyway."

————

At La Chaleur, the sidewalk café outside the Guilford, the after-work crowd was craning to watch the police activity. The sun had just gone down, and in the quieting darkness, the flashing lights from the cruisers and ambulances reflected in their cosmos and eighteen-dollar glasses of Sancerre.

Over between the café and the front steps of the apartment building, the lights strobed on the backs of two plainclothes cops facing Detective Heat.

One of them put away his notebook. They each shook her hand. Nikki leaned back against the warm stone façade of the Guilford and watched the shooting investigation team cross away to their black Crown Victoria.

Rook stepped over and joined her. " 'Go ahead, I need a new blouse anyway'?"

"I think that was cool for short notice." She tried to read him. "What, too girly?"

"Got Noah's attention." He followed her gaze to the incident investigation pair as they drove off for downtown. "Nobody told you to hand in your badge and gun, I hope."

"No, they expect this will clear just fine. They were actually amazed I didn't kill him."

"Didn't you want to?"

She thought a beat and said, "He's alive." The detective let that simple fact provide all the details. "If I need vengeance kicks, I just Netflix Charles Bronson. Or Jodie Foster." She turned to him. "Besides, I was aiming at you. You're the one I wanted to kill."

"And I even signed that liability waiver."

"Lost opportunity, Rook. It's going to haunt me."

Roach stepped out of the building and came over. Ochoa said, "Paramedics are bringing him out now."

Nikki waited until they carried Paxton's gurney down the steps and rolled it up to the curb before she walked over followed by Raley, Ochoa, and Rook. In the harsh utility light shining down from above the ambulance door, Noah's face was the color of an oyster. She checked with the paramedic standing with him. "Is he OK for a quick chat?"

"A minute or two, but that's it," said the EMT.

Heat stood so she loomed over him. "Just want you to know one good thing came out of that little hostage drama up there. Your gun. It's a twenty-five. Same caliber that killed Pochenko. We're running ballistics on it. And giving you a paraffin test for gunpowder residue. What do you think we'll find?"

"I have nothing to say."

"What, no spoilers? Fine, I can wait for the results. Do you want me to call you with them, or would you rather wait to hear them at your arraignment?" Paxton looked away from her. "Tell me, when you raced over here to get your hands on those paintings, were you going to use it on Kimberly Starr, too? Is that why you had the gun with you?"

When he didn't answer, she spoke to her team. "Kimberly owes me."

"Big-time," said Raley.

Ochoa added, "You probably saved her life when you arrested her."

Noah rolled his head back to face her. "You already arrested her?"

Heat nodded. "This afternoon, right after I found the paintings in the basement."

"But that phone call to me. The one you wire-tapped . . ."

"She was already in custody. Kimberly made that call for me."

"Why?"

"Why else? To get you to come to my art show." Nikki gave the sign to the paramedics and stepped away so the last picture the detective saw was the look on Noah Paxton's face.

———

The heat wave broke late that night, and it did not go quietly. As a front from Canada bullied its way down the Hudson, it collided with the hot, stagnant air of New York and spawned an aerial show of lightning, swirling winds, and sideways rain. TV meteorologists patted themselves on the back and pointed to red and tangerine splotches on Doppler radar as the skies opened and the thunder ripped like cannon fire through the stone and glass canyons of Manhattan.

On Hudson in Tribeca, Nikki Heat slowed down to avoid splashing the diners huddled under umbrellas outside Nobu, praying in vain for open cabs to get them uptown in the downpour. She turned onto Rook's street and pulled the police car into an open space in a loading zone up the block from his building.

"You still pissed at me?" he said.

"No more than usual." She put the car in Park. "I just get quiet after I clear a case. It's like I've been turned inside out."

Rook hesitated, something on his mind. "Anyway, thanks for the ride in all this."

"No problem."

Frankenstein lightning hit so close that the strobe flash lit their faces the same time as the thunder crack. Tiny hailstones began to pepper the roof. "If you see the Four Horsemen of the Apocalypse," said Rook, "duck."

She gave up a thin laugh that turned into a yawn. "Sorry."

"Sleepy?"

"No, tired. I'm way too cranked to sleep."

They sat listening to the storm rage. A car crept past with water up to its hubcaps.

At last, he broke the silence. "Look, I've been doing a lot of thinking and I just don't know how to play this. We work together—well, sort of. We slept together—most definitely. We have smoking hot sex one time, but soon afterwards, don't try holding hands, not even in the relative privacy of a taxicab.

"I'm trying to figure the rules. This isn't yin and yang, it's more like yin and yank. The past few days I've been going, OK, she doesn't mix the hot sex and romance so well with the single-mindedness of the police work. So it gets me wondering, Is the solution for me to give up our working relationship? Stop my magazine research so we can—?"

Nikki grabbed him into a deep kiss. Then she pulled away and said, "Will you shut up?" Before he could say yes, she grabbed Rook again, throwing her mouth back onto his. He wrapped his arms around her. She undid her seat belt and drew closer to him. Their faces and clothes became drenched in sweat. Another flash of lightning lit up the car through windows fogged by the heat of their bodies.

Nikki kissed his neck and then his ear. And then she whispered to him, "Do you really want to know what I think?"

He didn't speak, he only nodded.

The low rumble of thunder finally reached them. When it tailed off, Nikki sat up, reached for the keys, and killed the ignition. "Here's what I think. I think after all this, I've got energy to burn. Do you have any limes and salt and anything fun in a bottle?"

"I do."

"Then I think you should invite me up and see what we can get going tonight."

"Bite your tongue."

"Just wait."

They got out of the car and made a dash toward his building. Halfway there, Nikki took his hand and ran alongside him, giggling as they raced together up the sidewalk. They stopped at his front steps, breathless, and kissed each other, two lovers for the night getting soaked in the cooling rain.

ACKNOWLEDGMENTS

When I was an impressionable young latchkey lad, I had the good fortune of stumbling onto a National Geographic special on the accomplishments of Sir Edmund Hillary, the legendary New Zealand climber who was the first to scale Mt. Everest's snowy and mysterious heights. To say the show made an impression on me would be an understatement. For two glorious weeks of my tenth summer, I was fully committed to becoming the world's greatest mountain climber (never mind that at the time I had never seen a mountain in person, let alone left the urban canyons of New York City).

In my drive to surpass Sir Edmund, I enlisted my good friend Rob Bowman, whose older brother played Pop Warner football. I borrowed Rob's brother's cleats and swiped a hammer from the building super, believing I could use its claw-end as my pick-axe. I was halfway up the drywall when my mother arrived home. The treacherous and punishing slopes of Everest had nothing on my mother, and my distinguished climbing career ended well before I reached the summit . . . or the ceiling.

It wasn't until much later in life that I learned about Tenzing Norgay. And though Edmund Hillary is widely known as the first man to conquer Everest, he would never have reached the summit without Mr. Norgay. For those of you unfamiliar with that first historic climb, Tenzing Norgay was Sir Edmund Hillary's Sherpa.

Whenever I come to the acknowledgments section of a book, I often think of Tenzing Norgay, that unsung hero of Hillary's climb.

Like Sir Edmund, I, as this book's author, will receive just about all of the acclaim for whatever achievement lies within these pages. However, along the way I've had a lot of my own personal Tenzing Norgays to counsel me, guide me, lift my spirits, and carry my baggage (both emotional and physical). They have been there to keep me going, to inspire me, and to remind me not to look at the imposing summit, but at my own feet. As I take one step at a time, they have shown me the way.

The point is there are a number of people that I have to thank.

First and foremost on that list are my daughter Alexis, for always keeping me on my toes, and my mother, Martha Rodgers, for always keeping me grounded. In the extended Castle family, very special thanks goes to the lovely Jennifer Allen, my first reader always, and to Terri E. Miller, my partner in crime. May you, dear reader, be lucky enough to know women such as these.

Thanks are grudgingly due to Gina Cowell and the group at Black Pawn publishing, whose threats of legal action first inspired me to put pen to paper. And also to the wonderful folks at Hyperion Books, especially Will Balliett, Gretchen Young, and Elizabeth Sabo.

I'd like to thank my agent, Sloan Harris at ICM,

and remind him that if this book is a smash hit I expect him to improve my contract considerably.

A debt is due to Melissa Harling-Walendy and Liz Dickler in the development of this project, as well as to my dear friends Nathan, Stana, Jon, Seamus, Susan, Molly, Ruben, and Tamala. May our days, no matter how long, continue to be filled with laughter and grace.

And finally, to my two most loyal and devout Sherpas, Tom and Andrew, thank you for the journey. Now that we've reached the top, in your company it feels as though the stars are within my reach.

RC

July 2009

If you enjoyed *Heat Wave*,
be sure to catch *Naked Heat*,
the second book in Richard Castle's
Nikki Heat series.

An excerpt,
Chapters One and Two,
follows.

ONE

Nikki Heat pondered red lights and why they seemed to last so much longer when there was no traffic. The one she waited for at Amsterdam and 83rd was taking forever to change. The detective was rolling on her first call of the morning and probably could have lit up her gumball to make her left turn, but the crime was long since done, the medical examiner was on scene, and the body wasn't going anywhere. She used the interlude to peel back the lid of her coffee to see if it was drinking temp yet. The cheap white plastic cracked, and she ended up holding half the lid with the other half still seated on the cup. Heat cursed aloud and chucked the useless half on the passenger-side floor mat. Just as she was about to take a sip, desperately needing a caffeine jolt to lift her morning fog, a horn honked behind her. The light had finally gone green. Of course.

With an experienced hand tilting the cup so the momentum of her turn wouldn't slop coffee over the rim and onto her fingers, Nikki steered left onto 83rd. She had just straightened the wheel passing Café Lalo when a dog darted out in front of her. Heat slammed the brakes. Coffee sloshed onto her lap. It was all over her skirt, but she was more concerned about the dog.

Thankfully, she didn't hit it. She didn't even scare it. The dog, a small German shepherd or husky mix, boldly stood there in the street right in front of her, not moving, just staring at her over its shoulder. Nikki smiled at it and waved. And still, it just stood there. That stare unnerved her. It was challenging and intrusive. The eyes were sinister, piercing under dark brows and a permanent frown. As she examined it, something else seemed off about the dog. Like it wasn't a dog at all. Too small for a shepherd or husky, and the coloring of its rough coat was tan mottled by grey. And the muzzle was too thin and pointed. It was more foxlike. No.

It was a coyote.

The same impatient driver behind her gave another horn blast and the animal left. Not in a panic run, but a trot, displaying wild elegance, potential speed, and something else. Arrogance. She watched it reach the other curb, where it stopped, gave her a backward glance, complete with brazen eye contact, and then dashed off toward Amsterdam.

For Nikki, an unsettling way to start her morning: first the scare of almost hitting an animal; then the creepy look. She drove on, blotting herself with napkins from the glove box, wishing she had chosen a black skirt this morning and not gone with the khaki.

———

It never got any easier for Nikki to meet a corpse. As she sat behind the steering wheel at 86th and Broadway, parked behind the OCME van, observing the silent movie of a coroner at work, she once again reflected that maybe that was a good thing.

The medical examiner was crouched on the

sidewalk in front of the shared storefront of a lingerie shop and the newest gourmet cupcake bakery. A duo of mixed messages, if there ever was one. She couldn't see the victim he was working. Thanks to a citywide garbage strike, a waist-high mound of refuse started in the gutter and encroached on a good bit of the sidewalk, obscuring the body from Heat's view. She could whiff the two days of trash rot even in the morning chill. At least the mound formed a handy barrier to keep the looky-loos back. There were already a dozen early risers up the block and an equal number behind the yellow tape down at the corner near the subway entrance.

She looked at the digital clock flashing time and temperature on the bank up the street. Only 6:18. More and more of her shifts were starting like this. The downturn in the economy had hit everyone, and in her personal observation, whether it was the city cutbacks in policing or merely the sort of economy that fueled crime—or both—Detective Heat was meeting more corpses these days. She didn't need Diane Sawyer to break out the crime stats for her to know that if the body count wasn't up, the rate was at least quickening its pace.

But no matter what the statistics, the victims meant something to her, one at a time. Nikki Heat had promised herself never to become a volume dealer in homicides. It wasn't in her makeup and it wasn't in her experience.

Her own loss almost ten years ago had shredded her insides, yet in between the scar tissue that formed there after her mother's murder, there still sprung shoots of empathy. Her precinct skipper, Captain Montrose, told her once that was what made her his best detective. All things considered, she'd rather have gotten there without the pain, but someone else dealt those cards, and there she was, early on an otherwise beautiful October morning, to feel the raw nerve again.

Nikki observed her personal ritual, a brief reflection for the victim, forging her own connection to the case in light of her own victimhood and, especially, to honor her mom. It took her all of five seconds. But it made her feel ready.

She got out of the car and went to work.

Detective Heat ducked under the yellow tape in an opening in the trash heap and stopped short, startled to see herself staring up from the cover of a discarded issue of a *First Press* magazine poking out of a garbage bag, between an egg carton and a stained pillow. God, she hated that pose, one foot up on her chair in the precinct bull pen, arms folded, her Sig Sauer holstered on her hip beside her shield. And that awful headline:

CRIME WAVE
MEETS
HEAT WAVE

At least someone had the good sense to trash it, she thought, and moved on to join her two detectives, Raley and Ochoa, inside the perimeter.

The partners, affectionately team-nicknamed "Roach," had already been working the scene and greeted her. "Morning, Detective," they said almost in unison.

"Morning, Detectives."

Raley looked at her and said, "I'd offer you a coffee, but I see you've already worn yours."

"Hilarious. You should host your own morning show," she said. "What do we have here?" Heat made her own visual survey as Ochoa filled her in on the vic. He was a male Hispanic, thirty to thirty-five, dressed in worker's clothes, lying face-up in a pile of garbage bags on the sidewalk. He had ghastly flesh tearing and bite marks on the soft underside of his neck. More on his gut where his T-shirt was ripped away.

Nikki flashed on her coyote and turned to the ME. "What are all these bite marks?"

"Postmortem is my guess," said the medical examiner. "See the wounds on the hands and forearms?" He indicated the victim's open palms draped at his sides. "Those weren't caused by animal bites. Those are defense wounds from an edge weapon. I say knife or box cutter. But if he'd been alive when the dog got to him, he'd have bites on his hands, which he doesn't. And take a look at this." He knelt beside the body, and Heat dropped to a squat beside him as he used a gloved finger to indicate a piercing of the man's shirt.

"Stab wound," Nikki said.

"We'll know for sure after the autopsy, but I bet that's our COD. The dog was probably just a scavenger working the trash." He paused. "Oh, and Detective Heat?"

"Yes?" She studied him, wondering what other information he had for her.

"I enjoyed your article in this month's *First Press* immensely. Kudos."

A knot formed in Nikki's stomach, but she said thanks and rose up, moving quickly away to stand with Raley and Ochoa. "Any ID?"

Ochoa said, "Negative. No wallet, no ID."

"Uniforms are canvassing the block," said Detective Raley.

"Good. Any eyewitnesses?"

Raley said, "Not yet."

Heat tilted her head to scan the high-rise apartments lining both sides of Broadway. Ochoa anticipated her. "We've set up a check of facing residences to see if anybody saw or heard anything."

She dropped her gaze to him and smiled slightly. "Good. Also see if any of these businesses spotted anything. The bakery is a good bet to have staff around in the early-early. And don't forget security cams. That jewelry store across the way might have picked up something, if we're lucky." She side-nodded up the block to the man holding five leashed dogs on a sit command. "Who's he?"

"That's the guy who found the body. Made the 911 call at 5:37."

Nikki looked him over. He was about twenty, had a slim figure, tight jeans, and a theatrical scarf. "Let me guess. AMDW." Working a precinct on the Upper West Side of New York, she and her team had pet codes for some of the types who lived and worked there. AMDW was their acronym for actor-model-dancer-whatever.

"Close, Detective." Ochoa consulted a page from his notebook and continued, "Mr. T. Michael Dove, in the drama program at Juilliard, came upon the body while it was being bitten. He says his dogs made a mass charge and the other dog took off."

"Hey," said Heat, "what do you mean close? He's an actor."

"Yes, but in this case AMDW is actor-model-dog-walker."

Nikki opened her blazer to cover her hand from onlookers while she gave him the finger. "Did you get his statement?" Ochoa held up his notebook and nodded, affirming. "I guess we're covered here, then," she said. And then she thought of her coyote. She looked up the block at the AMDW. "I want to ask him about that dog."

Nikki regretted her decision immediately. Ten paces from the dog walker, he called out, "Oh, my God, it *is* you! You're Nikki Heat!"

Onlookers farther up the sidewalk pressed forward, probably just wondering what the sudden commotion was more than knowing who she was, but Nikki took no chances. She instinctively lowered her gaze to the pavement and turned sideways, adopting the pose she'd seen in the tabloids, of celebrities ambushed by the paparazzi on their way out of restaurants.

She stepped close and tried to clue the AMDW into the decibel level she wanted him to adopt by speaking in a low one herself. "Hi, yes, I'm Detective Heat."

The AMDW not only didn't pick up on the tone, he got more effusive. "Oh. My. God!" And then could it get worse for her? "Can I have a picture with you, Miss Heat?" He held out his cell phone to her two detectives.

"Come on, Ochoa," said Raley, "let's see what's happening with Forensics."

"Is that . . . Roach? It's them, isn't it?" called the witness. "Just like in the article!" Detectives Raley and Ochoa looked at each other, made no attempt to mask their disdain, and kept walking. "Oh well," said T. Michael Dove, "this will have to do, then," and he held his cell cam out at arm's length, leaned his head beside Heat's, and snapped the picture himself.

Like most people raised in the say-cheese generation, Nikki came factory-programmed to smile when her picture was taken. Not this time. Her heart was sinking so fast she was sure the pic came out looking something like a mug shot.

Her fan examined his screen and said, "Why so modest? Lady, you've got the cover of a national magazine. Last month, Robert Downey, Jr., this month, Nikki Heat. You're a celebrity."

"Maybe we can talk about that later, Mr. Dove. I'm really sort of focused on what you might have seen concerning our homicide."

"I can't believe this," he said. "I am an eyewitness for New York City's top homicide detective."

Nikki wondered if a grand jury would indict if she put a cap in him. Dropped him right there. But instead she said, "That's not really so. Now, I'd like to ask—"

"Not the top detective? Not according to that article."

That article.

That damned article.

That damned Jameson Rook for writing it.

It had felt wrong to her from the beginning. Last June, when Rook got his assignment from the magazine, it was to profile an NYPD homicide squad with a high rate of case clearance. The department cooperated because they liked the PR of cop success, especially if it personalized the force. Detective Heat was underwhelmed by the fishbowl aspect when her squad was chosen, but she went along because Captain Montrose told her to.

When Rook began his one-week ride-along, it was supposed to be in a rotation with the entire team. By the end of his first day he had changed his focus, claiming he could tell a better story using the leader of the squad as the eyes to cover the entire picture. Nikki's eyes saw his plan for what it was, a thinly veiled ruse to hang out with her. And sure enough, he started suggesting drinks, dinner, breakfast, offering backstage passes to Steely Dan at the Beacon and black tie cocktails with Tim Burton at MOMA to kick off an exhibition of his sketches. Rook was a name dropper, but he was also actually connected.

He used his relationship with the mayor to stay on ride-along with her weeks beyond his initial commitment. And over time, in spite of herself, Nikki started to feel, well, intrigued by this guy. It wasn't because he was on a first-name basis with everyone from Mick to Bono to Sarkozy. Or that he was cute, or looked good. A great ass is just that, a great ass and no more—although not to be discounted completely. It was . . . the total package.

The Rook of him.

Whether it was Jameson Rook's charm offensive or her passion for him, they ended up sleeping together. And sleeping together again. And again. And again . . . Sex with Rook was always smokin' but did not always represent her best judgment, she reflected in hindsight. However, when they were together, thinking and judgment took a backseat to the fireworks. As he put it the night they made love in his kitchen after dashing to his place through a torrential downpour, "The heat will not be denied." Writer, she thought. And yet, so true.

Things began to unravel for her around the stupid article. Rook hadn't shown her his draft yet when the photographer showed up at the precinct to shoot pictures and the first clue was that they were all of her. She held out for team shots, especially of Raley and Ochoa, her stalwarts; however, the best she could get out of the shooter were a few group photos with her team arranged behind her.

The worst of it for her were the poses. When Captain Montrose said she had to cooperate, Nikki indulged a few candids, but the photographer, an A-lister with a bulldozer approach, started posing her. "This is for the cover," he said, "the candids won't work for that." So she went along.

At least she did until the photographer was directing her to look tougher peering through the bars in the lockup and said, "Come on, show me some of that avenging-my-mother fire I've been reading about."

That night she demanded Rook show her the article. When she finished reading, Nikki asked him to take her out of it. It wasn't just that it made her the star of the squad. Or that it minimized the efforts of her team, turning others into footnotes. Or that it was destined to make her so visible— *Cinderella* was one of her favorite movies, although Nikki thought she'd rather enjoy it as a fairy tale than live it. Her biggest objection was that it was too personal. Especially the part about her mother's murder.

To Nikki, Rook seemed blinded by his own creation. Everything she mentioned, he had an answer for. He told her that every person he profiled freaked before publication. She said maybe he should start listening to them. Argument on. He said he couldn't edit her out of the article because she *was* the article. "And even if I wanted to? It's locked. It's already typeset."

That was the last night she saw him. Three months ago.

She thought if she never saw him again, it would be just fine. But he didn't go quietly. Maybe he thought he could charm his way back to her. Why else would Rook keep calling Nikki even in the face of serial no's and then a stonewall of no replies? But he must have gotten the message, because he'd stopped reaching out. At least until two weeks ago, when the issue hit the newsstands and Rook sent her a sonar ping in the form of a signed copy of the magazine plus a bottle of Silver Patrón and a basket of limes.

Nikki recycled the *First Press* and re-gifted the

booze at a party that night for Detective Levine, who was taking advantage of the early retirement buyout to trailer his boat to Fort Leonard Wood, Missouri, and start drowning worms. While everyone got lit on tequila shooters, Nikki stuck to beer.

It was to be the last night of her anonymity. She had hoped that, as Mr. Warhol predicted, her fame would only last fifteen minutes and be done, but for the past two weeks, everywhere she went, it was the same. Sometimes stares, sometimes comments, always a pain. Not only was the recognition aspect unpleasant for her, but each sighting, each comment, each cell phone picture, became another reminder of Jameson Rook and the busted romance she wanted to put behind her.

Temptation had gotten the better of a giant schnauzer, who started licking milk and sugar from Nikki's hem. She smoothed its forehead and attempted to steer T. Michael Dove back to the mundane. "You walk the dogs around this neighborhood every morning?"

"That's right, six mornings a week."

"And have you ever seen the victim around here before?"

He paused dramatically. She hoped he was just beginning his Juilliard drama work, because his acting was all dinner theater.

"No," he said.

"And in your statement you said he was being attacked by a dog when you arrived. Can you describe the dog?"

"It was freaky, Detective. Like a little shepherd but sort of wild, you know?"

"Like a coyote?" asked Nikki.

"Well, yeah, I guess. But come on. This is New York City last time I looked."

The same thought Nikki had had. "Thanks for your cooperation, Mr. Dove."

"You kidding? Am I ever going to blog about this tonight."

Heat stepped away to take a cell phone call. It was Dispatch reporting an anonymous tip on a home invasion homicide. She made her way to Raley and Ochoa as she talked, and the other two detectives read her body language and started to get ready to roll before she even hung up.

Nikki checked the crime scene. Uniforms had started their canvass, the remaining stores wouldn't open for a couple of hours, and CSU was busy running a sweep. There was nothing more for them to do there at the moment.

"Got another one, fellas." She tore a page off her notebook and handed the address to Raley. "Follow me. Seventy-Eighth, between Columbus and Amsterdam."

Nikki got herself ready to meet a new corpse.

———

The first thing Detective Heat noticed when she pulled off Columbus onto 78th was the quiet. It was just past seven, and the first rays of sun had cleared the turrets of the Museum of Natural History and were beaming golden light that turned the residential block into a placid cityscape begging to be captured in a photo. But the serenity was also odd to her.

Where were the blue-and-whites? Where was the ambulance, the yellow tape, and the knot of gawkers? As an investigator, she had grown accustomed to arriving on scene after the first responders.

Raley and Ochoa reacted, too. She could tell by the way they each cleared their coats from their sidearms as they got out of the Roach Coach and then clocked the surroundings on their walk over to meet her. "This is the right address?" Ochoa said without really asking.

Raley turned a swivel to scope out the homeless guy picking through the uncollected trash for recyclables up at the Amsterdam end of the street. Other than that, West 78th was still. "Kind of like being the first one to a party."

"Like you get invited to parties," came the jab from his partner as they approached the brownstone.

Raley didn't come back at him. The act of stepping onto the curb put an end to the chatter, as if an invisible and unspoken line had been crossed. They single-filed between a gap somebody had forged in the row of trash bags and refuse, and the two men flanked Detective Heat when she paused in front of the next-door brownstone. "The address is the A-unit, so it's that one there," she said in a hushed tone, indicating the garden apartment a half story below street level. Five granite steps led down from the sidewalk to a small brick patio enclosed by a metal railing trimmed by wooden flower boxes. Heavy drapes were drawn behind the ornate wrought iron bars covering the windows. Intricate stone-carved decorative panels were inset into the façade above them. Under the archway created by the stoop stairs leading to the apartment above, the front door stood wide open.

Nikki hand signaled and led the way to the front door. Her detectives followed in cover mode. Raley watched the rear flank, and Ochoa was an extra set of eyes for Heat as she put her hand on her Sig and took the opposite side of the doorway. When she was sure they were in position and set, she called into the apartment, "NYPD, if there's anyone in there, let's hear it."

They waited and listened. Nothing.

Training and working so long together as a team had made this part routine. Raley and Ochoa fixed eye contact on her. They counted her head nods to three, drew weapons, and followed her inside in Weaver stances.

Heat moved quickly through the small foyer and into the hallway, followed by Ochoa. The idea was to move fast and clear each room, covering each other but being careful not to bunch up. Raley lagged slightly to watch their backs.

The first door on their right gave on to a formal dining room. Heat rolled into it with Ochoa in tandem, each sweeping an opposite side of the room. The dining room was all clear, but a mess. Drawers and antique hutches gaped open above tossed silverware and china that had been raked out and smashed on the hardwood floor.

Across the hall they found the living room in the same state of disarray. Upended chairs rested on shredded coffee table books. A snow of pillow feathers coated broken vases and pottery. Canvas flags drooped out of frames where someone had torn or slashed the oil paintings. A pile of ashes from the fireplace blanketed the hearth and the oriental rug in front of it as if a critter had tried to burrow out through there.

Unlike in the front of the apartment, a light was on in the adjoining room toward the back, which from where she stood Heat made out to be a study. Nikki hand-cued Raley to hold his place and spot them as she and Ochoa once again took position on opposite sides of the door frame. On her nod, they rolled into the study.

The dead woman looked to be about fifty and was seated at the desk in an office chair, with her head tilted way back as if frozen in the windup to a huge sneeze. Heat signed a circle in the air with her left hand to tell her partners to keep alert while she navigated her way through the office debris scattered on the floor and went to the desk to check for any pulse or breathing. She released her touch from the corpse's cold flesh, looked up, and gave them a head shake.

A sound from across the hall.

They all spun at once when they heard it. Like a foot crunching broken glass. The door to the room where it came from was closed, but light was shining on the polished linoleum under the crack. Heat worked out the likely floor plan in her head. If that was the kitchen, then the door she'd seen at the back end of the dining room would also lead to it. She pointed at Raley and signed for him to go around to that door and wait for her move. She pointed to her watch and then made a chop on it to indicate half a minute. He checked his wrist, nodded, and went.

Detective Ochoa was already spotted at one side of the door. She took the opposite and held up her watch. On her third nod, they burst in large and loud. "NYPD! Freeze, now!"

The man sitting at the kitchen table saw three guns coming at him from two doors and shrieked as he thrust both hands high in the air.

As the flash of recognition hit her, Nikki Heat called out, "What the hell is this?"

The man slowly lowered one of his hands and pulled the Sennheiser buds out of his ears. He swallowed hard and said, "What?"

"I said, what the hell are you doing here?"

"Waiting for you," said Jameson Rook. He read something he didn't like on their faces and said, "Well, you didn't expect me to wait in there with her, did you?"

TWO

As the detectives holstered up, Rook breathed a sigh. "Man, I think you took ten years off my life there."

Raley came back with, "You're lucky you still have a life. Why didn't you answer us?"

Ochoa piled on. "We called out to see if anyone was here."

Rook simply held up his iPhone. "Remastered Beatles. Had to get my mind off the b-o-d-y." He made a wince face and pointed into the next room. "But I found that 'A Day in the Life' wasn't the most uplifting diversion. You guys crashed in on me at the end, just on that big piano bong. For real." He turned to Nikki and smiled meaningfully. "Let's hear it for timing, huh?"

Heat tried to ignore the undercurrent, which to her ear wasn't very much under anything. Or maybe she was more sensitive to it. As she scanned Roach for reactions and didn't see any, she wondered if things were more raw for her than she'd thought, or if it was just the shock of seeing him there, of all places. Nikki had crossed paths with old lovers before, who didn't? But usually it was in a Starbucks, or a chance glimpse across the aisle at the movies—not at a murder scene. One thing she was sure of. This was an unwelcome distraction from her job, something to be pushed aside. "Roach," she said, all business, "you two clear the rest of the premises."

"Oh, there's nobody here, I checked." Rook raised both his palms up. "But I didn't touch anything, I swear."

"Check anyway" was Nikki's answer to that, and Roach left to sweep the remaining rooms.

When they were alone, he said, "Nice to see you again, Nikki." And then that damn smile again. "Oh, and thanks for not shooting me."

"What are you doing here, Rook?" She tried to remove any hint of the playfulness that she used to hang on his last name. This guy needed a message.

"Like I said, waiting for you. I was the one who called in the body."

"Not what I'm trying to get at. So let me ask the same question another way. Why are you at this crime scene to begin with?"

"I know the victim."

"Who is she?" All the years on the job, Nikki still found it hard to go to the past tense when referring to a victim. At least not at the hour of discovery.

"Cassidy Towne."

Heat couldn't help herself. She half turned to look into the study, but from where she was standing, she couldn't see the victim, only the post-tornado effect of office supplies scattered around the room. "The gossip columnist?"

He nodded, affirming. "The buzz saw herself."

She immediately started calculating how the apparent murder of the *New York Ledger* 's powerful icon, whose "Buzz Rush" column was the ritual first read for most New Yorkers, was going to ratchet up the stakes on this case. As Raley and Ochoa returned and deemed the apartment clear, she said, "Ochoa, better reach out to the MEs. Give them a courtesy heads-up that we have a high-profiler waiting for them. Raley, you call Captain Montrose so he knows we're working Cassidy Towne from the *Ledger* and he doesn't get blind-sided. And see if he can put a hustle on CSU and also get some extra uniforms here, like, now." The detective could already project that the quiet, golden block she had enjoyed a few minutes ago would soon be transformed into a media street fair.

As soon as Roach left the kitchen again, Rook stood and took a step toward Nikki. "Seriously. I've missed you."

If his step closer was meant as body English, she had some nonverbal cues of her own. Detective Heat turned her back to him, got out her reporter's-cut notebook and a pen, and put her face to a new page. But she knew herself well enough to know the chill message she wanted to send was as much to herself as to him. "What time did you discover the body?"

"About six-thirty. Listen, Nikki . . ."

"How close to six-thirty? Do you have a more accurate idea of the time?"

"I got here exactly at six-thirty. Did you get any of my e-mails?"

"Got here, as in 'in the room to discover her,' or got here, as in 'outside'?"

"Outside."

"And how did you get in?"

"The door was open. Just as you found it."

"So you walked right in?"

"No. I knocked. Then called out. I saw the mess up the hall and went in to see if she was all right. I thought maybe a burglar had been here."

"Did you ever think someone else could have been in here?"

"It was quiet. So I went in."

"That was brave."

"I have my moments, you may recall."

Nikki looked as if she was focused on a notation but really she was replaying the night in the hallway of the Guilford last summer when Noah Paxton used Rook as a human shield, and how, even though he had a gun in his back, he still put a body slam on Paxton that gave Heat a clean shot. She looked up and said, "Where was she when you found her?"

"Right where she is now."

"You didn't move her in any way?"

"No."

"Did you touch her?"

"No."

"How did you know she was dead?"

"I . . ." He hesitated and continued. "I knew."

"How did you know she was dead?"

"I . . . I clapped."

Nikki couldn't help herself. The laugh shot out of her with a mind all its own. She was angry at herself for it, but the thing about a laugh like that was you couldn't take it back. You could only work to suppress the next one. "You . . . you clapped?"

"Uh huh. Loud, you know . . . to see. Hey, don't

laugh, maybe she was asleep, or drunk, I didn't know." He waited while Heat composed herself. And then a chuckle of his own fought its way out. "It wasn't like applause. Just . . ."

"A clap." She watched the way the corners of his eyes crinkled when he smiled, and she started to thaw in a way she didn't like, so she threw the switch. "How did you know the victim?" she said to her notepad.

"I've been working with her the past few weeks."

"You're becoming a gossip columnist now?"

"Oh, hell, no. I sold *First Press* on the idea of doing my next piece for them on Cassidy Towne. Not so much the titillating gossip thing but profiling a powerful woman in a historically male-dominated business, our love-hate relationship with secrets, you get the idea. Anyway, I've been shadowing Cassidy for the past few weeks."

"Shadowing. You mean like . . ." She let it fall off. This took Nikki down an all-too-uncomfortable road.

"Like the ride-along you and I had, yes. Exactly. Without the sex." He paused to read her reaction, and Nikki did her best not to let it show. "The editors got such a good response to my piece on you, they wanted to follow up with another like it, maybe turn it into an occasional series on kick-ass women." He studied her again, got nothing, then added, "It was a nice article, Nik, wasn't it?"

She tapped the tip of the ballpoint twice on the pad. "Were you here to do that today? Shadow her?"

"Yeah, she got an early start every day, or maybe

just continued from the night before, I could never tell. Some mornings I'd show up and she'd be at her desk in the same clothes as the day before, like she'd been working there all night. She'd want to stretch her legs so we'd walk up to H&H for some bagels and then next door to Zabar's for the salmon and cream cheese, and then come back here."

"So you did spend a fair amount of time with Cassidy Towne over the last few weeks."

"Yep."

"Then, if I need to ask you for cooperation, you may have some information about who she saw, what she did, and so forth."

"You don't need to ask, and yes, I know tons."

"Can you think of anyone who would want to kill her?

Rook scoffed. "Let's dig around this mess and find a New York phone book. We can start with the letter A."

"Don't be smart."

"Shark's gotta swim." He grinned, then continued. "Come on, she was a mud-slinging gossip columnist, of course she had lots of enemies. It was in the job description."

Nikki could hear footfalls and voices entering the front and put away her notes. "I'll have you give a statement later, but I don't have any more questions for you now."

"Good."

"Except one. You didn't kill her, did you?" Rook laughed, then saw her expression and stopped. "Well?"

He folded his arms across his chest. "I want a lawyer." She turned and left the room and he called after her, "Kidding. Mark me down as a 'no.'"

———————

Rook didn't leave. He told Heat he wanted to stick around in case he could be helpful with anything. She had the push-pull thing going: wanting him away from her in the worst way because he was such an emotional disruption; but then seeing the benefit of his potential insights as they went over the wreckage of Cassidy Towne's apartment. The writer had been to plenty of crime scenes with her during his ride-along last summer, so she knew he was scene-friendly, at least trained enough not to pick up a piece of evidence in his bare hands and say, "What's this?" He was also a first-person witness to the most profound element of his magazine story, the death of his subject. Mixed feelings or not, she wasn't going to begrudge Jameson Rook that professional courtesy.

When they went into Cassidy Towne's office, he returned her unspoken favor in kind, keeping out of her way by standing over near the French doors that led out to the courtyard garden. For Detective Heat it always began by slowing down and study-ing the body. The dead didn't talk, but if you paid attention, sometimes they did tell you things.

In getting a feel for Cassidy Towne, Nikki read the power Rook was talking about. Her suit, a tasteful, navy pinstripe over a French-blue blouse with starched white collar, would work for a talent agency meeting or premiere party. And it was expertly tailored to her, accenting a body that had seen regular gym time. Heat hoped that when she reached fiftysomething that she'd keep it that together. Nikki saw some tasteful David Yurman on Towne's ears and neck, potentially ruling out robbery. There was no wedding ring, so unless that had been stolen, Heat could also rule out marriage. Potentially. Towne's face was slack in death, but angular and attractive, what most would call handsome—not always the highest compliment to a woman, but according to George Orwell, she had had about ten years since forty to earn that face. Not making a judgment, but letting instinct talk to her, Nikki regarded her impression of Cassidy Towne, and the picture that emerged was of someone suited for battle. A hard body whose hardness seemed to run deeper than just muscle tone. A snapshot formed of a woman who was, at that moment, something she probably never was in life. A victim.

Soon CSU was there, dusting the usual touch points for prints, taking photos of the body and the roomscatter. Detective Heat and her team worked in tandem, but more big-picture than close-up. Wearing their blue latex gloves, they walked here and then there and then back again in appraisal of the office, the way golfers read a green before a long putt.

"All right, fellas, I've got my first odd sock." The detective's approach to a crime scene, even one in this much disarray, was to simplify her field of view. She pared everything down to getting inside the logic of the life that was lived in that space and using that empathy to spot inconsistencies, the small thing that didn't fit the pattern. The odd sock.

Raley and Ochoa came across the room to join her. Rook adjusted his position at the perimeter to follow quietly from a distance. "Whatcha got?" asked Ochoa.

"Work space. Busy work space, right? Big newspaper columnist. Pens everywhere, pencils, custom notepads and stationery. Box of Kleenex. Look at this beside her here." She stepped carefully around the body, still cast backward in the office chair. "A typewriter, for God's sake. Magazines and newspapers with clippings snipped out of them, right? All that stuff makes lots of what?"

"Work," said Raley.

"Trash," said Rook, and Heat's two detectives turned slightly his way and then back to Heat, unwilling to acknowledge him as part of this exchange. Like his season pass had expired.

"Correct," she continued, more focused on where she was going than on Rook now. "What's with the wastebasket?"

Raley shrugged. "It's right there. Tipped, but there it is."

"It's empty," said Ochoa.

"Right. And with all the tossing this room took, you'd think, OK, maybe it spilled out." She crouched near it and they went with her. "No clips, snips, Kleenex, or crumpled paper anywhere around it."

"Maybe she emptied it," said Ochoa.

"Maybe she did. But look over there." She side-nodded to the armoire that the columnist had used as a supply closet. It had been rifled, too. And among the contents scattered on the floor was, "A box of waste-can liners. Simplehuman, sized for this can."

"No liner in this can," said Raley. "And no liner on the floor. An odd sock."

"An odd sock, indeed," said Heat. "On the way in, I saw a wooden bin for trash cans in the little patio."

"On it," said Raley. He and Ochoa headed toward the front hall. Lauren Parry from the medical examiner's was making her way in the door as they went out. In the tight space between the tipped furniture, she and Ochoa ended up doing an impromptu dance step getting around each other. In her quick glance over, Nikki caught Ochoa lingering to check Lauren out as he left. She made a mental note to warn her girlfriend later about rebounding men.

Detective Ochoa was still fresh from a marital separation. He had hidden the breakup from the squad for about a month, but those kinds of secrets don't keep in such a tight working family. The laundry sitch alone gave him away when he started showing up in dress shirts with telltale "Boxed for Your Convenience" creases on their torsos. Over an after-work beer the week before, Nikki and Ochoa were the stragglers at the table, so she took the opportunity to ask him how it was going. A gloom settled over him and he said, "You know. It's a process." She was happy to leave it at that, but he finished his Dos Equis and half smiled. "You know, it's kind of like those car ads. What happened to the relationship, I mean. I saw one on TV in my new apartment the other night and it said, 'Zero interest for two years.' And I went, yep, that was us, all right." Then a sheepishness came over him about opening up like that. He left some money under his empty glass and called it a night. He didn't bring it up again, and neither did she.

"Sorry not to be here sooner, Nikki," Lauren Parry said as she set her plastic examination cases on the floor. "I've been working a double fatal on the FDR since four a . . ." The ME's voice trailed off when she spotted Rook leaning a shoulder against the connecting door leading to the kitchen. He pulled one of his hands out of his pocket and gave her a wave. She nodded and smiled at him, then turned to Heat and finished her sentence. ". . . four A.M." With her back to Rook, she was able to sneak a what-the-hell? face to Nikki.

Nikki lowered her voice and muttered to her friend, "Tell you later." Then, at full volume, she moved on. "Rook found the victim."

"I see . . ."

While her BFF from the ME's office set up to perform her exam, Heat filled her in on the discovery details the writer had provided in their kitchen interview. "Also, when you get a moment, I noticed a blood smear over there." ME Parry followed Heat's gesture to the same doorway she had just entered. Beside the jamb, the floral Victorian wallpaper showed a dark discoloration. "Looks like she might have tried to get out before she collapsed in the chair."

"Could be. I'll swab it. Maybe Forensics can cut a patch so we can lab it; that would be better."

Ochoa returned to report that both trash barrels in the patio hutch were empty. "During a garbage strike?" said Nikki. "Find the super. See if he disposed of it. Or if she had private pickup, which I doubt. But check anyway, and if she had it, find the truck before they barge it to Rhode Island or wherever it goes these days."

"Oh, and get ready for your close-up," said Ochoa at the door. "The news vans and shooters are lining up in front. Raley's working with the uniforms to move them back. Word is out on the scanners. Ding-dong the witch is dead."

Lauren Parry rose up from Cassidy Towne's body and made a note on her chart. "Body temp indicates a prelim TOD window of midnight to 3 A.M. I can do better after I run the lividity and the rest of the course."

"Thanks," said Nikki. "And cause?"

"Well, as always, it's preliminary, but, I think, obvious." She gently moved the office chair so that the body leaned forward, revealing the wound. "Your gossip columnist was stabbed in the back."

"No symbolism there," said Rook.

———

When Cassidy Towne's assistant, Cecily, reported for work at eight she broke down in sobs. Forensics gave Nikki Heat the OK, and she righted two of the chairs in the living room and sat with her, resting a palm on the young woman's back as Cecily leaned forward with her face in her hands. CSU had closed off the kitchen, so Rook gave her the bottle of water he had in his messenger bag.

"Hope you don't mind room temperature," he said, and then shot an oops look at Heat. But if Cecily made the connection to her boss's state in the next room, she didn't let on.

"Cecily," Nikki said, when she finished a sip of water, "I know this must be very traumatic for you."

"You have no idea." The assistant's lips began to tremble, but she kept it together. "Do you realize this means I have to find a new job?"

Nikki's gaze slowly rose to Rook, who stood facing her. She knew him well enough to know he wanted his water back. "How long had you been with Ms. Towne?"

"Four years. Since I graduated Mizzou."

"University of Missouri has an intern program with the *Ledger*," Rook injected. "Cecily transitioned from it to Cassidy's column."

"That must have been quite an opportunity," said Nikki.

"I guess. Am I going to have to, like, clean all this up?"

"I think our crime scene unit is going to be busy here for most of the day. My guess is the paper will probably let you take some time off while we do our thing." That seemed to mollify her for the moment, so Nikki pressed on. "I need to ask you to think about something, Cecily. It may be difficult at this moment, but it's important."

"'K . . ."

"Can you think of anyone who wanted to kill Cassidy Towne?"

"You're kidding, right?" Cecily looked up at Rook. "She's kidding, right?"

"No, Detective Heat doesn't kid. Trust me."

Nikki leaned closer in her chair to draw Cecily's attention back. "Look, I know she was a lightning rod and all that. But over the past days or few weeks, were there any unusual incidents or threats she got?"

"Oh, every day, like literally. She didn't even see them. When I sort her mail at the *Ledger*, I just leave them there in a big sack. Some of them are pretty random."

"If we gave you a ride there, could we see them?"

"Uh, sure. You'd probably have to get the managing editor to sign off, but fine with me."

"Thanks, I'll do that."

"She got calls," said Rook, "her *Ledger* extension forwarded to here."

"Oh, right, right." Cecily looked around at the mess. "If you can find it, her answering machine has some nasty shit on it. She screened." Nikki made a note to locate it and have the messages gone through for leads.

"I know something else that's missing," said Rook. "No filing cabinets. She had big filing cabinets in the corner near the door."

The idea of a filing cabinet hadn't occurred to Nikki. Not yet, anyway. Score one for Rook.

"There should be two in there," affirmed the assistant. She leaned forward in her chair to venture a look into the study but decided against it.

Heat made a note about the AWOL filing cabinets. "Other things that might be helpful would be her appointments. I assume you have access to her Outlook calendar." Cecily and Rook shared a look of amusement. "Am I missing something?"

Rook said, "Cassidy Towne was a Luddite. Everything was on paper. Didn't use a computer. Didn't trust them. She said she liked their convenience, but it was too easy for someone to steal your material. E-mail forwards, hackers, what not."

"But I do have her planner." The assistant opened her backpack and handed Nikki the spiral-bound datebook. "I have old ones, too. Cassidy had me hang on to them for documenting business meals and for tax prep."

Nikki looked up from a recent page. "There are two sets of handwriting in here."

"Right," said the assistant. "Mine's the one you can read."

"No kidding," said Nikki as she turned pages. "I can't make out her handwriting at all."

"Nobody could," she said. "Just part of the joy of working for Cassidy Towne."

"She was tough?"

"She was impossible. Four years of J-school to be the next Ann Curry, and where do I end up? Nanny to that thankless bitch."

Nikki was going to ask later, but with that opening, it seemed the perfect time. "Cecily, this is a routine question I ask everyone. Can you tell me where you were overnight, say between eleven P.M. and three A.M.?"

"In my apartment with my BlackBerry turned off so my boyfriend and I could get some sleep and without getting called by Her Highness."

On the short drive back to the precinct Nikki left voice mail for Don, her combat trainer, to rain check her busted morning jujitsu workout with him. The ex–Navy SEAL was probably in the showers by that time, no doubt having found another sparring partner. Don was a no strings, no worries guy. Same for their sex, when they had it. They both had no trouble finding other sparring partners there, either, and the no-strings relationship made for a mutually workable life design. If workable was your deal.

She had taken a hiatus from sleeping with Don during the time she was with Rook. Not a decision she made, it just worked out that way. Don never seemed bothered, nor did he ask about it when they resumed their occasional night sessions when summer ended and Jameson Rook was out of her life.

Now there he was again, Jameson Rook in her rearview mirror. Her ex-lover, riding shotgun with Raley, the two of them sitting wordlessly at the stoplight in the car behind her, looking out opposite windows of the unmarked like an old married couple with nothing more to say. Rook had asked to pool with Nikki back to the Twentieth, but when Ochoa said he wanted to accompany Cassidy Towne's body down to the OCME, Heat told Raley to play chauffeur for the writer. Nobody seemed thrilled with the arrangements but Nikki.

Her thoughts drifted to Ochoa. And Lauren. He fooled no one with his duty sense to stay close to the high-profile victim, calling it due diligence to see the delivery through from crime scene to morgue. Maybe she should butt out and leave Lauren to find her own way. When Ochoa had approached to suggest his plan, Nikki saw the masked smile on her friend's face as Lauren eavesdropped. As Nikki turned onto 82nd and double-parked in front of the precinct, she thought, hey, they were adults and she wasn't the den mother. Let them have whatever happiness there was to be found in this work. If a man is willing to ride with a corpse just to be with you, that's more effort than you get from most.

———

The coroner's van took a nasty pothole on Second Avenue, and in the back, ME Parry and Detective Ochoa took some air and came down hard on the seats flanking Cassidy Towne's body bag. "Sorry," came the driver's voice from up front. "Blame last winter's blizzards. And the deficit."

"You OK?" Ochoa asked the ME.

"Fine, I'm used to it, believe me," she said. "Are you sure this doesn't weird you out?"

"This? Nah, fine. No sweat."

"You were telling me about your soccer league."

"I'm not boring you?"

"Please," Lauren said. And after the slightest hitch, she continued, "I'd like to come see you play sometime."

Ochoa beamed. "For real? Nah, you're just being polite to me because I'm a live person in your day."

"True . . ." And they both laughed. His eyes fell away from hers for a second or two, and when he looked up she was smiling at him.

He gathered his courage and said, "Listen, Lauren, I'm playing goalie this Saturday, and if you're—"

The tires squealed, glass shattered, and metal crunched. The van crashed so hard to a sudden stop that its rear tires lifted and slammed down, tossing Ochoa and Lauren. The back of her head smacked the side wall of the cargo bay as the van came to rest.

"What the hell . . . ?" she said.

"You all right?" Ochoa unbuckled his belt to cross to her, but before he could get out of it, the rear doors flew open and three men in ski masks and gloves were filling it, holding guns on them. Two were Glocks, the third guy had a nasty-looking assault rifle.

"Hands!" shouted the one with the AR-15. Ochoa hesitated, and the shooter put a round in the rear tire underneath him. Lauren screamed, and even with all his range experience, the muzzle blast made Ochoa jump. "Hands, now!" Ochoa raised his high. Lauren's were already up. The other two masks belted their Glocks and went to work unlatching the hardware securing the gurney holding Cassidy Towne's body to the floor of the van. They made quick work of it, and as the rifleman adjusted his position to keep his aim on Ochoa, his crew rolled the gurney out of the cargo bay and wheeled it somewhere to the side of the vehicle where Ochoa had no view.

Behind them southbound traffic on Second was bunching up. The lane immediately behind the shooter was at a stop; the other lanes were crawling around the blockage. Ochoa tried to memorize all the details for later, if there was going to be a later. Not much to go on. He saw one passing driver on his cell phone and was hoping it was a call to Emergency when the crew returned to slam the cargo doors.

"Come out, and you're dead," called the AR-15 through the metal.

"Stay in here," said Lauren, but the detective had his weapon in his hand.

"Don't move," he told her and kicked the door open. He jumped out on the opposite side of where they had taken the gurney and did a cover roll behind the rear wheel. Underneath the van he could see broken glass, fluid streaming from the engine, and the wheels of the dump truck they had T-boned.

Tires burned rubber, and Ochoa booked it around the van in shooting position, but the big SUV—black, no plates—sped off. Its driver cut a sharp, evasive turn to put the dump truck between himself and Ochoa. In the seconds it took the detective to run up to the truck and brace, the SUV had turned off onto 38th Street for the FDR, the East River, or who knew where?

Behind Ochoa a driver called out, "Hey, buddy, can you move this?"

The detective turned. Sitting out there in the traffic lane was Cassidy Towne's gurney. It was empty.

––––––––––

Detective Heat returned to the bull pen from dropping off Cassidy Towne's phone message cassettes and datebook for analysis by Forensics. Raley strode to her as soon as she walked in. "Got an update on Coyote Man."

"Do you have to do that?" Heat objected to giving victims nicknames. She understood the economy of it, the shorthand it created for a busy squad to quickly communicate, sort of like naming a Word file something that everyone could easily reference. But there was also a dark humor component to it she didn't like. Heat also understood that—the coping mechanism on a grim job was to depersonalize it by making light of the dark. But Nikki was a product of her own experience. Recalling her mother's murder, she didn't want to think the homicide crew on that case had had slang for her mom, and the best way to respect that was not to do it herself. . . . And to discourage it in her squad, which she had always done, albeit with spotty success.

"Sorry, sorry," said Raley. "Re-set. I have some information on our deceased male Hispanic from this morning. The gentleman who you speculated may have been attacked by the coyote?"

"Better."

"Thank you. Traffic found an illegally parked produce truck a block from the body. Registered to . . ." Raley consulted his notes, "Esteban Padilla of East One Hundred and Fifteenth."

"Spanish Harlem. You sure it's his truck?"

Raley nodded. "Positive match to the vic in a family photo taped to his dashboard." Just the sort of detail that always made Nikki's stomach take an elevator plunge. "I'll do a follow-up."

"Good, keep me up on it." She gave him a nod and started to her desk.

"So you really think that was a coyote, huh?"

"Looked it to me," she said. "They do get into the city every now and again. But I have to go with the ME on this one. If it was a coyote, it came after the fact. I can't think of any coyote that would steal a man's wallet."

"Wile E. Coyote would have." Rook. Smart-assing from the old desk he used to sit at. "Of course, he would have gotten some ACME dynamite first and blown his nose and hair off. And then stood there blinking." He demonstrated. "I watched a lot of cartoons as a youngster. Part of my unsupervised upbringing."

Raley looped back to his desk and Heat stepped over to Rook. "I thought you were going to write a statement and go."

"I wrote it," he said. "Then I tried to make an espresso out of this machine I gave you guys and it's NG."

"We, um, haven't made a lot of espresso drinks since you left."

"Clearly." Rook stood and dragged the machine from the back of the desk toward him. "God, these things are always heavier than they look. See? It's not plugged in, the water reservoir is down . . . Let me set it up for you."

"We're good."

"OK, fine, but if you decide to use it, don't just put water in. It's a pump, Nikki. And like any pump it has to be primed."

"Fine."

"Do you want some help with that? There's a right way and a wrong way."

"I know how to—" She ended that thread of conversation right there. "Listen, let's forget all about . . ."

"Steamy deliciousness?"

". . . coffee, and look at your statement. Deal?"

"Done." He handed her a single sheet of paper and sat on the edge of the desk, waiting.

She looked up from the page. "This is it?"

"I tried to be concise."

"This is one paragraph."

"You're a busy woman, Nikki Heat."

"All right, look." She paused to collect her thoughts before she continued. "I was left with the distinct impression that your weeks—weeks—in the company of our murdered gossip columnist would mean you had more knowledge than this." She dangled the page at its corner between her thumb and forefinger so that it sold flimsy. The air-conditioning kicked on and it even waved in the breeze, a nice touch.

"I do have more knowledge."

"But?"

"I'm bound by my journalistic ethics not to compromise my sources."

"Rook, your source is dead."

"And that would release me," he said.

"Then pony up."

"But there are others I talked to who might not want to be compromised. Or things I saw, or confidences I was given access to that I wouldn't want to write down and have taken out of context at someone's expense."

"Maybe some time to think about this is what you need."

"Hey, you could put me in the Zoo Lockup." He chuckled. "That was one of the great take-aways from my ride-along, seeing you break down the newbies in Interrogation with that hollow threat. Beautiful. And effective."

She assessed him a beat and said, "You're right. I'm a busy woman." She took a half step and he blocked her.

"Wait, I have a solution to this little dilemma." He paused long enough to let her complete a rather unsubtle watch check. "What would you say if I told you we could work this case together?"

"You don't want to hear what I'd say, Rook."

"Hear me out. I want to see through this critical new angle of my Cassidy Towne piece. And if we were a team, I could share my leads and insights about the victim with you. I want access, you want sources, it's win-win. No, it's better than win-win. It's me-you. Just like old times."

In spite of herself, Nikki felt a tug on a level she didn't control. But then she thought, maybe she couldn't control the feeling, but she could control herself. "Do you have any idea how transparent you are? All you want to do is dangle your sources and insight so you can spend time with me again. Nice try," she said and moved off to her desk.

Rook followed her. "I was kind of hoping you'd like this idea, for two reasons. First, beyond—yes— the pleasure of your company, it would give us a chance to clear the air about whatever happened between us."

"That's only one reason. What's the other?"

"Captain Montrose already approved it."

"No . . ."

"He's a great guy. Smart, too. And the pair of Knicks tickets didn't hurt." Rook extended his hand to shake. "Looks like it's you and me, partner."

While Nikki stared at his hand, her phone rang and she turned away to answer. "Hey, Ochoa." Then her face lost color and her exclamation of "What?!" made heads turned in the bull pen. "Are you all right?" She listened, nodding, and said, "All right. Get back here as soon as you can after you make your statement."

When she hung up, she had an audience of the bull pen around her desk. "That was Ochoa. Somebody stole Cassidy Towne's body."

A stunned silence followed, which was broken by Rook. "Looks like we're teaming up just at the right time."

Heat's look didn't match his enthusiasm.

And be sure to look for *Heat Rises,*
Richard Castle's latest Nikki Heat thriller,
coming soon from Hyperion.

An excerpt, Chapter One, follows.

ONE

The thing about New York City is you never know what's behind a door. Homicide Detective Nikki Heat pondered that like she had so many times as she parked her Crown Victoria and watched police cruiser and ambulance lights lick the storefronts on Seventy-fourth off Amsterdam. She knew, for instance, the plain door to the wine shop opened into a faux cave done in soft beige and terra cotta tones with stacked bottles nested in wall grottos fashioned of riverstones imported from France. Across the street, the door of what had once been an FDR-era bank gave onto a staircase that spiraled downward to a huge array of indoor batting cages that filled with tween MLB hopefuls and kid birthday parties on weekend afternoons. But on that morning, just after four a.m., the most nondescript door of all, the frosted one without a sign, only a street number above it in gold and black foil stick-ons from a hardware store, would lead to one of the more unexpected interiors of the quiet block.

A uniform posted in front of the door shuffled to keep warm. Silhouetted by the industrial grade Crime Scene Unit work light from inside that transformed the milky glass into the blinding Close Encounters portico, Nikki could see his breath from forty yards away.

She got out and even though the air bit her

nostrils and made her eyes teary, Nikki didn't button her coat against it. Instead she fanned it open with the back of her hand by rote, making sure that she had clean access to the Sig Sauer holstered underneath. And then, cold as she was, the homicide cop stopped and stood there to perform her next ritual: A pause to honor the dead she was about to meet. That small, quiet, private moment lived as a ceremonial interval Nikki Heat claimed when she arrived at every crime scene. Its purpose was simple. To reaffirm that, victim or villain, the waiting corpse was human and deserved to be respected and treated individually, not as the next stat. Nikki drew in a slow breath and the air felt to her the same as that night a decade ago, a Thanksgiving eve, when she was home on college break and her mother was brutally stabbed to death and left on the kitchen floor. She closed her eyes for her Moment.

"Something wrong, detective?" Moment gone. Heat turned. A taxi rolled to a stop and its passenger was addressing her from his backseat window. She recognized him and the driver and smiled.

"No, Randy, I'm good." Heat stepped over to the cab and shook hands with Detective Randall Feller. "You keeping out of trouble?"

"Hope not," he said with the laugh that always reminded her of John Candy. "You remember Dutch," he said making a head nod to Detective Van Meter up front in the driver's seat. Feller and Van Meter worked undercover in the NYPD Taxi Squad, a special anti-crime task force run out of the Special Operations Division that roved New York's streets in customized yellow cabs. The plainclothes cops of the Taxi Squad had a foot in the old school. They were generally tough asses who took no crap and did what they wanted and went where they wanted. Taxi Dicks roamed freely to sniff out crimes in progress, although with more scientific policing, were lately assigned to target their patrols in areas where robberies, burglaries, and street crimes spike.

The cop at the wheel rolled his window down and nodded a wordless hi, making her wonder why Van Meter had bothered to open it. "Careful, Dutch, you'll talk her ear off," said Detective Feller with the Candy chuckle again. "Lucky you, Nikki Heat, getting the middle of the night call."

Dutch said, "Some folks have no manners getting killed at this hour." Heat didn't imagine Detective Van Meter paused a lot for reflection before meeting a corpse.

"Listen," she said. "Not that I don't like standing in twenty-five degrees, but I've got a vic waiting."

"Where's your ride-along?" said Feller with more than a little interest. "The writer, what's his face?"

Feller, fishing again. Just like he did every time they crossed paths, testing to see if Rook was still in the picture. Nikki had been on Feller's radar since the night months before when she escaped from a hired killer in Rook's loft. After Heat's battle with the Texan, he and Dutch were in the first wave of cops who raced to her aid. Ever since, Feller never missed a chance to pretend he didn't know Rook's name and take a sounding on her. Heat rolled with it, she was no stranger to interest from men, even liked it if they didn't cross a line, but Feller . . . In the Rom-Com he'd be more Com than Rom; the joshing brother rather than the love interest. Detective Feller was funny and good company but more for beers in the cop bar than Sancerre by candlelight. Two weeks ago she saw him come out of the men's room at Plug Uglies wearing a sanitary tissue ring around his neck, asking everyone if they'd also like a lobster bib.

"What's his face?" repeated Nikki. "He's off on assignment." And then to send the message, she added, "He's back at the end of this week, though." But the detective read something else in her voice.

"That a good thing or a bad thing?"

"Good thing," Heat said a little too abruptly. So she flashed a grin trying to reset her tone. "Real good." And then, to convince herself, added, "Really good."

————

What Nikki found on the other side of the door was not an urban shrine to oenology with artfully stacked green bottles, nor did she hear the ping of an aluminum bat followed by the thud of a ball into padded netting. Instead, a throat-catching mixture of incense mixed with vapors from a harsh cleaning solvent rose up to greet her as she descended a flight of stairs to the basement. Behind her, Detective Van Meter moaned a low, "Whoa," and as Heat rounded the landing to make her turn down the last flight, she heard Dutch and Feller snapping on gloves. Van Meter muttered to his partner, "I catch an STD down here, I'll sue till I own the damn city."

At basement level they arrived at something that

only charitably could be referred to as a reception
area. The crimson painted brick walls behind the
Formica counter and the Internet catalogue chairs
reminded her of a small, private gym lobby, and not
a very high-end one. Four doors were spaced along
the far wall. They were all open. Three led into dim
rooms, lit only by the spill of harsh radiance from
the CSU light stands set up to illuminate the lobby
during the investigation. More light, punctuated by
strobe flashes came from the far doorway, where
Detective Raley stood watching the activity, latexed
hands by his side. He saw Nikki out of the corner
of his eye and stepped out to her.

"Welcome to Pleasure Bound, Detective Heat,"
he said.

Copsense made Nikki scope out the other three
rooms before entering the crime scene itself. She
knew they'd have been cleared by Raley and the uniforms who responded first, but she poked her head
in each doorway for a quick glance. All she could
make out in the murkiness were the shapes of
equipment and furniture of the bondage trade and
that each chamber was themed. In order: a Victorian boudoir; an animal role-play parlor; and a
sensory deprivation room. In the coming hours
these would be swept by CSU and forensic evidence gathered, but for now she was satisfied with
her survey. Heat took out her gloves and walked to
the far doorway where Feller and Van Meter waited
deferentially behind Raley. This was her case on
her turf and unspoken etiquette dictated she go in
ahead of them.

The corpse was naked and bound at the wrists

and ankles to an X-shaped vertical wooden frame known as the St. Andrew's Cross. The structure was bolted to the floor and the ceiling in the center of the room and the dead man's body sagged downward, bent at the knees, his buttocks hovering above the linoleum. The bulk of his weight, which Heat put at almost two hundred fifty pounds now unsupported by muscle, strained the wrist straps high over his head and pulled his arms into a taut Y.

Detective Feller whisper-sang the chorus of "YMCA" until Nikki scalded him with a glance. Chastened, he folded his arms and looked away at his partner, who shrugged.

"What have we got, Rales?" said Heat to her detective.

Raley consulted a single page of notes. "Not much, as of yet. Check it out." He swept the room with his arm. "No clothes anywhere, no ID, no nothing. After-hours cleaning crew made the discovery. They're not English speakers so Ochoa's doing the honors in the office getting their statement. Prelim, though, is they say the place closes about one, sometimes two, that's when they come in. They were doing their usual janitor stuff, figuring they were all alone, and came in here, to the, ah . . ."

"Torture chamber," said Nikki. "The rooms are themed. This one's for torture and humiliation." She read his look and said, "I worked vice once."

"So did I," said Raley.

"I worked it harder." Heat arched a brow and watched him blush. "So nobody else was here at the discovery. Did they see anyone leaving?"

"Negative."

"There's a bubble for a surveillance cam in the lobby," said Van Meter.

Raley nodded. "On it." And then he turned to Nikki. "There's a locked closet in the manager's office where the cleaners say she keeps the recorder."

"Wake up the manager," said Heat. "Tell her to bring in the key but don't tell her about the body. Just say there was an attempted break-in. I don't want her making calls on the way here and I want to see her reaction when she finds out."

When Raley stepped out to make the call, Heat asked the CSU technician and the police photographer if they had looked for any clothing or a wallet or ID anywhere else on the premises. She knew what the answer would be—these were professionals—but the base had to be covered. The obvious, if thought to be too obvious, is what got overlooked and left holes in an investigation if you start assuming and stop checking. They confirmed no clothing, ID, or other personal effects on their initial sweep.

Detective Feller said, "How about Dutch and I cruise the neighboring blocks, see if anyone who's up saw anything?"

Van Meter nodded. "At this hour not many people around but we can hit the diners, garbage collectors, delivery trucks, whatever."

"Sure," said Detective Heat. "Appreciate the assist."

Feller gave her the puppy eyes again. "For you, Nikki? C'mon." He took out his cellphone and knelt to get an angle of the dead man's face with its camera. "Won't hurt to show this around to see if anyone knows him."

"Good thinking," she said.

On his way out Detective Feller paused. "Listen, sorry if I was out of line with the Village People thing. Just breaking the tension, you know?"

As much as she couldn't abide disrespecting a victim, she looked at him and read his embarrassment. As a veteran NYPD detective, she knew it was just misplaced cop humor and not meant to be callous. "I don't even remember it," said Heat. He smiled, gave her a head nod, and left.

———

Lauren Parry knelt on the floor beside the victim and, as she filled in each box in her report, the medical examiner recited to Nikki, "OK, so we have a John Doe, late-forties, approximately two-fifty to two-fifty-five." The ME pointed to her nostrils. "Obvious smoker, definite drinker."

It was always tough with the Does, thought Nikki. Without a name to go on you were hobbled at the starting gate. Precious time in the investigation would be spent just figuring out who he was.

"Preliminary T.O.D. . . ." Lauren Parry read the thermometer and continued, ". . . Eight to ten p.m."

"That long ago? You sure?" Heat's friend looked up from the clipboard at her and stared. The detective said, "OK, so you're sure."

"Preliminarily, Nik. I'll run the usual tests when we get him down to Thirtieth Street, but for now that's a good window for you."

"Cause of death?"

"Well, you just want every little thing, don't you?" said the ME with a twinkle behind her dead-pan. Then she grew pensive and turned to consider the corpse. "C.O.D. could be asphyxiation."

"The collar?"

"That's my best first guess." Lauren stood and indicated the posture collar biting into the man's neck, drawn so tight by the strapping at the back it caused his flesh to roll over its edges. "Certainly enough to restrict the windpipe. Plus the broken blood vessels in the eyeballs are consistent with choking."

"Let's rewind. 'Best first guess?'" asked Heat.

"Come on, Nikki, you know I always tell you first shot is preliminary." Then Lauren Parry looked back at the body, pondering again.

"What?"

"Let's just mark it 'choking' as a prelim until I do my autopsy."

Nikki knew better than to press Lauren for conjecture, just as her friend knew not to push her for speculation. "That's fine," she said, all the while knowing that her pal from the Office of the Chief Medical Examiner was mulling something.

Lauren opened a plastic drawer in her kit for some swabs and resumed her testing while Nikki did what she always did at a death scene. She clasped her hands behind her and slowly walked the room, occasionally squatting or bending, eyeing the corpse from all angles. This wasn't just a ritual, it was a fundamental procedure to clear her head of all conclusions and projections. The idea was to open her mind to impressions, to just let in whatever came in and, most of all, simply to notice what she was noticing.

Her sense of the victim was that he wasn't a physically active person. The sizable roll of soft fat around his midsection suggested a lot of sitting, or at least an occupation that didn't involve movement or strength like sports, construction, or other manual labor. Like most people, the skin on his upper arms was pale compared to his forearms but the contrast wasn't great; no farmer's tan. That told her he not only was indoors a lot but that he either wore long sleeves most of the time or didn't likely tend a garden or play golf at a club. Even this long after summer there would be more residual tanning. She stepped close to examine his hands, being careful not to breathe on them. They were clean and soft, underscoring her feeling about his indoor life. The nails were neat but not manicured; she usually saw that among middle-aged men who were wealthy or young urban groomers who were more fit. The hair was sparse up top, befitting the age Lauren had fixed, as were the strands of white mixed in with its dull, iron filings color. The brows were wildly bushy, sometimes an indicator of a bachelor or widower, and his salt and pepper goatee gave him an air of academia or arts and letters. Nikki looked again at his fingertips and made note of a bluish tinge that looked to be within the skin itself and not topical, like from oil paint or ink stains.

Bruises, welts, and abrasions were everywhere, front, back, and sides. Torso, legs, and arms. In keeping with her open mind approach, the detective tried not to ascribe the marks to a night of sadomasochism. Possible, even likely, given the setting but not a for certain. There were no obvious cuts, punctures, bullet holes, or bleeding she could see.

The rest of the room was immaculate, at least for a torture dungeon. The CSU vacuuming and print dusting might yield some forensic evidence but there was no visible trash, cigarette butts, or any clues such as a conveniently dropped hotel matchbook with a killer's room number on it like you saw in old movies on TCM.

Again, keeping an open mind, Nikki refused to conclude there even was a killer in the classic sense. A homicide? Possibly. Murder? Still just possibly. The door had to be left open for an accidental death from a consensual torture session gone too far resulting in a panic flight from the Dom in the relationship.

Heat was sketching her own diagram of the room layout, something she always did as a personal companion to the one filed by the Crime Scene Unit, when Detective Ochoa came in after his interview of the cleaning crew. He had a sober tone as he quickly greeted Nikki but softened when his gaze fell on the ME.

"Detective," said Lauren with a little too much formality.

"Doctor," he replied, matching her reserve. Then Nikki caught Lauren taking something out of the side pocket of her suit and slipping it into his hand. Detective Ochoa didn't look at it, just said, "Right, thanks," and stepped across the room, where he turned his back and fastened his watch to his wrist. Nikki could do the math on where The Oach was when he was awakened by the dead body call.

Seeing these two go through this charade of non-intimacy gave her a twinge. She lifted her pen above her diagram and paused, reminded of how not long ago she and Rook had similarly conspired to low key their affair—also fooling no one. That was back in the summer heat wave when he was a ride-along journalist researching Nikki's homicide squad, and ultimately Nikki, for the feature story he was writing for *First Press*. Having her picture on the cover of a respected national magazine was a mixed blessing for the publicity-shy Heat. Bundled with the annoyance and unhappy complications of her fifteen minutes came some unexpectedly hot times with Jameson Rook. And now, some form of a relationship. Well, she thought—something she had been doing a lot of lately—not so much a relationship but a . . . what?

After the heat of their romance ratcheted up and rose to even greater intensity, something else happened over time and togetherness. It deepened into what began to feel to Nikki like a Real Deal that was headed somewhere. But where it ended up heading was off a cliff into an abyss where it suspended midair.

He had been gone four weeks now. A month of Rook disappearing on his investigation of international arms smuggling for a *First Press* exposé. A month off the grid while he bounced around mountain villages of Eastern Europe, African seaports, airstrips in Mexico, and God knows where else.

A month to let Nikki wonder where the hell they were with each other.

Rook's communications sucked and that didn't help. He told her he would be going deep undercover and to expect some radio silence, but come on. Going all this time in isolation without so much as a phone call was chewing at her, wondering if he was alive, rotting in some war lord's jail, or what? Could he really be out of communication this long, or had he simply not made a good enough attempt? Nikki denied it at first but after days and nights of trying not to think the thought, she now struggled with the notion that perhaps the charm of Jameson Rook, the rogue globetrotter, was wearing thin. Sure, she respected his career as a two-time Pulitzer-winning investigative journalist, and knew intellectually what came along with all that, but the way he blew out of Dodge, the way he blew out of her life so easily, had her questioning not just where they stood as a couple but where he stood with her anymore.

Nikki looked at her own watch and wondered what time it was where Jameson Rook was. Then she looked at its calendar. Rook had said he would be back in five days. The question for Nikki was, by then where would they be?

———

Heat mulled resources and decided it would be more productive for her to wait for the manager of the underground sex club to arrive and unlock the video closet. That way she could free up her own pair of detectives to snag some uniformed officers and canvass the neighborhood on foot. Since the taxi team had volunteered to hit the diners, all-night workers, and delivery guys, she charged Raley and Ochoa (collectively and always affectionately known as "Roach") to concentrate on finding an ID or a wallet. "You should do the usual checks. Trash cans, dumpsters, subway grates, under apartment stoops, or anyplace else that's a handy place for a dump and run. Not a lot of doorman buildings in this neighborhood but if you see one, ask. Oh, and check out the Phoenix House up the block. Maybe some of our friends in recovery were up and heard or saw something."

Roach's cell phones chimed about two seconds apart. Heat held up her own mobile and said, "That's a head shot I just emailed you of our vic. If you get a chance, flash it, you never know."

"Right," said Ochoa. "Who doesn't love to have a picture of a choking victim shoved in their face before breakfast?"

As they started up the stairs to street level, she called after, "And make note of any surveillance cams you see with a street view. Banks, jewelry stores, you know the drill. We can drop in and have them do a check when they open for business later this morning."

———

Detective Heat had to shake off a foul mood after dealing with the manager of Pleasure Bound. Nikki doubted the woman had been awakened by Raley. On the contrary, Roxanne Paltz vibed having been up all night, heavily and severely made up and arriving in a tight vinyl outfit that creaked whenever she moved on the chair in her office. Her granny glasses had blue lenses matching the tips of her spiky, bleach-damaged hair, which gave off the unmistakable scent of cannabis. When Nikki told her the real reason they were there, the dead man in her torture chamber, she lost color and reeled. Heat showed her the picture on her cell phone, and the woman nearly got sick. She sat down unsteadily and drank a sip of the water Nikki gave her from the cooler, but after she recovered, said she'd never seen the guy.

When Nikki asked if she could have a look at the surveillance video, it got contentious and Roxanne Paltz was suddenly all about Constitutional rights. Speaking with the authority of someone who has been hassled for running a sex trade business, she cited just cause, unlawful search, client confidentiality, and freedom of expression. Her lawyer was on speed dial, and even though it wasn't even six in the morning, she called and woke him up, Nikki having to deal with her raccoon mascara glare while she parroted back his certainty that no cabinets could be unlocked or video screened without a judge's warrant.

"I'm just asking for a little cooperation," said Nikki.

Roxanne sat there listening to the attorney on her phone, nodding and nodding, vinyl creaking with each head bob. And then she hung up. "He says to go fuck yourself."

Nikki Heat paused and gave a slight smile. "Judging from some of the equipment you've got here, this would probably be the one place I could actually do that."

The detective knew she would get the search warrant and had just ended her call downtown to get the wheels turning on one when her phone vibrated in her hand. It was Raley. "Come topside, I think we got something."

She arrived back up on the sidewalk expecting sun but it was still dark. Nikki had lost a sense of time and place down there and reflected that was probably the whole idea.

Detectives Raley, Ochoa, Van Meter, and Feller stood in a semicircle across the street under the green canvas canopy of the corner grocery. Crossing Seventy-fourth to meet them, Nikki had to pause so she didn't get run over by a delivery guy on a fat-tired bike. She watched his trailing breath as he passed with somebody's order-in breakfast bouncing in the wire basket and figured maybe she didn't have the hardest job in the city. "Whatcha got?" she said as she stepped over to the crew.

"Found some clothes and a shoe wedged in the space between the two buildings here," said Ochoa, training the beam of his Streamlight Stinger in the wall gap separating the grocery and the nail spa next door. Raley held up a pair of dark trousers and a black tasseled loafer for Heat and then slipped them into a brown paper evidence bag. "Spaces like this? Classic place to stash," said Ochoa. "Learned that in Narco."

"Give me the light, Crime Dog, think there's more here." Raley took the mini from his partner and squatted in front of the gap. A few seconds later he pulled out the mate to the other loafer then said, "Well, what do you know?"

"What?" Ochoa asked. "Don't be a dick, what is it?"

"Hang on a sec. If you weren't packing on the weight, you could have done this instead of me." Raley twisted his shoulder to get a better angle for his reach into the narrow opening. "Here we go. Another collar."

Nikki expected to see something in a leather gimp rig with sharp studs and stainless steel D-rings but when Raley finally stood and held it up in his gloved hand, it wasn't that kind of collar at all. It was a priest's collar.

In 2005 New York City funded eleven million dollars to modernize the NYPD's high tech capability by building the Real Time Crime Center, a computer operations hub that, among numerous capabilities, provides crime reports and police data to officers in the field with startling immediacy. That is why in a city of eight and a half million people it only took Detective Heat less than three minutes to get a likely ID on the victim in the torture dungeon. The RTCC accessed records and spit out a Missing Persons Report filed the night before by a parish rectory housekeeper for a Father Gerald Graf.

Nikki assigned Roach to stay and continue their canvass while she made the drive uptown to interview the woman who filed the MPR. Detectives Feller and Van Meter were off their shift, but Dutch offered to help Roach continue knocking on doors. Feller appeared at her car window and said if Heat didn't mind the company, he'd be happy to ride shotgun with her. She hesitated, figuring this was about Feller engineering his opportunity to ask her to catch a drink or dinner later. But a veteran detective was reaching out to help with a case on his own time and she couldn't say no to that. If he tried to bend it into a date offer, she'd simply deal with it.

Our Lady of the Innocents was on the northern border of the precinct, mid-block on Eighty-fifth between West End Avenue and Riverside. At this early end of the morning rush hour, a five minute drive, if that. But as soon as she pulled onto Broadway, they caught a red in front of the Beacon Theater.

"Glad to finally have some time alone with you," said Feller while they waited.

"For sure," said Nikki, who then hurried to steer the topic away. "Appreciate the assist, Randy. Can always use another pair of eyes and ears."

"Gives me a chance to ask you something without the whole world around."

She looked up at the light and considered breaking out the gumball. ". . . Yeah?"

"Any idea how you did on your exam for lieutenant?" he asked. Not the question she expected. Nikki turned to look at him. "Green," he said and she drove on.

"I don't know, seemed like I did all right. Hard to know for sure," she said. "Still waiting for the results to be posted." When the department's civil service test was offered recently, Heat had taken it not so much out of a burning desire for the promotion, but because she wasn't sure when it would be given again. Budget cuts from the economic crisis had hit New York as much as any other municipality and one response the year before had been to cut back on raises by postponing the scheduled rank advancement tests.

Detective Feller cleared his throat. "What if I told you I hear you aced it?" She gave him a sideglance and then concentrated on the driver of the bread delivery truck who had stopped to double park in her lane without flashers. While she hit her blinker and waited for the passing lane to clear, he went on. "I know this to be a fact."

"How?"

"From some inside sources. Downtown." He reached for the dashboard. "Mind if I back off the temp? Starting to bake in here."

"Help yourself."

"I try to keep myself connected." He turned down the knob one click then decided on one more before he settled back in his seat again. "Not planning on riding in back of that cab forever, ya hear what I'm saying?"

"Sure, sure." Nikki made her swing around the bread truck. "I, um, appreciate the info."

"So when you get by your orals and all the other hoops they make you jump through—like teach you the secret handshake, or whatever—do me a fave? Don't forget your friends on your way up."

Whoomph there it is, thought Nikki. She felt a little embarrassed. All this time thinking Feller wanted to date her when maybe what he really wanted was to network her. She replayed her mental picture of him at the cop bar clowning in his ass gasket lobster bib and wondered if the jester in him was all in fun, or if he was really just a skilled glad-hander. The more he talked, the more that picture emerged.

"When you get your gold bar it's going to be a piece of good news in your precinct for a change. And you know what I mean."

"I'm not sure I do," she said. They hit another red at Seventy-ninth, and unfortunately this was a long one.

"Not sure, that's a laugh," he said. "I mean Captain Montrose."

Nikki knew full well what he meant. Her skipper, her mentor, Captain Montrose was under increasing pressure from One Police Plaza over his performance as commander of the Twentieth Precinct. Whether it was the bad economy, increased unemployment, or a reset to the dark days of the pre-Giuliani disorder, crime statistics were edging up throughout all five boroughs. And worse, they were spiking in election season. Gravity rules, so in response, the shit roll was all downhill to the precinct commanders. But Heat could see her captain was taking an extra pounding. Montrose had been singled out, called down separately for extra meetings and ass chewings, spending as much time at HQ as he did in his office. His personality darkened under the pressure and he had grown atypically remote—no, more than remote, secretive. It made Nikki wonder whether something else was going on with him beyond precinct perf stats. Now what bothered Heat was that her boss's private humiliation was Out There as department gossip. If Feller knew about it, others did, too. Loyalty made her deflect it, back up her boss.

"Listen, Randy, who isn't getting squeezed these days? I hear those weekly CompStat meetings at 1PP are brutal for all the skips, not just mine."

"Seriously," he said with a nod. "They should put a drain in the floor to let the blood run out. Green."

"Jeez, it just turned." Nikki pressed the accelerator.

"Sorry. Drives Dutch crazy, too. I tellya, I've got to get my ass out of that cab." He powered down his window and spat. When he closed it again, he said, "This isn't just about the performance figs. I have a bud in Internal Affairs. Your man is on their radar."

"Bull."

"No bull."

"For what?"

He made an exaggerated shrug. "It's IA, what do you think?"

"No. I don't buy it," she said.

"Then don't. Maybe he is clean but I'm telling you he's got his neck on the stump and they're sharpening the ax."

"Not maybe. Montrose is clean." She made a left onto Eighty-fifth. A block and a half ahead, she could see a cross on the church roof. In the distance, across the Hudson, the apartments and cliffs were pinking from the rising sun. Nikki switched off her headlights as she crossed West End Avenue.

"Who knows," said Feller, "you get rank, maybe

you'll be in position to take over the precinct if he goes down."

"He is not going down. Montrose is under pressure but he's straight as they come."

"If you say."

"I say. He's unassailable."

As Nikki got out in front of the rectory, she wished she had made the drive alone. No, what she wished was that Feller had just asked her for drinks, or bowling, or for sex. Any one of those, she would rather have dealt with.

She reached for the bell but before she could press it, she saw a small head through the stained glass window in the door and it opened revealing a minute woman in her late sixties.

Nikki referred to her notes from the RTCC message. "Good morning, are you Lydia Borelli?"

"Yes, and you're with the police, I can tell."

After they showed ID and introduced themselves, Nikki said, "And it was you who called about Father Graf?"

"Oh, I've been worried sick. Come in, please." The housekeeper's lips were quaking and her hands fluttered nervously. She missed the doorknob on her first attempt to pull it closed. "Did you find him? Is he all right?"

"Ms. Borelli, do you have a recent photo I could look at?"

"Of Father? Well, I'm sure somewhere . . . I know."

She led them over thick rugs that muted their footfalls through the living room and into the pastor's adjoining study. On the shelves of the built-in above the desk several photos in glass frames were perched between books and knick-knacks. The housekeeper took one down, swiping her finger along the top of the frame to dust it before she handed it over. "This is from last summer."

Heat and Detective Feller stood beside each other to examine it. The shot was taken at some sort of protest rally and showed a priest and three Hispanic protesters, with arms linked, leading a march behind a banner. Father Graf's face, frozen in mid-recitation of a chant, was definitely the same as the one on the corpse at Pleasure Bound.

The housekeeper took the news stoically, blessing herself with the Sign of the Cross and then lowering her head in silent prayer. When she was done blood vessels showed through her temples and tears streamed down her cheeks. There were tissues on the end table near the couch. Nikki offered her the box and she took some.

"How did it happen?" she asked, staring down at the tissue in her hands.

Fragile as the woman appeared, Heat thought better of giving her the details at that moment about the priest's death in a BDSM torture and humiliation dungeon. "We're still investigating that."

Then she looked up. "Did he suffer?"

Detective Feller squinted at Nikki and turned away to hide his face, suddenly making himself busy replacing the photo on the shelf.

"We'll have more details after the coroner's report," answered Nikki, hoping her dodge was artful enough to be bought. "We know this is a loss for you, but in a while, not just now, we're going to need to ask you a few questions to help us."

"Certainly, anything you need."

"What would be helpful now, Ms. Borelli, is if we could look through the rectory. You know, search through his papers, his bedroom."

"His closet," said Feller.

Nikki moved forward. "We want to look for anything that would help us find out who did this."

The housekeeper gave her a puzzled look. "Again?"

"I said, we'd like to search the—"

"I heard what you said. I mean, you need to search again?"

Heat leaned closer on the couch to face the woman. "Are you saying someone searched here already?"

"Yes. Last night, another policeman. He said he was following up on my missing person report."

"Oh, of course, sometimes we cross signals," said Nikki. That could well be the case but her uneasiness was growing. She caught a look from Feller that said his antenna was up, too. "May I ask who this policeman was?"

"I forgot his name. He said it but I was so upset. Senior moment." She chuckled and then stifled a sob. "He did show me a badge like yours, so I let him roam free. I watched television while he looked around."

"Well, I'm sure he filed a report." Nikki flipped open her spiral reporter's notebook. "Maybe I could cut through some red tape if you described him."

"Sure. Tall. Black, or do I say Afro American these days? Very pleasant, had a kind face. Bald. Oh, and a little birthmark or mole or something right here." She tapped her cheek.

Heat stopped writing and capped her stick pen. She had all she needed. The housekeeper had just described Captain Montrose.

A Conversation with Richard Castle, author of *Heat Wave*

Hyperion: Your last book was pretty controversial. I don't think I'm giving away any spoilers here since this made newspaper headlines all across the country: You decided to kill off your most beloved character, Derrick Storm. A lot of your fans were outraged. What was the rationale behind killing off your main character? Was this something you'd planned since the start of the Storm series? Was it an emotional decision for you?

Richard Castle: I think the reason Derrick Storm is so beloved is that he lived the life we all wish for . . . danger, romance, adventure. And I loved writing him, but after so many books, I ended up knowing him too well. There were no more surprises for me. So rather than inflicting on him the slow death of literary mediocrity, I gave him the ending he deserved. Derrick went out in true Derrick Storm style, a man at the top of his game. It was obviously emotional to let go of him and he's still very much a part of me. A handsome, charming, roguish part of me. But I know for a fact that he'd be a big fan of Nikki Heat and *Heat Wave*—particularly Nikki's pose on the cover. Who wouldn't be?

Hyperion: Your new book features a female main character, NYPD detective Nikki Heat. Rumor has it that she's based on the real-life NYPD homicide detective Kate Beckett. In fact, you arranged for a series of official civilian ride-alongs with Beckett over the past few months to observe how she works and what goes into a real murder investigation. Were you surprised at all by anything you saw on your ride-alongs? What was your most eye-opening experience?

RC: My time with Detective Beckett and the other detectives in the 12th precinct has been very informative. For instance, I never knew how bad coffee could taste until I tried theirs. My admiration for the work police officers do has only grown from the experience, because I had no idea they were doing it while drinking such bad coffee.

As for the most eye-opening experience, rather than give away anything that ended up in the book, I'll simply say that being shot at is not as much fun as it looks in Tom Cruise movies.

Hyperion: You originally met Detective Beckett when you were asked by the NYPD to consult on one of their cases, a series of copycat murders based on the murders in several of your novels, a series of murders that you were actually instrumental in helping to solve. As a writer, how did it affect you to have the line between imagination and reality blurred like that?

RC: Well, besides the fact that the killer focused on my truly lesser works, I was glad to be a part of the investigation. Ultimately, Detective Beckett was able to clear the name of a true fan, a man whom the killer set up to take the fall.

It was a fascinating case, and yet another example of how life can be stranger than fiction. In fact, if I'd written that story myself, everyone would accuse me of being self-aggrandizing. And, clearly, I'd never want to do that . . .

Hyperion: Has Detective Beckett read the manuscript for *Heat Wave*? If so, what was her response?

RC: I haven't had a chance to show Beckett the manuscript yet, but I'm looking forward to hearing her thoughts. Hopefully it'll live up to the high standards of thorough police work and professionalism that she's established. As well as being, obviously, a sexy, exciting murder mystery with chills and thrills on every page.

I think she'll like it. I hope she'll like it. Oh God, what if she doesn't like it? What if she gets mad? Did I mention the sex scene?

Hyperion: As a single dad, did your exposure to the reality of everyday violence make you worry more about raising your daughter in New York City? Did you ever discuss what you saw with her after your ride-alongs?

RC: I worry less about Alexis growing up in New

York City than I do about her growing up with me. After all, given my line of work, our dinner table conversation usually centers around plot twists like whether a self-cleaning oven could incinerate a body. I do discuss cases with her sometimes, but I usually leave out the gory details.

Although she's still my little girl, she's a native New Yorker and has a great head on her shoulders—I can only be thankful that she is far wiser than I was at her age.

Hyperion: In your new book, *Heat Wave*, Detective Nikki Heat also has a ride-along civilian, journalist Jameson Rook. He is a bit of a smart-ass. How much of his personality is based on the real Rick Castle? (And are you really that much of a loveable smart-ass?)

RC: Rook? Castle? Absolutely no connection. Rook's pretty cool though. I mean, the guy's got a Pulitzer Prize! Plus, he's so brilliant and handsome. Well, now that you mention it, maybe I did base him on someone . . .

As to whether I'm a lovable smart-ass, it depends on who you ask. My daughter thinks I'm lovable and smart. My exes just think I'm an ass.

Hyperion: So 'fess up: Did you want to be a cop when you were a kid?

RC: Actually, I wanted to be a lion tamer or the ice

cream man. How cool would that be? Driving a funky truck and ringing a bell. Bringing joy and happiness to millions of kids. I like to think of my books as little ice cream bars for my audience. That's why the covers are so colorful.

Hyperion: The sense of place in your novels is powerful; the city of New York comes across almost like a character. What kind of relationship do you have to New York City and how does that influence your writing?

RC: I love New York because it has all the contradictions of a truly fascinating protagonist. Amazing wealth and utter poverty, noble intentions and terrible greed, young love and age-old hatred living side by side. Plus, there's a beautiful woman on every street corner in this city. What more can a writer ask for?

Hyperion: Will we be seeing more of Nikki Heat in future books?

RC: That's up to the readers of America. I can only hope they'll enjoy reading Nikki as much as I've enjoyed writing her.

Look for the next thrilling book in the bestselling
Nikki Heat series in September 2011!